THE
RULES
OF
US

THE
RULES
OF
US

JENNIFER NISSLEY

LR LABYRINTH ROAD | NEW YORK

Text copyright © 2023 by Jennifer Nissley
Jacket art copyright © 2023 by Salini Perera

Visit us on the Web! GetUnderlined.com

Educators and librarians, for a variety of teaching tools, visit us at RHTeachersLibrarians.com

Library of Congress Cataloging-in-Publication Data
Names: Nissley, Jennifer, author.
Title: The rules of us / Jennifer Nissley.
Description: First edition. | New York: Labyrinth Road, 2023. |
Audience: Ages 14 & up. | Audience: Grades 10–12. | Summary: Jillian and
Henry do everything together, but when they come out as gay to each other
and become interested in other people, the former couple must figure out
how to move on without losing each other.
Identifiers: LCCN 2022055394 (print) | LCCN 2022055395 (ebook) |
ISBN 978-0-593-48489-0 (trade) | ISBN 978-0-593-48491-3 (ebook)
Subjects: CYAC: Interpersonal relations—Fiction. | Friendship—
Fiction. | LGBTQ+ people—Fiction. | LCGFT: Novels.
Classification: LCC PZ7.1.N584 Ni 2023 (print) |
LCC PZ7.1.N584 (ebook) | DDC [Fic]—dc23

The text of this book is set in 11-point Sabon LT Pro.
Interior design by Michelle Crowe
Interior art used under license from Shutterstock.com

Printed in the United States of America
10 9 8 7 6 5 4 3 2 1
First Edition

FOR MY STUDENTS

1.

I KNOW CARLA GETTING up to dance with Bea Nabarro has nothing to do with us.

Nothing.

But.

There they are. Carla Kaminski. Beatriz Nabarro. A flailing approximation of some dance everybody's been copying off social. Which, by the way, is all prom is. Approximations. Flailing. My dress tighter and pinker, the back dizzyingly lower, than anything I've ever worn. And the DJ's pumping his fist and the music hurts my teeth and carrying these cups across the gym without getting splattered has sweat pooling under my pits, but somehow every song that's played since we arrived has been okay—verging on tolerable. And I actually kind of love sweating. I love this dress.

Funny how high triumph can fling you.

Back at our table, I flop sideways into Henry's lap, sloshing punch all over us.

"Jillian!" Henry squawks. Light strobing off the dance

floor catches the edge of his enormous tortoiseshell glasses. His dad's. That's why they don't fit. "I'm on the hook for excessive damage." He smooths his vest, one of several components that apparently make up a tux, our decision to attend prom so last-minute that we got stuck with whatever the mildewy shop on Booker had left over. Ergo, his bow tie isn't quite the same pink as my dress. More bronchial. And off by just the teeniest bit of a centimeter? I plunk our cups down to adjust it for him, and he smiles. The first Henry smile I've seen all night. "Thanks. How red does this stuff taste?"

"Hmm . . ." I tip a drop over the soggy paper rim and smack my lips. "Gory." Henry laughs.

Scooting lower, I rest my head on his and survey the prom committee's efforts. Unlike the seniors, who get everything—prom at a fancy hotel in Albany with glittery fish tanks, a lobby practically shrink-wrapped in gold leaf—juniors have festivities confined to the gym. Our school's cathedral to forced teamwork has been transformed with sloughs of blue streamers and lights so billowy that you almost can't see the hairs shellacked into the floor. Could be worse. This is Elmerville, after all. Upstate New York. If not for prom, we'd be celebrating at Applebee's.

I nudge him. He's blinking into his punch.

"To our emergence from the flames of essay hell," I say. Henry toasts like he kisses. Fly-by gentleness that makes every part of me blush.

No need for Carla whatsoever.

Henry sets his cup on the table, which isn't *ours*, just abandoned enough to feel like it, strewn with plasticky aquamarine plates and anonymous tux jackets, the table-cloth splotched with grease from the buffet we missed because Henry wasn't ready when he said he'd be. Nested on a nearby chair are a minimum of five pastel purses, each large enough to conceal a single tampon or vape pen. Henry sinks against me. I rest my chin in his dark hair.

"You like *this* song, don't you?" I bellow over the relentlessly pulsing dubstep. He grunts. My eyes skip over the dance floor behind him.

Carla is tall. Not extremely so, but storky enough that I could pick her out if I had to. Then there's her hair. When she and Bea reeled past me at the punch bowl, I noticed she'd changed it again. Buzzed part of one side so her curls zigged spectacularly, her own personal fireworks show as she danced.

Henry would deem it all pretty ridiculous.

He'd say, *And you care about them because . . . ?*

But I don't care.

Not about Carla's new hair or Bea's hand enfolding hers. The way Carla's dress has wrinkled in the back, like lines on a pillowcase.

"What time is it?" Henry shouts.

"Um"—I check my phone—"just after nine." Prom ends at eleven. My dad said to call if we wanted out earlier, but . . . "Why? Do you want to go already?"

He shakes his head, like I don't know what he's thinking. Of course we don't need prom.

It doesn't need us.

But our junior year also wasn't like everybody else's. A

barrage of mentor check-ins and short essays and deadlines so torturous they surpassed even our academic pain thresholds. *That's what it takes,* Henry kept saying. Every time I sobbed over my laptop, ground my nails into my sides, and howled, his reminder echoed through me. *What it takes, what it takes* . . . Because, let's be real, the Lucille M. Purdy Memorial Scholarship isn't just *the* most prestigious and coveted scholarship in New York State. This scholarship awards ten students of exceptional merit up to $85,000 for tuition and school-related expenses. More money than my parents make in one year, combined. So much money that when I think about it, light pulses behind my eyes.

Because $85,000 means more than tuition. For Henry and me, $85,000 buys our only opportunity to attend the same school: Oneida Polytechnic Institute, the top in-state university for video game design. We've been gnawing our way toward this moment, haunting the Purdy Scholar subreddit for application strategies, since we were thirteen. Practically infants. Since submitting our applications last night, I haven't stopped grinning. So, contrary to every other social instinct in our possession, prom isn't pointless. Just this once. It's not pointless, after the year we've had, to want to dance with my boyfriend, my face in his neck for the slow songs. They've played two already.

My chin's planted in Henry's hair. It takes a second to realize he's on his phone.

"Hey." I grind my butt bones into him. "You okay?" South Korea is a million hours ahead of New York. Texts from his dad come at inconvenient times.

"It's not . . . shit." The tux jacket Henry slung across the back of his chair starts to slide, and as he lunges after it, I decide the pink on his bow tie is so jarringly *not* like mine that we maybe should've gone with the second option the shop owner showed us. "Not my dad," Henry goes on. He glances toward the DJ booth, likely calculating whether the number of writhing bodies violates the gym's 310-person occupancy limit. "It's Yuna."

"Yuna?" Henry's achingly cool older half sister, who lives with their dad in Daegu. Or, as Henry refers to her, Preferred Spawn. "You never talk to— Wait. Is that why you're in such a shitty mood?" His eyes widen, like the perfectly obvious also pains him. I slap his phone onto the tablecloth. "Okay, no, not tonight. We agreed. No bullshit, no drama. We're celebrating. And"—I dip my head toward the dance floor—"if talking about Purdy's too risky, can you at least rejoice in the fact that we're not Carla and Bea right now?"

Henry's brow scrunches, his dress shirt damp where I'm gripping his shoulder. "What do you mean?"

I'm dripping with sweat myself, thanks to my punch bowl expedition. Shrugging, I splay my fingers through the sopping ends of my curls.

So much for not mentioning her.

"Just that they're back together." I try to swallow. It never helps. "Or seem like they are. I give them, mmm . . . forty-eight hours before they're fighting publicly." I expect a smirk, one of Henry's seismic eye rolls, but the crease in his forehead only deepens. "Henry." I sandwich his face between my hands. A must for imparting emphasis. I trash-compact those glorious cheeks together until his lips bunch, and then I boom, "APPLICATIONS ARE DONE. WE CAN ENJOY OUR LIVES AGAIN!" As he twists away, angling for a glimpse of Elmerville High's most reliably combustible couple, I drop my chin back to his hair.

The dance floor glows like a wish, and Bea has Carla backed into a subwoofer, their mouths zippered together. Carla's hair hangs lank over both their faces. A color you can't quite call blond. She breaks the kiss, laughing, and I see her pink tongue.

"Oh," Henry says. "Oh, yup, I see. I'm going to go ahead and give this"—he consults the watch he doesn't wear—"twenty-four hours. Based on current conditions, forty-eight is looking generous."

"Twelve," I whisper.

He gasps. "Brutal."

A fist pushes up into my throat.

IT'S COOLER OUTSIDE, the sidewalk littered with tree sperm and kids pretending to smoke. Mr. Nett, who was undoubtedly born to teach freshmen racket sports, threatens detention even though the sidewalk isn't school property, as Annabel Western promptly reminds him. Then Preston Kline shouts, "This is a high school, Nett-o, not a fascist state!" which gets a big OOOOOOHHHHH. Henry steers me through the melee, toward a set of concrete steps where, incredibly, nobody's barfed yet.

"Thanks," I get out.

We sit, and his lips brush my ear.

"I suck," he says.

"Don't apologize. I'm the one who needed air—"

"No, you were right. We deserve to actually have fun for once, and I'm ruining our good time, but it's . . . it's just that . . ." He looks at me, his Adam's apple jerking. "Aren't you even a little scared?"

"Scared?" I laugh. "Of what?"

He tugs his bottom lip for, like, a minute.

Theoretically I could tell him, *I've been so stressed for so long that not having pressure feels like pressure.* I could confess to accidentally microwaving my Golden Grahams again this morning, obsessing over a thousand fatal misinterpretations of an application tip we'd picked off Reddit.

"I'm not scared," I say.

He leans his head on my shoulder, and I wrap my arms around him, inhale his sweaty hair. "Summer," he murmurs.

"Soon." That's why the air smells like tulips.

"Yeah." His fingers sneak back to his lip. "But . . ."

I get it. If high school were a video game, this would be the part where we eject the disc and never touch it again, standard protocol when we're one level away from beating the whole thing. Henry struggles with endings. I squeeze his arm, and we watch the gym doors across the street. Music thumps gently.

He hasn't asked why I suddenly had to get out of the gym so badly. I don't know what I'll say if he does.

"Next time," he says, turning toward me so I can make out the murk of his glasses lenses, smudged by what I'm certain is my nose grease, "when you start hauling ass for the exit, a warning might be nice? Otherwise, I endorse this change in scenery. You're not the only one who wanted a break."

He says that last part under his breath, the way he apologized when we picked him up, his hair wet and bow tie flapping, so hopelessly jumbled my dad had to stop taking pictures to help him fix it. Now I almost don't notice when the music pulsing from the gym thins out, gets soft and drippy. Slow dance number three. Before I can suggest going back inside, the doors thwack open and Carla slips out, towing Bea behind her. They hop onto the brick wall ringing the entrance no more than one hundred fifty feet away from us. Carla giggles, her dress hiked up to reveal disco ball Converse. Bea pinches Carla's thigh.

"The Call," I say.

Henry snaps upright.

"Is that what you're worried—"

He clamps a hand over my mouth. "Don't!"

"I was only—"

"*Shhh!*" His eyes bulge.

Every applicant knows The Call is merely a formality. An invitation by the Purdy people to some final-round "interview" to prove you're as impressive in their crosshairs as you are on paper. According to the subreddit, every student who receives The Call ultimately gets selected. Every. Single. One. I didn't bring it up to jinx us. Just the opposite.

The surest thing I could pull into the light.

Now Bea's whispering in Carla's ear. Her contact with

Carla's body has transitioned from a pinch to stroking a spot on her thigh best described as *inner,* and the moment I see that, *my* body—from forehead to kneecaps, my cheeks squeezed against Henry's palm—goes molten. I pull back. But Henry noticed.

Naturally.

"Um," he says, "you're staring at Kaminski and Beatriz . . . ?"

"I am?"

Henry squints at me through his plastic lenses, convincing nobody that he can actually see out of them. I fight the urge to look away. "Oh-kay, then." His fingers tiptoe over my kneecap. It's stubbly. But there's this thing Henry does when he touches me. The parts I miss shaving don't feel like misses at all.

At least, they didn't used to.

The breeze picks up, crueler and colder than it has any right to be, given that it's practically June. Neither of us makes any move to go back inside. I stare at the concrete steps, forcing my head as vacant and cool as the moonlight spilling over them.

He exhales. "Anyway, we can't talk about The Call."

"Right," I say. "Totally. That's fine." Superstition is Henry's most infuriating stress reflex. Some are Korean— like eating sticky foods before tests—but just this week he lost it over a cracked mirror. On his mom's car. That he didn't even break. I sat on him in the ShopRite parking lot until he stopped hyperventilating. "I mean, maybe that's not the kind of energy we want to be beaming into the universe yet. On a scale of one to ten, ten being the most certain we've ever been about anything, we're what now, do you think? A solid nine? So once we do get the—" He bites my collarbone. "Ow! Jesus! I wasn't going to say it!"

And I'm not jealous of Bea Nabarro. Bea—pronounced *bee* for no reason other than to make you mess it up. A girl who live-streamed herself piercing her own tongue with a sewing needle and has worn the same tattered jacket with DYKE patched onto the back since ninth grade. Coincidentally, as long as she and Carla have dated. Or their tortured equivalent of dating: breaking up and screaming while obstructing, like, an entire row of lockers every other week. Besides mumbling, *Excuse me, sorry, I just need to . . .* , I only know Carla from occasionally smiling at her at the rock-climbing gym Henry and I go to.

Now she's pressed so close to Bea they could kiss again if they wanted. My throat narrows.

I need to think of something else.

But that's exactly my problem.

There's no thought that won't end with Carla's hands in my hair, her breath on my cheek.

I pluck Henry's hand from my knee and spread it over my face, reveling in his smothery boy warmth that smells like a basketball, even though he hasn't touched one in ages. This is the only way to clear my mind. The only way to— "Wait." His phone is in his lap. The case, textured to resemble redwood, only makes it look more fake. I hover the screen at him so his face will unlock it. "You're sure there wasn't—"

"Jillian!" He snatches his phone back. "I literally just looked, and besides, it's ten p.m. on a random Friday in May. Why would Purdy contact us now?"

"Shouldn't we double-check that our applications uploaded?" Once The Call comes and we've been anointed, there'll be no more inspections to pass, no more nights tipping from triumph to this other place where Henry and I have no future, no anything.

Henry touches his phone on his chin. Then he slides it into his tux pocket. "You're on the subreddit. According to the posts, we probably won't hear about the interview until August. You know, to maximize our suffering."

Accurate. "But—"

"Remember when Cooper Wertz farted and blamed it on me, and even Mr. Shapiro low-key believed him? I would rather talk about that than Purdy. Please. *Please*, Jilly."

His hand stayed draped over my face this whole time. Now I push him off and fold my arms, chilled from my drying sweat and wishing we were home, except retreat is its own betrayal, the same as giving up. And I don't give up.

Ever.

Henry sucks his lip. Annabel Western, ascending the steps with her drunken entourage, trips over us without saying sorry.

I wait until they're gone, clopping through the senior lot, to mash my eyes shut. All I need is to hear him say it. I need to hear him say, *We've got this, Jilly, don't worry.* Because at the end of the day, my want is nothing without his. It's limp, powerless—no better than a wish. Put ours together, though, and what have you got? Destiny. I don't know why he's scared of saying so.

"Could you maybe," I say, "go back to believing in us?"

His face collapses. "What?"

The way you're supposed to. The way I'll squash every last doubt tapping at my skull, so when The Call does happen—once we go to OPI, where we'll found our own video game studio and go on to win every developer award and never be pried from each other's sides—our lives will become like those puzzles we already know the answers to, no surprises, no blanks. One letter per space.

2.

MY DAD PICKS US UP in his bathrobe and stops at 7-Eleven for the usual sleepover provisions: goldfish. Gummy bears. Prepackaged nachos with "salsa" and plastic cheese. At home, we peel our damp clothes off and shower. Individually. Dad stays up, so the alternative's not an option. When I'm finished, I bundle Henry's sweaty tux with my sweatier dress and leave them on the bathroom floor, then spend, like, five minutes inspecting the marks my strapless bra bit into my nipples.

In my bedroom, I move faster. Throw on pajamas and pocket a condom from the stash at the back of my sock drawer. I don't hide them because I'm scared of my parents finding out I'm ready for sex. Obviously not—Mom gave me these. It's just that hiding them beats admitting she guessed anything right about me.

Except Henry is . . . nowhere? Not in the bathroom, or— God help me—Garrett's room, across the hall. But I squeak his door wider to be sure.

"Hey," I say. Honestly, the fact that he's allowed to be awake past ten is criminal. When I was his age, our parents put me to bed when it was still light out. Yet here he is, flopped in his beanbag chair playing *The Legend of Zelda: Twilight Princess* on the old Wii U console I so benevolently donated to him at Christmas. Heaped nearby are pillows and a sleeping bag that Henry will burrito himself into for the night. To me, it's all kind of excessive. Who's going to tell his mom if he gets into bed with me? But she only tolerates sleepovers because my parents promise we'll sleep apart, and he hates deceiving her. I step onto the crinkly sleeping bag, nearly blocking the TV.

"Have you seen Henry?" I ask.

Garrett slashes a Shadow Beast without blinking. "Am I your boyfriend's keeper?"

Suddenly it feels super obvious I'm not wearing a bra. I cross my arms. "Garrett, come on. Was he in here? At all?" A very generous pause, and then I tilt closer. "Helping you?"

He glares. People think Garrett and I look alike, which is impossible, since he's a twelve-year-old boy and I'm not. Piss him off, though, and it's hard not to see the resemblance. There's just this quality we share. Lightning cleaves our foreheads whenever anybody dares to challenge, daunt, defy us. Also, our hair is brown and curly. But it's not like we did that on purpose.

"Henry doesn't help," Garrett says. "He advises. Maybe he's hiding from you."

On the ride home, Henry was so quiet as we nibbled gummy bears that I unbuckled my seat belt, stroked his thigh as high as I could with Dad humming Fleetwood Mac in the driver's seat. *Hey,* I murmured. *You good?* A tear skipped down his cheek.

I snort at Garrett. "Please."

The Shadow Beasts he's been hacking away at regenerate with throat-splitting howls. Feeling charitable, I pull the Zelda wiki up on my phone, toggling on audio narration so Garrett won't accuse me of ambushing him with reading. The robotic lady voice drones blankly on, and all I can think of is kissing Henry's wet cheek in the back seat. He wouldn't say why he was crying. But I know whatever's wrong, it's my fault.

"So . . . kill them in batches," Garrett summarizes.

"Right. Exactly." I shove my phone into my waistband, almost dropping it. "If you don't, the survivor will just resurrect the dead ones and you'll be trapped in the Twilight Realm for eternity. Next time you get stuck, repeat after me: the wiki is your friend." And the developers' idea here was kind of genius, so he should be taking notes.

Garrett nods. "Gotcha."

I steady myself on the stairs just past his room, digging my toes into the ratty carpet our landlord won't let us replace. There's a window like a porthole above the landing that overlooks our creaky swing set and the tent we haven't ventured into since I don't know when. When I spot this oasis of orange light in the otherwise unlit backyard, the silhouette inside, I don't move. Certain I'm hallucinating.

I've got a lot to make up for tonight. So much that I almost thought, in between grabbing the condom and stopping here, that Henry had figured it all out, that he was gone. But Henry would never run from me. According to my parents, stress breeds *unhelpful coping mechanisms*, which must explain his anxiousness lately. This doubt I can't shake.

Of course Henry believes in us.

Our first night in the tent, we were twelve. Henry was trying to prove farts weren't water soluble, and I leaned close and fantasized about kissing him while he googled furiously. Only, there wasn't any kissing then. No runaway dads or girls' smiles lighting up places within me I can't name. Just us and a bag of sour worms. iPhone moonlight on his face.

Now I brush the pocket of my pajama shorts, making sure the condom hasn't fallen out. I bite my lip and think of Henry, warm and hard and on top of me. Not a coping mechanism.

The real thing.

"GOD." HENRY REACHES OVER me to zip the tent flap, sealing us into our sacred cocoon of Nintendo and high-fructose corn syrup. "Tell me this is not better than watching everybody get wasted and barf on their own shoes."

It's too chilly for wet hair. Naturally, I realized this the second after I successfully edged onto the deck, too late to whirr the sliding door open and get a towel without alerting my parents, whose bedroom is downstairs by the laundry area. Like, as cool as my parents are with Henry and me messing around, we didn't get permission to be out here, which is their big thing. Communication. *Trust.* Shivering, I take the flashlight from Henry, muffling the beam with my knees.

The light goes red from the press of my skin, cupping Henry at random angles and making it impossible to tell whether he's done crying or just trying to act like it. He nibbles a sweatshirt string, awaiting my answer.

Watching Carla and Bea trade hits off a vape pen when my dad drove up. Minty smoke and the burn of their laughter. "Um. Sure . . ." We're facing each other, knee to knee, backs rounded to compensate for the tent that has undoubtedly shrunk since middle school. "Surprised you came out here. I mean, good call. But the spiders—"

"I checked the premises thoroughly." Henry sucks the string, peering into the tent's eaves. "And daddy longlegs aren't really spiders, are they?"

"Arachnids, yes. Spiders, no."

"I figured we must've looked that up at some point. But, yeah." Tentatively, he pushes a curl behind my ear. "I was hoping for privacy."

Privacy? Meaning . . .

Okay.

Okay, yeah. "Same," I say, my heart starting to race.

The condom crinkles as I take it from my pocket. Henry's eyebrows fly up.

"It's kind of cliché," I admit. "Everybody loses their virginity on prom night." But I want this—want *him*—so badly, I'm okay with being everybody for once. We can be everybody, can't we, and still be us? "It's only that . . ." I shrug. "We've been talking about waiting until we're ready, and now I just, I feel like I am. Ready, I mean. So ready. But only if you are," I add. "Only if you want to."

The string slides from his lip. "Of course I *want* to."

"Right! But if you'd rather wait, or you're just not feeling it tonight, that's fine. I totally understand. No pressure!" I laugh a little too loud.

And then he grabs my face in both hands and kisses me. It's so startling I make a noise, accidentally bang my nose on his glasses. But I kiss back. How could I not? His mouth isn't like a boy's. At least not how you'd think kissing a boy would feel, like sucking a closed fist. His lips are so soft. As the making out intensifies, I slowly, carefully, lift the glasses off and set them on the dewy tent floor.

Either Henry doesn't notice I've freed him from his glasses or he doesn't care. He's on top now. Heat leaps from him, our mouths smashed together, and wherever the condom tumbled is temporarily irrelevant because one feel of him through his fleecy sweatpants has me guiding his hand lower so he can feel me. Our hands move. Keep moving. Only when I'm fumbling for the condom, gasping against Henry's ear, do I realize what's happening.

"Shouldn't we . . ." I say to him. "Don't you want to . . ." Because we're so close, *I'm so close,* and what we're doing isn't sex at all. Or at least not the health-class definition of sex, the condom on and him inside me. This is watching Netflix in my living room, rubbing each other under a blanket with my parents down the hall. It's staring at pre-algebra notes while Henry nibbles my neck because his mom isn't home and I laugh like *stop* when what I mean is *don't stop*. Never stop.

So we don't.

We don't stop.

I finish first, Henry soon after, our wrists pinned, and as we whimper and sigh, I hook my other arm around him, hold on tight as I can. God.

We haven't gotten each other off using *that* particular method since we became eligible for AP classes. How come . . . why did I . . .

"Wow," Henry says into my neck. "What's the scientific explanation for why touching through our clothes can feel even better than when there aren't any?"

"Mmm, pretty sure that's called friction." My voice sounds far off, pooled in the back of my head.

Henry pulls himself up to look at me. "I thought we were going to—"

"We still can," I say quickly.

"*You* can." His blush deepens. "I need a minute."

"More like fifteen," I correct him, poking his hip. Henry reaches for the condom, setting it on me as he eases back down, the gold packet pressed between our chests like the seal on a fancy letter.

"Maybe we should wait," he says. "That felt really great just now. Didn't it?"

Objectively, but that wasn't our intention. I stroke Henry's biceps, down his back, the muscles pliant and firm from all our climbing. Soon he'll be ready again, and this time, I won't mess us up. In one instant, I'll become a Girl Who's Had Sex with Her Boyfriend. A girl who never second-guesses who she is, who she wants. So powerful and sure, nothing—nobody—can derail her.

Nearby, Henry's phone pings, lighting up with another text from Yuna: Let me know how it goes baby brother ♥. Prom, she must mean. It's 10:49. We could still be there.

As Henry scrambles for his phone, I push onto my elbows. "Do you not want to have sex because you're too freaked out about Purdy?"

"No, I . . . Hold on." He pushes his phone into his hoodie pocket. "I was down for sex. Or thought I was. You're the one who initiated the rubbing—"

"But isn't that why you wanted to leave prom early, too? It's okay. Here—" I twist my legs through his. "Climber?" Naturally, there are rules for our version of cuddling, and code names: *climber* for the person on top, *wall* for the one being smothered. Henry oofs when I pull him onto me, our bodies squashed tight and the tip of his nose icy where it lodges against my shoulder. "Next time I won't be so hard on you. About Purdy. I get that you want to be cautious. And that's good," I go on, realizing I'm babbling into his hair, that he's caught his breath but hasn't said anything. "Really good. When we revisit this conversation, after we've gotten . . . that thing you won't let me say, and we've won the scholarship and been accepted to OPI and picked out all our classes together, this will all seem hysterically funny. We'll have had plenty of sex by then. And been to senior prom, which we both know is superior anyway. Right?"

Wind paws the tent. I smooth the back of his sweatshirt. Showing him, like always, how unafraid we are. "Henry?"

I don't feel his shoulders jerking. Not until they do again. And again, and—go figure. "Hey." I pat him. Henry's most legendary bout of hiccups clocked in at exactly thirty-two minutes, but they usually strike only before exams or dentist appointments. "Do you want me to get you some water?" We shouldn't be out here much longer regardless. As he shakes his head, a drop of wet pricks my neck, and I peek instinctively at the ragged canvas above us. It's . . . raining? His shoulders heave again.

Oh.

"It's okay." Seeing is impossible, the flashlight's rolled away, lost, but I manage to find his slippery face in the dark, push back his bangs. "Shh, shh, it's okay. I'm so sorry. We don't have to—"

"Jilly . . . I—I think . . . I think that . . ." His words garble, washed away by a bellowing sob. All I can make out is ". . . gay."

Gay.

It slams into me. Knocks the breath from my lungs. Why does he think I'm . . . Because he caught me gawking at Carla? Anybody would gawk at Carla. She's got an undercut, and a gap between her front teeth that she tongues when she's thinking, and a smile like she's just woken up. *Carla* is into girls. Carla Kaminski. Congrats to her.

But I can't be gay. I'm with Henry.

I love Henry.

Henry's bawling. I haul him to me by his sweatshirt

strings. "You're wrong. I'm not gay, and I wasn't staring at Carla! I mean, I was. She's hot. It's okay for me to think another girl is hot. That doesn't mean I have"—dreams about sliding my hand between her legs and kissing—"*feelings* for her." Henry gapes. I'm clutching the strings, but he pulls away, wiping roughly at his cheeks.

"Jillian," he wails.

My breathing falters once more. *Feelings,* I said.

Feelings for her.

From the day she walked into the climbing gym. Feelings so big and new, I'm afraid I'll never know where to put them.

"Just because I want . . . I mean, I'm not . . . Even if I was . . . gay," I stammer. "A little. I mean . . . maybe. Maybe I have been questioning a little. But that doesn't mean I'd ever date a girl." I can hear my voice getting shriller, boiling up into my ears. "If I wanted that, I wouldn't be with you—"

"*I'm gay!*" Henry screams. "Me!"

I sit back. "What?"

"For fuck's sake, that's what I'm trying to tell you! Have been trying to tell you for months. Literally months. But the time was never right, and then it started feeling like it was too late, but ever since we submitted our Purdy applications, I just . . . I couldn't . . . And now you're telling me that you're also— Hey!"

I don't know where he found the flashlight, but he shouldn't have it. Not now. I wrestle it from him and fold over. This is not happening. Not like this, with too many gummy bears swimming in my stomach and my parents doz-ing to *Saturday Night Live* reruns, like, a hundred feet away. "Okay," I start murmuring. "Okay, okay . . ." I'm working out where to put this new information, probing for its right-ful place in the story of us that has only ever been right. Only been safe.

Except now I'm laughing. Smearing at the hair snagged across my eyes. "That's fine," I howl.

We're going to be so fine.

There's this look Henry gets when he's feeling especially terrible. A look I haven't seen since his dad moved out this past fall and texted him the news while we were filing into the cafeteria. One glance at him then, the hollowed-out white-ness of his face, and I knew he was going to barf. Threw my lunchbox down and lunged, caught the splatter in my hands.

Tonight there is no splatter. No shrieks from grossed-out freshmen or playing with his hair in the nurse's office, waiting for his mom to pick him up. He whips the tent open—*zzzzzzzttttttttt*—

And runs.

3.

WHEN I CREAK INTO the kitchen the next morning, my parents' heads snap up instantaneously.

"Jilly!" Mom beams. "How was prom? I tried so hard to stay up and wait for you, but you know how it goes. The second my head hits the pillow . . ."

Caffeine calls. I spoon as many grounds into the coffee maker as the basket can hold, then fill the pot with water. Mom stares at me instead of at the case notes fanned across the table. Inconvenient. But then, if I hadn't come down of my own free will, she would've barged into my room to have this conversation anyway. My parents—I swear, sometimes making an appearance is the only way to avoid them. "Great," I say. Then, since maybe that didn't come out so convincing, "Really great."

"Is Minjun still upstairs?" Mom asks, careful to pronounce the second syllable *june*.

I slam the coffeepot down.

"Jillian! Don't—"

"Mom, for the last time, call him Henry." The only people who don't are subs calling roll on their first day. I set the coffeepot back gently, willing myself smooth. No cracks as I say, "That's what he prefers."

"Well, what does his birth certificate say?"

"Minjun, but—"

"So that's his name, then. Case closed."

Without looking up from his files, Dad says, "Calling him Henry is imperialist, honey."

Mom nods. "There's no reason we can't make an effort to pronounce his Korean name correctly."

My parents are social workers. Obsessed with allyship, but in this overeager-progressive-white-people way that can ignore Henry's needs and wishes. As the coffeepot fills, drip by agonizing drip, my sticky eyes roam across dishes, streaked with syrup and waffle tufts, stacked in the sink. I peek at my phone.

Nothing.

HENRY???? I text.

"What was the theme again?" Mom asks.

My fingers squelch on the faucet knob, also coated in syrup. Thanks, Garrett. "Theme . . . ?" Oh. We've swerved back to prom. "A Night Under the Sea," I recite. Water clatters over the dishes. I blast the petrified sponge with Dawn and start scrubbing.

"That's right!" Mom says. "I keep forgetting. Did anybody compliment your dress? I still can't believe what a

25

bargain that was. You couldn't have looked more beautiful. And Minjun! So handsome. It's a shame he was running late. We barely had any time for pictures. I was thinking we could print one of them out, get it framed. Wouldn't that make such a nice gift for Henry and his mom?"

I slot the last plate into the drying rack, grinding my soapy palms against the counter where she won't see.

Last night, after Henry ran, I did, too. Screamed for him to wait, to stop, to just . . . *anything*. But he's so fast. He's always been so fast, and the road has no shoulder. I was in my bare feet. No surprise he hit the trees before I did, or that they swallowed him up. But he'd be back any second. That's what I told myself. I told myself, *He won't leave me here.* Not in the middle of a blacked-out road, where headlights could come blasting at any second. *Gay.* The word knocked around inside me. *Henry. Gay.* Gnats ricocheted off my cheeks.

I remembered what I'd blurted first, the hugeness of it. More enormous than I could ever take back.

And then I did the unthinkable. The second most unprecedented move, after his.

I surrendered. Tapped out.

Quit.

At home, I snatched up our prom clothes and shoveled them into my room, certain they were evidence of something, except I was sobbing by then, so it was hard to know what. Now, as my parents burrow back into the paperwork, I confront the tent, framed neatly by the window above the sink. The flap lolls open.

Okay. Henry ran. Ran away from *me,* and maybe I reciprocated, but there's no problem we can't solve by turning to each other. No reason to tell my parents what happened, when their relentless insistence on Garrett and me *feeling our feelings* makes everything an emotional emergency. I'll figure this out on my own. If I could just find Henry . . .

"Perfect," I choke out.

Wryly, Dad says, "Seems like somebody had a little *too* much fun."

Mom shoots him a look as she gets my favorite bunny mug down from the cabinet. "Ohh, so that's why you didn't wake me up when you got home."

"Dad," I say. "You picked us up. We weren't drunk—"

"Oh, honey, you're teenagers. It's normal. Next time, drink vodka. We won't smell it on your breath." Mom winks.

I shut my eyes. Soon my parents will pack up their files. While Mom heads to the clinic, Dad will take Garrett to his climbing class to spare me from what my father thinks is just the pain of post-prom functioning, and by then Henry will have returned my texts. We'll get into my bed and press our noses close like nothing happened, because we're in love and cosmically bound by Purdy, and what I told him last night—what we told each other—contradicts these basic facts.

Shakily, I text: pls pls pls call me so I can at least know you're not dead?!?!?!?!?

27

This is the Hudson Valley. Land of careening turns and black bears.

Mom sets my mug on the counter beside me and gathers my hair back from my face, her smile a little sadder now. "Are you sure you're okay? Where *is* Minjun? I hope he's not too hungover."

Right. No escaping the inquisition. The most I can do is try not to flinch as Mom strains my fuzzy curls through her fingers. This is what I get for sleeping on them wet. "I'm fine, Mom. Just tired. And Henry left already. He . . . had to go do something. For his mom."

She frowns. "His sneakers are still here."

Which, I don't know, seems like the inevitable consequence of blasting from a tent in sweatpants and crew socks, but what does she expect me to say? *Sorry, Mom, but we just came out to each other simultaneously?* Henry can't use the bathroom at school without telling me where he'll be. He's the most accountable kid on the planet.

Also, I didn't come out for real.

Did I?

My phone buzzes and I jerk away, plunging a hand into my sweatshirt pocket. "It was an emergency. But don't worry! Everything's good now. Prom was just so magical!"

"Well . . ." Mom forces a laugh. For a therapist, she's having an outrageously difficult time *processing* how not into this conversation I am. "Alcohol has been known to inflame passions. If you got into a fight—"

"*Mom.*"

"—you can fill me in on all the details after you've recovered."

Once she returns to the table, I swipe frantically at Henry's reply.

🍕 🍕 🍕 😵 😤 😿 ☠️

Great.

4.

HENRY DOESN'T SEEM SURPRISED when I ambush him on the sidewalk outside the pizzeria. Why should he be? Five p.m. is when he always gets off work. But my heart makes the *most* extreme racket as I follow him to Ms. Yoo's beat-up Civic, aka Purple Monster, aka Big Purp. Tootsie Pop wrappers tumble from Henry's apron while he moves his mom's crap to the back seat.

"You know I can't use my phone at work."

I blink. Henry's walked around to the driver's side, bangs smashed to his forehead beneath a backward Atlanta Dream cap. "What?" I say.

"You think I was ignoring you, but my breaks are, like, barely anything, and we got slammed for lunch, and—what was I going to do? My boss is strict as hell."

"I didn't say you were ignoring me." Haven't said a word, in fact, since I spotted him slumping out of the pizzeria, his face the color of wet paper.

"Okay." He swings the door open, startling a bunch of

crows on the I LOVE NEW YORK PIZZA sign behind him. "Not out loud, but whatever."

Tonight's too cold for being almost June, the sky over the strip mall stiff blue. A glimpse at the rearview mirror suggests I've shredded my lips, even though that's more Henry's style.

I take a breath. "You haven't answered my texts since your emoji onslaught at ten-forty-two this morning. The last time you went that long without answering, you were having your appendix removed. And your boss isn't that much of a jerk. He doesn't care when you sneak me free onion rings. Or that we make out constantly in the break room."

Henry flushes. Crows caw and flap.

"Whatever," he repeats.

My shorts are sucked into my crotch. I tug them free as Henry plops sideways in the driver's seat, toeing off his ragged Pumas. "Tell me you didn't run here," he says.

"What if I did?"

He recoils.

"That's only five miles. Five and a quarter, tops." Except I forgot to rub coconut oil on my thighs, so now I'm basically bleeding. I stand with my legs apart, ventilating, while he chucks his shoes in the back and produces sandals, swatting sock fuzz from his toes. "My parents needed the car for some social-worker banquet thing, and I couldn't wait around my house for you anymore, and . . . I needed to see you. So."

Henry bends to slip on his sandals, and I pin my finger to the bridge of his glasses. Sometimes only teamwork keeps them on his nose. "What's the plan, then?" he murmurs as my finger stays put. "You're here. Now what?"

My tongue thickens. Like it isn't obvious why I'm here. I'm going to pull him into the back seat and whisper all the reasons last night can't change us. He'll agree because . . .

Because he has to.

Henry waits, his expression one of polite disdain reserved for complaints about insufficient pepperoni. "Let me guess," he says when I don't answer. "More secrets you're burning to tell me?"

Secrets? I take my finger away. "You're one to talk."

But then, who cares who said what when the whole night felt so wrong? Slapping after him through the wet grass. The darkness slashed with my shouts and the white banner of his hoodie. Henry must be thinking the same. He softens.

Something goes limp inside me, too.

"You ran," I say. "You ran. And now you're being . . ." He rises from the driver's seat. "You're being a colossal asshole—"

"Jill." He grabs my shoulders. "I was trying to come out to you and learned we might both be gay instead. What did you want me to do?"

We might both be gay.

Last night, it wasn't like the significance skidded past me. But hearing him say it now makes me start roaring all over again. The same wild, heaping laughter that spilled from me in the tent. Am I gay? And if he is, too . . .

"It would make sense." I say this a bunch of times.

"Wouldn't it just make so much sense?" We've always been sealed together. Every beat of us the same.

His grip loosens when I tell him so.

"We're not always the same," he says.

"Yes, we are! I mean," I stumble, as his eyes narrow, "I'm white and you're Korean, and we've had some very different experiences because of that, but that's not what I'm talking about. I'm talking about *us*. This can't—it's not going to affect our relationship. Tell me you understand that." He backs up. "Henry."

A tectonic shiver through my chest.

"Henry. Please."

I've told him this, and can't now, but he resembles Ms. Yoo way more than his dad. They have the same wide-set eyes and tousled hair and way of sucking their lips when they're thinking. Finally he steps close again. A breeze brushes between us, carrying the slithery green stink of the river.

"Let me take you home," he says.

5.

"CLIMBER OR WALL?"

Evening sun sears my eyes.

"Jillian?"

My hands a soggy tangle in my lap.

"Hello?"

Henry hovers in front of me. I count, then recount, the climbing ribbons tacked to the corkboard behind his head. Thirteen.

"Wall," I answer.

It feels strange to be doing this after our fidgety car ride home. Henry also seems uncertain, and fear flares through me, like he's only offering out of obligation, not because he wants to. But my bed grumbles and creaks as I lie back. Creaks even more raucously once I'm situated and Henry spreads his full weight on top of me. His legs cover mine, arms too, so heavy and familiar that the darkness of not knowing squeezes right out of me. He twines our fingers together, and it's like growing roots. I turn my head, exposing a cheek for him to squash under his. One to one. That's the rule. The way everything should be.

On the nightstand, just visible over the ridge of my pillow: Henry's crumpled tux jacket. Nintendo Switch controllers. Notebooks and ChapStick. A tiny sapphire ring Grandma B got me for my seventeenth birthday that I like but never wear, since jewelry isn't really for me anymore, but I haven't gotten around to telling everybody. Maybe by September, when Henry and I turn eighteen.

He sighs. Or I do. This rush of warmth across my lips.

"You smell like a grease trap," I inform him.

"Fun fact. Like, forty percent of I Love's revenue comes from mozzarella sticks alone."

"Sorry—*alone*?"

"Right, let me amend that. Mozzarella sticks with"— an alarmingly convincing dry heave—"raspberry sauce. Oh God." He shudders. "Nope. Can't do it. I still can't pretend that's acceptable."

Carefully I tip his sweaty hat up with my finger and flick it to the carpet. I run my knuckles down his neck, which must feel good, because he doesn't stop me.

"I'm sorry," Henry says.

I can sense the breath he's holding—my own is hunkered in my belly.

"You're right. I shouldn't have run from you. I could've made more of an effort to text you back while I was at work. That was intensely crappy of me. But it's not like I was trying to ice you out."

"Really." I drop my hand to the mattress. "What was the plan, then?"

If Henry realizes I'm mocking him, he doesn't call me on it. "I don't know."

"Bullshit. There's always—"

"A plan, I know, but this time there wasn't. For the record, I didn't *want* to run. Too much was happening all at once. My feet made the decision without me." He looks away, and . . . it could be my imagination. A trick of the blaring sunlight. But stiffness flickers over him, just like in the I Love's parking lot. "I think I just needed space."

"Yeah," I say. When what I mean is, *Look at us. My little bed.*

We don't do space.

Across the hall, Garrett's playing *Zelda*. His sword clanks as he dies and restarts the dungeon again and again. I shift up slightly, confirming that the door to our shared bathroom is closed. Words come rushing. "You should've seen my parents this morning. I did my best to fend them off, but my mom's convinced we came home wasted and got into a fight." Saying one thing while my eyes ask another: *Are we?*

"God," he huffs. "That's so not what this is. We never fight."

Of course we don't. Of course we wouldn't—that's the first rule of us, and the second and the third, so I don't exactly require confirmation.

But it's nice to hear him say it.

"Anyway," Henry says. Real Henry. "I'm ready to talk now, if you are."

I nod against the pillow.

"Great. So." He nibbles his lip. "How long have you known you're into girls?"

I've been staring at Henry's jacket putrefying on my nightstand. My dress on the carpet, pearly-pink fabric lapped with deodorant stains. Then Henry turns my chin, and it's only him I'm seeing.

"You first?" I wince. Then I'll know precisely what to say. I'll know how to reveal the truth without exposing myself as a fraud.

"See, it's funny, because I thought the whole reason we were here is because I'm *not* into girls—"

I sock him.

"Okay, okay, ow." He shrugs, miserable. "It's hard to say. I mean, my family's kind of traditional, so it's not like I've been exposed to legions of positive gay role models throughout my childhood or whatever, let alone met another gay Korean person in real life. But I've sort of always had this idea that I might be gay, to be completely honest. Even longer"—his voice wobbles—"longer than I've known you." Somehow I resist pointing out why this is inaccurate. We've known each other forever. Met literally the day he moved to shitty, pointless Elmerville from Savannah, Georgia. I've only been questioning for—

"Your turn," he says.

I press my eyes shut. "Three months."

Which is precisely what makes this such a mistake. Exactly one of many reasons I wish I could cram every last word I said about Carla back where it came from. Henry hasn't said he wants that, but he must. We don't *do* messes. We don't do mistakes.

Or so I believed.

"That's why you've been so weird about Purdy," I say hoarsely, changing the subject. "You regret doing it. After all our hard work, the plans we've made, you never actually wanted—"

"No, Jillian, Jesus! It's just the opposite! Why do you think I've been so scared to come out to you? Because of this. Exactly *this*. I love you. You're everything. Purdy is everything, but the farther we got into the process, the more my anxiety ramped up because . . ." He wipes his eyes on my pillow. "I don't know. It felt so huge. Plotting out the rest of our lives before we've gotten the chance to fully explore who we are. That's why I asked if you were scared."

Plotting . . . ? Purdy isn't a plot.

Purdy is destiny.

It has to be.

"I told you," I say. "I don't want a girlfriend."

Henry nibbles his lip for another moment. Then he leans so our noses are touching. "Stop."

"Stop what? I'm—"

"When the daddy longlegs took over the tent, you claimed you weren't afraid of them but didn't help me pick a single one of them off. You *say* you like mung bean sprouts, but when my mom serves them, it's like you suddenly can't see that they're on the table. You've never tasted a mung bean sprout in your life, Jillian Leigh Bortles. That's a fact. And, yeah, maybe you've never admitted that out loud, but

I know you better than anybody else does. I know that a lot of the time, the stuff you sound most certain about secretly indicates the opposite. So don't act like you don't have a crush on Carla Kaminski. Don't act like when I called you out for staring at her at prom, that was the first time I ever noticed it. Because when you say"—his legs lasso me—"that you don't *want* to date a girl"—I yank free to whack his shoulder—"what you really mean is—"

"*Fine!*"

"Fine what?"

I say it.

I whisper, "I want to date a girl."

Henry eases off, and we sit up, my mind reeling.

This curiosity I've been fighting could become more than daydreams. More than movies my hands play when they're roaming and I can't sleep. I could be with a girl. Her hands could be under my clothes. I could kiss a girl on the mouth and press as close to her as Henry and I just were, even though admitting to that want a moment ago nearly atomized me and there's no telling where it might lead. If I didn't come out all the way in the tent, I absolutely have now. "Okay, so . . ." I look at Henry, my smile wilty. "What's next?"

"Jillian." He swallows. "You know what."

And then my bedroom tilts and his lips are against mine and it's almost a real kiss, with spit and everything, because I drool when I cry. I wrench my phone from my waistband, summoning the lock screen. *Purdy scholars are college-bound* . . . "And sometimes," Henry's saying, "I feel like

I'll forget how to breathe if you're not right beside me, but the truth of the matter is that you have these feelings for girls, right? And I have feelings for boys." . . . *high school students and residents of New York State who demonstrate exceptional well-roundedness and merit* . . . "Feelings we haven't been able to explore because we're so wrapped up in each other . . ." I mouth *Purdy,* blotting him out, my lungs no longer functioning, but that's okay, it's perfect, since this is the only oxygen I need: *Purdy scholars are self-starters, motivated, ambitious, and curious. The ideal candidate possesses these and other immutable characteristics consistent with—*

"Domination," Henry finishes, covering my screen. "Of college and life." I scrub at my nose, grateful he at least quit speechifying to finish the Purdy Creed with me. Including our improvised ending.

My bed gives a fantastic creak as he rolls closer. We rope our arms around each other and he pushes his face into my neck and we just . . . breathe. His socks chafe my ankles. He put them on inside out again.

"We have to do Purdy," I say.

Henry tips back, studying me. "How?"

"I . . ." Don't know. I don't know I don't know I don't know. Just that the alternative is impossible: a world without Henry. A world where us splitting means breaking up with the future, too. "Think about it. We've worked our asses off. And wanting to go to the same school, majoring in game design—none of that's changed."

"Okay . . ." Henry pushes onto an elbow, getting pumped.

"Okay, right, that's true. We'd never be able to attend OPI without that money, anyway."

"Exactly."

"And no matter what, we'll always be best friends," he says.

Softly, I add, "Everything like it was."

Henry nods, and I burrow against his chest where the fryer smell is particularly pungent, zested with armpit. He tucks my hair behind my ear as best he can with most of it snarled beneath me. Doing what he couldn't yesterday—joining his want with mine to heal the galactic rift that coming out tore between us. As scary as it is, I can already see the new world taking shape between our stitching.

Henry and me as friends. *Best* friends.

A girl.

With me.

Gradually our breathing slows. We gaze at each other across the daisies that dot my pillowcase.

"You really mean it," I say. "Nothing else will change between us."

His lips part, but before he can answer, I'm remembering the summer before seventh grade. The summer Henry moved here. The summer my family started renting this house. We were between leases, crashing with my parents' colleague Ms. Henderson on the way other side of town, when she mentioned the new family across the street from her. *A mom and a dad*, she said. *And a boy who seems about your age, Jilly.* She paused, then added, *I'm not sure they speak much English.*

Except I'd already spied on the boy and his dad playing basketball in their shady new driveway, the dad demonstrating how to arc a shot so the ball went in every time. *You can do this,* he kept saying, ruffling his son's hair. *You'll get it if you practice.*

Obviously, Ms. Henderson was racist.

That afternoon, I was scraping at the sidewalk with chunks of old chalk Ms. Henderson kept for her grandkids, when I glanced up and found him there. Toes lined up with the curb, a grin tugging shyly at his face, like he knew it was rude to watch over my shoulder but couldn't help himself.

Now Henry smiles this ragged smile and says, "I mean, obviously, we should . . . We can't keep messing around. Getting each other off and stuff. So there is one more change."

I think of us in the tent. The condom I pushed back into my sock drawer, one more piece of us flung away. "I can . . . I can live with that."

"Same." A spluttery laugh. "Like, I'm pretty sure *not messing around* is the definition of being broken up?"

"You'd think? But tell that to our illustrious peers." I sit up. "Promise me, Henry. Promise we'll make this work and won't turn into an absolute conflagration like every last couple at school becomes after they break up. Wait"—I reach around him, scrabbling for a notebook on my nightstand—"we'll write it down. No fighting—that's a given. No messing around . . . no more running. Um, what else? We've got to prioritize Purdy—"

He clasps my hand. "That's perfect. Remember what you asked me at prom? If I believed in us? Here's the deal:

We're awesome. Nothing like those fools. I have more faith in us than anybody, anything else. We can totally be normal friends."

When we met, he didn't make fun of me for playing with chalk, even though we were way too old. He grabbed a piece to finish the line I'd just started—the beginning strokes of a dog. But I could see that what he had in mind was better. *A kappa*, he explained. *It's a type of demon—I saw it on YouTube. When you go into the water, it swims up and yanks your soul out of your butthole, so now I'm not going swimming anymore unless I one hundred percent have to.*

That's when I knew we were the same.

It's simple. Other kids at school fuck up their relationships because they're not us. Not Purdys. They won't look out their bedroom windows tonight and think, *There aren't as many stars as we have plans.*

Sucks for them.

I push Henry back onto the bed, lowering myself toward him until our noses bend.

"One hundred percent," I say.

#1—NO FIGHTING

#2—NO MESSING AROUND

#3—NO MORE RUNNING

#4—PURDY FIRST

6.

THE ROUTE TO SCHOOL goes like this: Trees. Driveway.
Trees.

Trees.

Trees.

Elmerville is irrefutably the worst part of New York. Too
far north for day trips to the city, but perfectly situated to
receive metric fuck tons of snow through April. Henry texts
that he's running late (my mom's gonna drop me off on her way
to the hospital sry!!!!!!), and my parents have already left with
Garrett, so I jog to avoid taking the bus alone. Another cool
morning. Pavement laced with pollen, clouds wispy like a
word you've forgotten, fizzing on your tongue. I stick to the
road's edge, safe from potholes but not multiple plowed-over
mailboxes, looming in my peripheral vision with major guy-
hitting-on-me-at-a-gas-station energy. Around here you're
never safe from winter.

A block from the school, I force myself to walk. It's awkward enough being one of, like, five almost-seniors without

a car; getting spotted running in jeans, my backpack bouncing off my butt, would only cement my reputation.

I hit the drop-off circle just as Henry emerges from Big Purp, juggling his backpack and two trifolds and speaking Korean. I take one of the posters, then wave to Ms. Yoo, who smiles and toasts me with her giant Thermos, her seat belt wrinkling her scrubs.

"Morning, Jillian," she says. Like this is any other day.

"Morning," I say back.

Like I believe her.

Once she drives off, Henry turns to me. His smile ragged like yesterday, and shy, but . . . trying. He's trying. Air inches back into my lungs.

"So," I say.

He hefts his backpack. "So."

"First day back since we . . ."

"Dumped each other?" he finishes quietly.

"Yeah." Yesterday, Sunday, was easier. Our designated homework day. Projects for AP Rhetoric and AP US History, and on top of that Henry booked with church and youth group. At school, distractions aren't so abundant. These last days before summer are painful enough without every step toward the entrance whittling another layer of my skin away. Our classmates are in there—kids who probably saw us at prom, who have only known me with Henry. I grab his wrist. "Wait."

The other late drop-offs filter past us until we're alone save for a groundskeeper and one extremely persistent Weedwacker. Henry's eyebrows prick expectantly.

I say, "You're identifying as gay now."

"Yes?" He looks perplexed.

"What about me? What do I call myself?" Over the weekend, there were moments when the labels I tried on—*gay, bi, pan*—seemed to fit, and other moments when they squeezed and slipped like Grandma's ring. How could he identify as gay so readily? We're in love with each other. We've been physically intimate. And obviously that doesn't mean he can't be gay any more than it means I'm not, but this is all so new and confusing, and I've never felt so unsure. "What if 'gay' isn't right?"

"It doesn't have to be," Henry says. "You don't have to call yourself anything until you're ready. Or even have any label at all, if that works for you. I'm going with 'gay' because it feels right for me. That might change someday. I really can't say for certain. But there's, like, a million different accounts and subreddits devoted to this stuff. I'll send you some links." He takes his poster from me, bundling it under his arm. "Shall we?"

I get that by offering resources, he's trying to help. But the fact that he's done research on his own is extra disorienting.

You don't have to call yourself anything. I picture Henry's proclamation bannering the poster—*That might change someday*—in his crowded lefty writing.

When will I know? I want to demand. *How? Tell me the steps.* "I'll be gay," I say.

"You don't have to—"

"No, for real. If that's what you're comfortable with, then, yeah. Me too." The same.

47

Henry tugs me forward—"Great, sure, if that's what you want"—and I realize with a jolt we're holding hands.

Is *that* okay . . . ?

When I ask, Henry replies, "Hmm, let's find out. Hey, Siri?" he says into his phone. "Is holding hands sex?"

I shove him. "The rule is broader than sex—"

"Wow, Siri, thanks." He looks to me. "She says it's cool as long as nobody gets a boner."

Okay. Yeah. Maybe I *am* being overly technical. We just don't know how to walk into school any other way, and it is probably simpler—for processing purposes—if we don't overhaul our *entire* existence any more than we already have. Better to let the newness build so microscopically that we won't notice the pain. "I hate when you're right," I say. Henry pulls me after him.

On the last step, his phone chirps. Probably an ad for a Nintendo Switch Online subscription our parents won't let us get anyway, but whatever. We're unfailingly fastidious about email. Grinning, he thumbs the screen. "You *love* me. Thus our continued endeavor."

As I roll my eyes, a girl strides around us—one of, like, three freshmen who stand out enough to consistently identify. Her pink hair's in French braids, and she's wearing a sweatshirt that says HEY THERE. And a rainbow choker that catches at my own throat.

When I glance back at Henry, his grin's vanished with her.

"What's wrong?" I ask.

He's staring at his phone.

"Henry?" I say nervously. "What is it? Come on. Let me . . ." Prying his phone from him requires less force than expected. I almost punch it through my teeth.

The email begins, Dear Scholarship Candidate, we regret to inform you . . .

From the depths of my backpack, my own phone dings.

7.

WE'VE ENDURED BOTH PRESENTATIONS, a fire drill, and one extremely unnecessary rainbow-flame chemistry demonstration before we're able to reconvene for lunch. We huddle in the back of the library, where we've eaten since the barf incident, unnoticed in the Reference section's dusty wilderness.

"I give up." Henry tosses his phone into his bag. "If there was a way around the school's content blockers, everybody would know it."

I refresh my browser only to confront the same message: *WEBSITE UNAVAILABLE.* "Okay, this is exactly why Albany County Community College's coding camp should offer financial assistance— *Don't,*" I warn. Henry sucks his cheeks, clearly in agony. But a speech on why hacking and coding are different skill sets is not what either of us deserves right now. "What kind of school doesn't trust their own students to access *any* apps or websites? Do our parents' tax dollars pay for this? It's freaking diabolical."

Henry says, "If we can't access Purdy's website to double-check the criteria—"

"There's no *double-checking*," I insist. "It's a mistake. There must've been some kind of processing error on their end."

"We could get passes to the guidance office," he goes on, not listening. "But we'd need an appointment. . . . Wait." He lunges for his phone. "The computers. I heard the guidance computers' filters are more lenient—"

"You need an appointment for the lab, too." All we can access on school grounds, besides our student portals, is Beaver Mail, which seems like the worst part of having a beaver for a mascot until you meet somebody from another school and remember the entire county calls you the Crotches. While Henry mauls his lip, I surrender once more to the message on my screen:

Dear Scholarship Candidate,

We regret to inform you that, based on your current academic and extracurricular credit status, you are among the disproportionate number of students applying this year who have failed to adequately demonstrate WELL-ROUNDEDNESS, a core tenet of the educational philosophy of our founder, the late Lucille M. Purdy. All applicants have until September 5 to furnish proof that this requirement has been met. Until then, you will remain ineligible for the Lucille M. Purdy Memorial Scholarship.

Please be aware that the Purdy Foundation celebrates the uniqueness of every student. Therefore, what constitutes "well-roundedness" will vary tremendously among applicants. For a sampling of approved classes, clubs, and activities that might fulfill this need, click _here_.

Henry taps the link over my shoulder.
WEBSITE UNAVAILABLE.
"Fuck," he says.

I bury my head between my knees, scouring my mental Purdy index for any restrictions or parameters we could've overlooked. "There's no way. We've taken so many different classes—*two* English electives in addition to all the cores. And Human Physiology . . ."

"All those recommendations," Henry whispers, dangerously close to tears. "The interviews. Our final essays. All that amounts to shit now? Because of some random technicality? The school year ends in two weeks, and after that . . . in August we're supposed to . . . We don't have *time* to take more credits."

I stay folded over, working so hard not to cry in public that I don't point out he nearly broke his own rule about The Call. Blood beats at my temples. "I told you, it's got to be—"

A burst of laughter from Nonfiction, wispy and husky all at once. I don't need to look up to know whose it is.

But I do.

"Oh my God, stop." Carla rounds the shelves with a giant art portfolio slung over her shoulder, flanked by Libby

Joseph, who's fumbling to tie back her locs. Both girls are less than twenty feet away, oblivious to us hunkered behind a table of freshman ceramics projects. Through my swaying curls, I can just make out the little whorl of hair on the back of Carla's head. Paint on her fingertips red as my face must be.

Henry plucks my sleeve. I can't tell if he's been watching me. "Got to be what?"

"A *mis . . .*" The word gives way. "Mistake." Our lunches—sweaty off-brand sports drinks from the cafeteria vending machines, the noodles and veggies Henry didn't touch—are strewn around us like unfinished thoughts. Mechanically, I pile my yogurt cup into a Ziploc. "We'll just have to wait until we get home to write back. Remember when we needed help understanding our parents' tax documents? That lady was a Purdy oracle."

Carla and Libby stray closer, their giggles pinging off the shelves. Henry's mouth tightens. He whips out his trig notebook and scrawls: *Next we'll??????* Then the pencil's in my hand: Wat

LIKE IF THAT DOESN'T WORK

IF IT ISN'T A MISTAKE

"A for effort, Libs," Carla's saying, "but you know I can't tell Bea that."

"Why not?" Libby asks.

This angle is ideal. Bisected by ceramic bowls and table

legs, only chunky vegan boots visible until I tilt my head to catch the girls' faces, too. Carla frowns, her upper lip wrinkling. "It's rude."

"Bea is rude," Libby says. "She's ignoring you."

Carla pushes a hand through her choppy hair. I clutch my jeans.

How does she identify? Gay? Something else? As far as I know, she's only dated girls. And if I'm gay, the next person I date will probably have to be a girl, so . . .

Case closed?

"Jillian," Henry hisses.

I drag my focus back to the notebook open across our knees, its spill of triangles and formulas somehow more coherent to me than what I thought, until seventy-two hours ago, was the only intelligible part of my life. Henry scribbles onward, not bothering to hide his frustration. The steadiest, most dependable person I've ever known. As Carla turns away—this graceful slide toward Libby, who's calling her name—I command myself to breathe.

Purdy first, we said.

Henry's pencil scratches determinedly across the paper. I snatch it from him and write: WE WILL FIGURE IT OUT TONIGHT! He reads the words and nods, his sweatshirt cuff pressed to his mouth.

If breaking up couldn't stop us, one email certainly won't.

8.

I'M MAKING A LIST of symbols in *The Awakening* when Dad pops in. "Hey, Jilly Bean. Dinner in thirty, okay?"

"Okay." My desk faces the wall. I keep my head down, extremely busy.

"It's ziti night."

My parents alternate evening shifts at the methadone clinic they run in Albany, meaning dinner duty alternates between them. "Sounds great, Dad." Every night is pasta night when he cooks. Not because he's bad at cooking but because Grandma B ordered family DNA kits and now he's convinced we're Italian instead of whatever Bortles actually is. Not that I'm complaining. I'll take ziti over Mom-versus-microwave any day.

I cap my pen. This list is going exactly nowhere. You shouldn't be allowed to have your hero die on the last page. That's worse than learning it was all a dream. Worse than not finishing the story at all.

Dad reads my laptop screen over my shoulder. "Kate Chopin." He smiles. "Don't know her."

"*Chopin,*" I correct his pronunciation, all phlegmy and French. He laughs. I'm shit at languages. The one *W*, for *withdrawn,* on my transcript proves it.

I should be having nightmares in Mandarin.

"Minjun had to go?"

"Dad, it's Monday. He just came by to get his tux and help with that email." An exquisitely persuasive letter to Purdy's administrative assistant explaining her error, which, knowing her response time, she's bound to answer any—Wait. I haven't checked my email in at least five minutes.

A furtive tap on my phone reveals only my lock screen. The Purdy Creed.

My eyes burn.

If only Henry could've stayed.

Except of all Ms. Yoo's rules, *No Jillian on school nights* has the fewest workarounds. During his last bout of strep throat, she left the hospital early to pick up his schoolwork instead of letting me bring it over. So.

"Ah," Dad says. "Sorry to hear about your scholarship trouble. Sounds like you two have that covered, though."

"Yup." I type some more. Random key stabbing. Translation: *Go away*. But a glance over my shoulder reveals that Dad's escalated from hovering to sitting—*fully* sitting on my bed. Legs crossed, slipper dangling off one foot and everything.

Softly he asks, "Is that all that's bothering you?"

My teeth clench. In the Bortles household, there aren't invitations to share. More like expectations. And while I get how lucky I am to have parents who listen, their exuberant embrace of whatever I tell them, their commitment to being a *safe space*—whether affirming the tantrums I spontaneously developed when I was ten and sick of moving so much, or supporting Garrett's exploration of veganism that ended faster than we learned to pronounce *tempeh*—suffocates me.

"There's a girl," I say, realizing as the words muscle out that they're not at all Carla-related, but instead about the freshman with the rainbow choker. "She . . . It's that . . . She had this . . ."

"What is it?" Dad frowns. "She likes Minjun? Is that why you guys fought?"

"No!" I cry. "We didn't—"

"What, then? I'm here for you. Tell me."

Which is all I need to hear to know exactly where this conversation is headed. I'll explain about the rainbow choker and he'll ask why that matters and I'll say, *Well, I kind of like girls, too,* and he'll go on Amazon and order one for me immediately. After he tells my mom. And she tells Garrett. And next I know, they'll be adding not just a choker to the cart but pride flags and rainbow stickers and GAY AF T-shirts to plaster on all our beings. Not that there's anything objectively wrong with that stuff. But I just acknowledged to *myself* that wanting anybody but Henry was a possibility. Now that I have, I deserve a chance to figure out what that means on my own, without my parents deciding for me.

I swivel back to my computer. "Nothing. We're doing a group project. I wanted to tell you in case I need to stay after."

Dad pats my shoulder. I can tell he's disappointed. "It's good to see that you and Minjun have made up. Maybe he can join us on Friday."

I nod.

He presses my door shut on his way out.

Once I'm sure Dad's actually gone, not lingering in the hall like some weirdo, I push my notebook aside and refresh my in-box.

Empty.

I might not make it until we hear back lol, I text Henry. He replies instantly, and the power of that alone pushes a grin onto my face.

> Yeahhhh
>
> U look at the link btw?

> > What link

> omg the one in the email
>
> With all the "well-roundedness" options or w/e

> > Oh.
> >
> > Nope.
> >
> > I told u
> >
> > We've taken so much freaking English
> >
> > We did NOT read heart of darkness for nothing

Ok but I JUST checked

And Purdy defines well-roundedness as exploring

something DIFFERENT from all the other stuff you do

So our billion English credits don't count.

In fact we took too much English

Sry to tell you

He picks up on the first ring. "Jilly—"

"Too much? What are you talking about?"

"Just look at the—"

"I'm going!" I pull the email up on my laptop, then jab here. Nothing screams URGENT like abusing a touch screen. "Okay, it says: 'Well-roundedness comprises a vast array of content areas available to students across New York State seeking to expand their horizons academically, creatively, and/or recreationally through various school-sanctioned offerings.' . . . Blah blah blah . . ." I scroll and scroll, back-handing to the very bottom of the page, where content areas are displayed. A blaze of terms like *Drama* and *Creative Writing* and *Club Sports*.

"This is ridiculous. How can the same requirement be fulfilled by a class *or* an extracurricular?" I close my laptop and rest my cheek on top, consoling myself with its heat and stench of burnt dust. From the sound of Henry's voice, he's gone horizontal, too.

"I don't get it, either, but I just got an email from Ms. Vincent." Henry's guidance counselor, who advises students whose last names start with *N* to *Z*. "She's squeezing me in for an emergency appointment first thing tomorrow."

"How?"

"Jillian, she got her parakeet's birthday added to morning announcements last month. Does she seem like a prime candidate for 'having a life' to you?"

"No, I mean . . ." My jaw aches. "The requirements. We read them all. We were so sure."

"Yeah, so I'm going to go ahead and declare that officially irrelevant at this point? Yes, we screwed up, but it's not like a terminal screwup. According to Vincent, we have plenty of options, so you should email your guidance dude now. I got lucky. Maybe he can fit you in, too."

Because that's exactly what I need. The same guidance counselor who told me in freshman year that I'd make an *exceptional nurse* advising me on well-roundedness. A concept that, according to Purdy, can mean anything, and yet literally nothing we've done.

My cheek remains glued to my laptop. The fan buzzes, billowing dust at me. I can't tell if I'm supposed to be crying or just really have to sneeze. "Right," I say.

After that, we're both quiet—almost. There's the faintest shifting on his end. This click his throat makes when he's working up to something.

"Jill? Can I ask a question?"

"Climbing's out," I answer. "The website explicitly says 'school-sanctioned.' "

He hesitates. "More like an unrelated question. Now that we've gotten Purdy out of the way."

We emphatically haven't, but whatever. I wish he could

be here. I wish we could be playing video games, losing ourselves in some other world with boundaries that the developers have already defined, where none of our choices leak into reality.

Sure, I tell him.

"Great. Okay." His breath whooshes in my ear. "So I'm just going to say it. Kaminski. Are you thinking of asking her out? Because—I mean—you were staring at her again today, and—it's not a big deal," he barrels on. "You're allowed to like her. Totally allowed. Or, sorry, 'allowed' isn't the right word. You never need my permission to do anything. Ever. I—"

Since he started talking, I've been stretched across my laptop, absently stroking the fuzz on my arms. "Are you jealous?"

"I'm not jealous," he says quickly. "Not at all! Really! Jillian, I *want* this for you. It's just . . . you know. Kind of weird to see. That's all."

"What about you?"

"Me?"

"Yeah. Any guys you're into?"

He coughs. "Not really."

It's a bit like slipping off a wall at the gym. Not the fall itself, but when the rope jerks and you squeal because you know it's got you.

"Don't get me wrong," Henry says. "There are definitely guys at school I think are hot."

"Like who?"

"Like, um, Parker Evans."

"*That*'s your type? The captain of the basketball team? The kid who got in-school suspension for spreading—"

"Wow, first of all? Rude. Second, it'll never happen, so no need to panic. Parker's straight as hell."

The tenderness in my jaw accelerates to a throb. I make sure my mouth guard is on my nightstand, certain I'll be wearing it tonight. "Maybe you and I aren't the right people to be making those assumptions." Probably nobody is.

But.

"Guess not," he says tightly.

My room got dark when I wasn't looking. I flip open my laptop and start to type, guided by the glow of the screen.

Henry asks if I'm still there.

"Yup. Emailing guidance."

"Oh. Sweet."

"As we said, Purdy first."

And that entails composing this email without picturing him and Parker Evans sweating all over each other.

After some perfunctory phrasing advice, Henry says he's got to go—he still has the entire outline for our lab report to do. I say goodbye, then slap my phone under my notebook. The cursor blinks.

Odds are dinner's ready. I should wash my face, pull my hair back in that way that looks just so put together.

As if people who truly are put together must stoop to making the effort.

Shorts and a tank top drape my desk chair, stinky from my run to I Love's the other night. I throw them on and grab my Nikes from the rack downstairs, and then I'm out the door. Flying. The sun got strong on our walk home this afternoon, and at nearly eight o'clock, the heat's only starting to lift away. My shoes spark off the sidewalk, the breeze like cool hands to my cheeks.

Anybody in the string of passing cars might think, *That girl's running from something huge.* A reasonable assumption, except that I'm officially done running from my problems.

I'm running to catch up.

DAD DOESN'T SAY A WORD about my impromptu 5K, even though by the time I get back and shuck my sopping clothes, the table's been cleared, dishes washed and put away. My phone has seven missed calls from Henry.

Garrett glowers as I emerge from my room, wrapped in a towel. "Where the hell did you go?" he demands.

"None of your business. And don't say 'hell.'"

"You just did."

I close the bathroom door and crank the shower until steam clouds the mirror. I step in gingerly, sparing my curls, only to misjudge the distance and soak half my bun anyway. Garrett calls something *Zelda*-related from the other side of the door.

"Leave me alone!" I scream.

If everybody would just leave me alone.

Safely back in my room, I lock both doors—Garrett-proofing—and put on the tarp-size T-shirt I've worn to bed since last week. I shut off the lights and get into bed and grind my face into the comforter, immersed in . . . boy smell. Henry's neck and his hands. Backward WNBA caps and that pink detergent his mom buys.

I grab my phone off my nightstand.

"Hey." He sounds strange—relieved, but maybe kind of evasive at the same time. "Thanks for . . . I was afraid you wouldn't . . . hi."

Technically, withholding calls is his move. But since we're past that, I don't say so. I curl onto my side, mashing my wet hair against the pillow. "That *was* weird before, right? Talking about our crushes like we're . . ." I swivel my tongue. The words need a push. "Friends."

"Yeah," Henry says.

"But that's the end of it. The weirdness."

"Right," he affirms. "Of course. Obviously." Springs squeak. He must be in bed, too. Maybe in his Yoshi sweatpants.

Maybe not.

He says, "Can I ask one more question, though? Not to be weird. Just because all this is so new."

I nod, then remember he can't see. "Go ahead."

"When did you first realize you were into girls? I know when I asked the other day, you said three months, but that's not long at all. I guess I was curious if you could pinpoint the moment."

Not long at all.

That ache again.

Not long at—

"Jillian?"

A tooth just pulled.

I might as well explain. "You know how I've been taking Garrett to his Saturday climbing class? Well, Carla's little sister is in it, too. You were with me, actually, the first day she came in." It was pouring. Early March. Just before Purdy hijacked our existence and we could still climb every weekend and on Wednesdays after school, volunteering religiously at the reception desk to maintain our discounted memberships, which mostly involved lounging on each other's laps and flicking through social until a day-passer approached to ask about shoe rentals. But that morning, when I glanced up from the meme Henry was showing me, Carla was there. Carla Kaminski. A junior like us, except we hadn't had a single class together since sixth grade, and there was no explanation for why that suddenly seemed so unacceptable. Her blondish hair was in tatters, face as bare as my thumbnail. She held up a pair of size fours. *So, do I, like, leave these here, or . . . ?*

As I finish telling this story, there's Henry's silence, wide in my ears.

That moment upended me.

And he doesn't remember.

"Huh," he says. Then, after I don't know how many minutes: "I think I'm falling asleep."

Me too, I could lie.

Instead I drizzle my fingertips down my belly, listening to him breathe. "I wish you were here."

"Same."

"You could lie on top of me again." I hear myself laugh. "Or you could be the wall this time. Whatever you want."

"*Whatever* I want?"

"Mmm."

Sleep might not be a bad idea. Nature's anesthetic. It's only been three days, but I'm ready for coming out to stop feeling like the lid's been torn off me. I think of myself in the tent, how fiercely I wanted to believe that sex with Henry was all I needed to be whole. Now I'm farther from that girl than I ever was, my mind drifting to the most unhelpful places. A wrinkled black dress and pride pins. This gnawing inside that has nothing to do with skipping dinner.

Are you thinking of asking her out? Henry wanted to know. I just realized I never answered. And my fingertips have gone from absently stroking my belly to making circles on my thigh. I imagine the tickle of Carla's pink lips. Her head shaved on one side.

"What you asked me before," I say. "About Carla? The truth is, I don't know if I *can* ask her out." If he asks why not, I'll tell him, *She hardly knows me.* I'll say, *I'm terrified.*

Thankfully, Henry doesn't pursue it, and I don't pry about boys anymore, either. Our breathing muted and bare, like all the words we can't say.

9.

FIRST PERIOD DOESN'T START for fifteen minutes, but when I stumble into trig, Henry's seated amid the sea of empty chairs, tapping his mechanical pencil—two mechanical pencils, actually, in a surprisingly intelligible rendition of the original Pokémon battle theme—against his desk. He jumps when he sees me.

"Guidance is useless." I squeeze into the seat next to him. "Literally useless. I waited around the office for, like, half an hour only to find out Mr. Winn doesn't come in until *ten* on Tuesdays. What kind of crap is that? What if you and I elected to just not come in until ten on Tuesdays? We'd be expelled. God. What about you? What did Vincent say? You never texted me."

Mr. Purnell's up at the board, scribbling an equation we'll supposedly be able to solve by the end of the period. Now he whips around, aiming the dry-erase marker at us. "Whoa! Have you guys been in my class all year?"

"Nope," I say, my eyes all over Henry.

"Didn't think so. See, I knew you two must've graduated and become president already." Purnell turns back to the board, muttering, "If anything, you should be sharing credits with the less fortunate."

We both sort of smile. Mr. Purnell has a beard and tells funny stories, which makes him cool. In teacher-adjusted terms, anyway. Why can't our scholarship be in his hands, instead of some faceless committee's?

"We're taking AP Stats with you next year," Henry announces, clearly stalling.

Purnell makes a *praise Jesus!* gesture, palms up. "What else?"

"Only AP Physics, AP European History, and AP Lit." He smooths his palms over his shorts as Mr. Purnell staggers against the whiteboard and pretends to defibrillate himself.

"Henry," I hiss. He turns warily. "What. Did. Vincent. Say?"

"Well . . . it's kind of . . ."

"What? Not good?"

"Um. I'll be comfortable declaring it neutral. Eventually."

"Then *what*?"

He jiggles his pencil on his desk, looking pained, like when a math problem is hard enough to qualify as a personal affront.

The jiggling subsides. "Summer school."

I stare.

"Not *school* school," he says, correcting himself. "A

class . . ." The explanation's just as rushed, but apparently, Purdy maintains agreements with community colleges all over the state for students whose high schools don't offer enough courses or activities to satisfy scholarship requirements. "That's not quite our situation, but it isn't like Elm-High offers many summer classes regardless, and Vincent assured me it's all the same for the people in charge of final decisions. At the end of the day, they just want to see that their criteria were met—"

"Their criteria don't make any sense! We're at the top of our class. We run and climb and destroyed the SAT. You work, like, twelve hours a week. That's the epitome of well rounded—"

"None of that *counts*. Don't you see?" He smears his bangs back. "Look. The SAT's a perfect example. Remember when the teacher who taught those classes told us the SAT doesn't measure anything about us that actually matters, just how good we are at taking this one specific test? That's more or less what we're going through with Purdy. If we want this scholarship, we need to play by their rules. Meet *their* criteria for well-roundedness. It's not, like, an objective measure of whether we really are."

I hear what he's saying, and I get it, but honestly, this well-roundedness requirement doesn't feel like playing by any sort of rule at all. It feels like kissing Henry with a head full of Carla, every rule you've ever stuck to switched up midgame. All the more reason mine and Henry's must stay intact.

"So," I grit out, "what's the plan?"

"Well, Vincent said the class I picked at A-Triple-C"—Albany County Community College, nearly forty minutes north of Elmerville—"runs on a compressed schedule, and it'll wrap up way before the September deadline, so I won't have any problem submitting my updated transcript. Boom. Eligibility restored." He clicks his pencil, *clickclickclick,* against his thigh. "Big relief, right?"

"Okay . . . ," I say slowly. Not to be a jerk. This is just a lot of information to metabolize before first period. "Half our summer will be obliterated, and getting to Albany and back will undoubtedly suck, but okay, yeah. Whatever. Small price to pay." I dig my phone out of my bag, pulling up the Google Doc I've been tending to all morning. *NOTES FOR GUIDANCE MEETING.* "What class is it? Interpretive Horticulture? Intro to Puppeteering? I'll have Winn put me in the same one."

"Mandarin," he tells his lap.

Around us—commotion. Classmates encroaching. When did the bell ring? My stomach gets tighter—Henry, paler—until every desk is occupied and Purnell's marching us through the solutions to last night's homework.

Once we've transitioned to today's tortures, Henry pokes my arm. "Can we revisit this?"

My pencil wobbles. It's extremely difficult to copy an equation with the teacher standing in front of it.

"Jill. Jilly. Jillian Leigh—"

"Stop!" I whisper back. "You'll get us in trouble."

"It's important!"

My notebook's the kind with graphing paper. Assault-ingly white. I flip to last month's formulas—wouldn't be trig without an ungodly amount of backtracking—only to confront doodles depicting mech-suited chickens with special scanners embedded in their breasts to detect crumbs. Sketches for a game concept we won't have the skills or tools to make until college. Probably coding camp at ACCC would've made us impeccably well rounded, if we'd been able to afford it.

My pencil strokes fuse beneath the fluorescent lights.

Mandarin.

I tear off a corner of the page, neatly decapitating a chicken. Welp, I write, that was a miscalculation. I mean, of what must've been infinite options, he chose the one class we almost failed? I fold and fold—all school's taught us by blocking apps is to text like our forebears—then swipe the note onto Henry's desk. He flares his eyes at me. I shrug. And that's as far as we get because Purnell's calling people to the board, and any movement could be mistaken for volunteering.

Henry's fourth up. He stands between Wilson Long-champs and Annabel Western while Purnell walks us through precisely how and why Henry got thirty instead of three, which is the correct answer. Then Henry passes the marker to Wilson, who might resemble Parker Evans under certain conditions. Light brown skin, slightly overlapping front teeth.

As Henry makes his way back, navigating carefully to

avoid Nalgenes and backpack straps, I let my ponytail fall forward.

Henry drops into his seat. "I hate math." He leans to inspect my notebook. "What'd you get?"

"Nothing," I say, and he frowns, so I show him my notebook, the problem half-copied.

"You didn't try?"

"No," I answer as Purnell goes, "Miss Bortles?"

And the room contracts around me.

"I—I'm sorry, I didn't . . . I actually. Um. Pass. Please." Passes happen every class, and Purnell respects them, so there's no reason to panic, except that I am. I've never, *ever* passed.

Once everybody's moved on, laughing at Purnell's rendition of Wilson's molecularly tiny handwriting, Henry slaps our note, unfolded, onto my desk. A speech bubble springs from the chicken's severed neck.

who's bein an asshole now, it says.

"WE'RE HORRIBLE AT MANDARIN."

"I know," Henry says. Class is over, and we're pressed against the cinder-block wall outside Purnell's room, whispering despite the stampede.

"Did you forget what happened when we tried it last year? 'Take a world language,' they said. 'Prepare yourselves for the global economy.' We had to withdraw, Henry. Total retreat! We ended up in study hall with a bunch of—"

"I *know*," Henry says through his teeth. "But . . . listen." He shifts his bag to his other shoulder. "It was the only option that wouldn't conflict with my schedule at I Love's over the summer. My boss and I have been ironing that shit out for weeks. What choice did I have?"

Second bell trills, and the crowds disperse. Quiet creeps back into the halls like new growth after some sort of cataclysm, broken only by the occasional giggle or shoe squeak. It feels exposing. I cross my arms.

"Since when does a world-language class count as *well rounded*?" I say this because it's the only thing to say. Because there's no use arguing against a job Henry can't leave. If my parents weren't so maniacal about me helping out at the clinic, I'd be mopping up marinara with him. God knows we could use the money.

"The fact that we dropped it sophomore year is exactly why it counts. There are no language credits anywhere else on my—on our transcripts." He gnaws his lip.

The classroom door swings open, and a handful of kids shuffle out, Wilson Longchamps among them. A group always hangs back to joke with Purnell after class, as if math is just that thrilling.

Henry doesn't spot Wilson; his back is to the door, his eyes on mine, pleading, and—wow, he's moody today. I think of falling asleep last night on the phone. Waking up at two a.m. to discover my battery near death but the two of us still breathing. Henry needs to know I'm with him. Is that it? He needs to know I'm not about to let the *prospect* of failure scare me into exactly that? As Wilson passes us, handsome, Parkerish, I stroke a strand of hair behind Henry's ear. It's getting long enough to do that again.

"Away, lovebirds!" Purnell jangles his keys at us. "Late passes are not granted for canoodling."

We die. Flail apart to inspect whatever inch of wall is closest to our respective heads until Purnell rounds the corner. Then we surge back together, more cautiously.

"I need to—" Henry begins, just as I say, "If this class is the only thing standing between us and Purdy, then, yeah, it might be hard, but we can do it. We lasted long enough that we probably remember the basics, anyway." I'm lying. All I recall from Mandarin I is Ms. Chen's plum lipstick and nonstop soliloquizing about the school's dysfunctional copy machines, but we can't give up, can't allow our plans one more opportunity to disintegrate. We owe this to ourselves. As friends.

Normal friends.

"I'll go to guidance during lunch," I tell him. "Winn hasn't answered my email yet, but I'll chain myself to the door until he agrees to see me—"

"You can't!" Henry screeches.

"Huh?"

There's no word to describe the look he's giving me. Not one that would fit into any puzzle.

"Mandarin is full." He squeezes his palms together. "I took the last seat."

10.

A SIGN ON WINN'S DOOR says *BACK AT:* with felt clock hands pointing at 4:30. It's 4:33. I perch on my chair, leg jiggling, sweat dripping between my boobs. On the wall, a poster encourages students to TAKE INITIATIVE. The whole office smells like the inside of my family's old refrigerator.

My demands are simple. Namely, Winn must call Albany County Community College regarding my interest in Introductory Mandarin for Non-native Speakers, and in turn ACCC will increase the student count by one or create a new section or do whatever needs to be done to make this happen before I call the *Albany Times-Union* and inform the paper that a local college is sabotaging the future of an extraordinarily high-achieving student over something as arbitrary, as freaking tyrannical, as an enrollment cap. How's that for initiative?

4:43. My thighs sound like masking tape as I tear them from the seat.

Okay. Normally, if I was looking for a teacher, I'd scour their subject wing, but Mr. Winn isn't a teacher, and school ended almost two hours ago. My best bet is to proceed systematically from wing to wing. Flush him out. First up is English, where Ms. Bacon, who made Ryan Heinegg and me lie on the floor together when we acted *Romeo and Juliet* in freshman year, is watering cacti on her desk. She asks if she can help me, but I cruise past like I don't hear, peeking in classroom after classroom until I'm satisfied Winn isn't around. On to social studies, then science, still reeking of formaldehyde after the sophomores' final rite of passage: dissecting sheep brains. Winn's not here, either. I double back, ponytail slapping between my shoulder blades.

It's weird being at school this late in the afternoon. Like in those video games where you're the first to set foot on an alien planet, centuries after its inhabitants got wiped away. Only the stubbornest marks of civilization remain: partially disassembled bulletin boards that teachers have started taking down for summer. A granola bar wrapper stuck to the floor. Even the air has lost its charge, smelling as beige and dull as the walls as I get farther from the science wing. I do a lap of the library, including the study cubicles, but it's hard to check properly with the lights off and doors locked. When I pass the table of ceramic lumps that sheltered Henry and me all year, my hand reaches automatically for my phone. I owe him a status update.

Winn MIA :/

Henry's shift started a few minutes ago, but he'll see my email when he's on break. Better yet, I'll take the bus to I Love's, deliver word of my victory personally. Few wings remain. Winn's got to be in one of them.

I veer out a side door.

Except it's quiet. Too quiet for what should be the way to the gym, where the walls thrum after school with the force of a thousand JV try-hards dribbling. This floor has scuffs I don't recognize. One row of ceiling lights has been cut off, and the rest glint strangely off glass cases. Projects line the walls. Mostly watercolors. One collage appears to be a human face made entirely of trash salvaged from the cafeteria. *Fellow Beaver,* it's called. And in the middle of it all, a roar of color. Whipping lines. A painting so vast, with reds so layered, I hold my breath trying to follow the brushstrokes, making myself dizzy. My eyes dart to the signature at the bottom. *C. KAMINSKI.*

Carla.

I reel back and nearly smack into a case, my reflection smeared across threads of wire jewelry. Crumpled shirt, hair all thistly. An intrepid explorer wrenched from her air supply.

Obviously, I'm aware of Carla's art. You can't crush on somebody this rabidly without absorbing the hottest fact about them, but I've never seen her work up close before. Her Instagram is private. I check over my shoulder first, then step back to the painting. Press my thumb to a ridge of paint so red I can practically feel it beating.

Light emanates from a door at the end of the hall. I pull my hand away and hurry toward it.

Nobody's here. The classroom as unoccupied as the canvases twinkling in the corner, so blank my eyes sizzle. Is that . . . cat piss I'm smelling? I turn abruptly.

And see oranges.

Purples.

Yellows.

A whole tray of pastels left where anybody could take them. Emboldened, I pick one up. Aquamarine worn to practically nothing. Tiny knucklebone.

"Do you want those?"

I yelp. The pastel skips from my grasp.

Carla Kaminski pokes her tongue between the gap in her top front teeth, watching me from the doorway.

"Oh, um . . ." The pastel detonated. I crouch to sweep it up, only to smear an aquamarine blood trail. "I'm sorry. I was . . . I'm just trying to find my guidance counselor, but then I . . . And there were . . . I'll have this fixed in no time, don't worry." I gather the remains as best I can with bare hands—penance—and ferry them to the sink. I finish scrubbing and deplete, like, half a roll of paper towels smudging blue around my palms. Carla hasn't moved. Her shaggy bob's scraped into a bun, her septum pierced, her cheeks the sort of pink that looks like permanent sunburn. A portfolio, more compact than the one she toted around the library, dangles from her index finger.

She says, "We left those out on purpose. They're pretty

busted, but you can take them if you want. Natalia hates throwing supplies away."

"Natalia?"

"The teacher . . . ?" She leans her portfolio against the jamb.

"Oh, *Natalia*. Right."

The pastels were . . . a mishap. But I recovered, initiated a competent cleanup. My next task? Introduce myself. Easy. Except that this is the closest we've ever stood, the first time we've been alone together outside my head. As I sweat, rooted to the floor, Carla approaches the worktable closest to the window. She scoots the stool aside and kneels at what must be a storage cubby, her back to me. Gold letters on her windbreaker spell out ELMERVILLE CREW. "I'm . . . ," I try. "I'm . . . uh . . ." Hair swirls up the back of her head like a Van Gogh sky.

With Henry it was different. When we met, we understood each other instantly, through pure soul mate osmosis. He said his name and I told him mine and that was that. We were ours. I squeeze my tongue against the roof of my mouth, searching for words that'll paint me in the boldest blues—colors Carla might notice. Never mind I can't draw for shit and the odds she saw me fondling her painting are fifty-fifty.

The intensity of her rummaging eats up my chance. My fingertips burrow into my palms, slippery from the pastels.

"Who's your guidance counselor?" she asks.

The question startles me. Her voice, thinner than it ever

sounded in the cavernous gym, doubles, then fades as it bounces around the metal cubby.

"Winn," I stammer. "Mr. Winn."

"Damn. He's elusive."

"*So* elusive. For real, and the worst part is he . . ." I stop, refusing to let my rambling give away how relieved I am this interaction isn't over. "There's just a problem I'm trying to sort out. A really minor problem with a class I'm taking this summer. I'm getting it fixed, though. I mean, *we*'re getting it fixed, my"—I almost say *boyfriend*. "It'll all get taken care of. Today."

Carla stands. It's late enough that the sun's begun to slant, the room flushed with light in a way no room ever is during school—the way no classroom should be capable of, honestly. When she turns, her tongue between her teeth again, sparks blitz my belly. Proof there might be no justice in the world.

Henry's everything.

But how could *everything* leave out this feeling?

"I'm Jillian," I say.

Carla gathers her spoils from the cubby. A withered tube that she taps against her palm, her expression vague as a cloud that hasn't taken shape just yet. "Okay."

My chest twists.

She slips past me, sweeping her portfolio off the floor.

I scramble to add, "From the climbing gym? And you're Carla!" Which is what you'd think I'd be doomed to relive forever, besides the pastel explosion and flash sweats—my awful voice shrieking *And you're Carla!* on and on to infinity. It's not until she's left, with nothing more than a casual *Thought you looked familiar,* that I glance down and see . . .

Aquamarine.

All over my shirt.

And I was just *talking* to her. Looking like some weird bird shit on me.

11.

MS. YOO ISN'T HOME when I sneak over later. Her car's gone, sensible nursing shoes missing from the rack on the screened-in porch. Panting, I toe off my Nikes, slip them carefully into an empty space.

Shadows carpet the stairs. I slip past doors that guard rooms I've never seen, including Yuna's, uninhabited since she decided not to renew her visa and returned to Daegu years ago. My memories of her are vapor now. The photo outside her old room so outdated—Yuna's our age, grinning from the side of her mouth. Henry, looking faintly startled like he still does in pictures, grips her dress in his chubby fist. One of four decorations in the entire upstairs.

Hard to say what's more mind-blowing: Henry's sister having fourteen years on us, or his house, twice as big as mine, containing half as many things.

His bedroom door is cracked. A scrap of moon hangs in the window, not bright enough to see by. Activating my flashlight app reveals Henry submerged in goose down, glasses hinged off his nose.

"Henry?"

He forgot an alarm again.

"Henry." I switch on the brontosaurus lamp. "It's almost eight o'clock. You know what happens when we exceed standard napping hours." No response. I crouch in front of him, and when he fails to acknowledge even *that,* I rest my cheek on the bed. Sweat rolls down my kneecaps. His breath grazes my lips.

I sit up, wiping my tangled hair back. Piled alongside his phone on the nightstand are a paperback novel with dragons on the cover—I seriously doubt it counts for AP Lit—and a teacup whose shine seems dental under the brontosaurus's glow. I peer inside. Full. And prickly-smelling. Ginger, as expected. The photograph tucked behind it is the same one of him smiling with his dad that's been there for a while. There are still Nintendo figurines—Pikachu, Kirby, Diddy Kong, Sheik—arranged in battle formations around the TV on his dresser. A fan splutters, ruffling dark plaid curtains. They're the same, too. I'm not sure why I thought his mom would've changed them.

It's risky. Who knows when Ms. Yoo will finish up her class, but that's part of what makes being here so exciting— the exact reason I clapped my notebook shut to run over. I mean, Henry and I dated for four years, but we've known each other almost five, and I've hardly ever witnessed how the weekday darkness presses into his room. Headlights from a passing car wash across his desk, revealing stacks of textbooks, his backpack slumped over the floorboards. More new sights, yet still . . . predictable. Unlike everything that went down today. As I crawl under the covers, Henry activates, wriggling until our foreheads meet on his pillow.

"Oh my God," he groans. "I thought you were my mom."

"Wow."

"For a second—before you got into bed. It was harrowing. Is she here? Are we dead?"

"Nope." He's just as sweaty as I am. And . . . shirtless, his chest glimmering. I pry my gaze up. "What's wrong? You coming down with something?" This is a reasonable question asked by somebody who is reasonable. Somebody who can fail spectacularly at introducing herself to a girl and can love her best friend, love him completely, without needing his strong boy arms or soft boy lips.

He sniffs. "You know, my mom thought so when she picked me up from work. I feel fine."

"You don't look it." Cheeks flushed, eyes and nose all gummy.

He laughs. Barely. "She already knows you're here. You're aware of that, right? You know she can sense your presence from afar? Oh, and you're already pregnant." He *sounds* gummy. I push his head back onto the pillow.

"You're not going to ask how it went with Winn?"

Henry seems to just be realizing he's overheating. He kicks the blankets off and rolls onto his back. "How'd it go?" he asks, echoing me.

I sigh. "It didn't. It might be time to pursue alternate strategies, considering he's, like, a hologram programmed to appear wherever I'm not."

More headlights go by, sidling over Henry's cheekbones. Hip bones. "Yeah."

"I will find him."

"Yeah," he says again.

"I'll get into class. No question. Just a waiting game," I say, my laugh all watery.

Regardless, I'm not here to burn up any more dendrites obsessing over the nonproblem that is Mandarin. I'm here because Ms. Yoo's taking a nursing final and my parents think I'm on a run. Because falling asleep on the phone is okay and all—just not as good as this. You can't get drunk off somebody's germs, sink into their arms, with your faces in different zip codes.

Henry curls toward me, our sweat seeping down into the mattress. My finger on his lip.

"Do you ever wonder," he says, "how my parents messed up so bad?"

"Uh. No?" Don't mean to snarl. But. Conversational whiplash. "We're fully aware. Your mom kicked your dad out last year."

"Right . . ." Henry's mouth twists. "But before that. They're supposed to be adults, aren't they? Older, wiser, and all that? Why bother being forty if you can't avoid all the shit they did? Like arguing all the time. Or getting married when they knew they weren't really in love. Anyway," he says, edging his eyes across my face, the expression I seem to have stuck there but can't quite feel, "I've been thinking about that. A lot." What Henry needs when he brings up his parents can be impossible to decode. Sometimes I doubt even he knows. So I don't remind him how his dad used to yell at him. I don't tell Henry how, eight months ago, when he found out his dad was leaving, the arms I folded around him felt numb with relief. I don't say anything. He moves closer, nibbling my finger in the half dark. "Why did my mom need my dad to leave before she went back to school? She's always talked about becoming a registered nurse. He would've supported her. He could've fought harder to stay. Or moved back down south so I could visit him, instead of fucking off to Korea—"

I shake my head. "We're more prepared, Henry. We'll have Purdy—"

"You don't think my parents had plans?"

"Not good ones," I say fiercely.

"What if that's how it happens, though? What if . . . ," he starts to warble. My finger drops from his lip. "I'm just saying, ultimately, plans are decisions, too, right? Our plan. Anybody's. You make a series of choices the best you can, with the information you've got, and that's it—everything that comes after gets left to chance, and you don't know what's next. No matter how tempting it is to believe you do. But that doesn't have to be terrible. Right? Wouldn't logic dictate that if bad consequences happen unexpectedly, then . . . then happy accidents could, too?"

"Happy accidents."

"You know." He sucks his cheeks. "Like how I met you."

Chalk grit under my fingernails. August heat leaning hard on my shoulders until I turned and he was there, his head where the sun should've been.

An accident.

If we hadn't stayed with Ms. Henderson.

If the Yoos hadn't picked the house across the street from her because the school was good, and the previous owners forgot their basketball hoop.

"Is this about Mandarin?" I counter, recovering my nerve. "Because I told you—I'm getting that seat. Not 'by accident.' There's no other option."

He reaches for me, and we lapse into quiet, his chest a blur of heat like we're twelve years old again, cuddled in this exact bed. Our arms will never be long enough to stretch around all he's lost. But together, we give ourselves plenty to hold on to. One thing that won't fall apart.

Tonight, Henry's not wearing Yoshi sweatpants. Different ones. His hair feathers against my lips. "You changed your shirt," he murmurs.

I stiffen. "I ran here."

"So? All your clothes are running clothes."

"So I . . ."

Can't tell him.

I cannot tell Henry about Carla. Other than my crush revealing that she has, in fact, been touched by knowledge of my existence, nothing happened.

Nothing.

Besides, bringing her up would only make things weird again. We swore off weird. Period. And I haven't recovered from this latest Henry spiral. His anxiety always goes for the throat.

As if words like *happy* and *accident* belong in the same universe.

"I—I was strategizing," I say. "For Winn. My pen blew up all over me." Not technically a lie. When I got home, I opened my trig notebook, stared at the wide empty page for what felt like hours. I flipped to our chicken drawings, waiting for some sort of sign that, yup, flailing with Carla equals gay, and it's okay I didn't start figuring this out until just now, it's okay not to be certain, to keep wondering. . . . The thought made my belly jump worse than when she looked at me. "I—"

His tongue flickers over mine.

Neither of us pulls away. This kiss there, then not. "We can't," I whisper. Henry shrugs, embarrassed, but also like, *Making out isn't much riskier than holding hands . . . ?* Valid point. I walk my fingertips over his smooth bare shoulders, wishing I had just told him about Carla. The shirt I slapped into the trash when I got home, knowing the oils wouldn't budge. I'd confess, *There's no shape, no edges, to what Carla does to me.*

Henry's apologizing when I say, "Do it again."

"You sure?"

"Kiss me. Please."

The only line getting crossed between who we are and what we'll be.

#1—NO FIGHTING

#2—NO MESSING AROUND????????

#3—NO MORE RUNNING

#4—PURDY FIRST

12.

HENRY INHALES DEEPLY WHILE I spin my combo. "Think we'll miss this?"

"Lockers? No."

"Not lockers. I mean"—he does it again, a deep, summoning breath—"*this*. The high school smell."

"Um." My locker pops open. We have only a couple of minutes until first period, the hallways choked with students lugging final projects and band equipment. I saw my nose on my sweatshirt cuff and ditch books I won't need until after lunch, smelling only beaten-down wills and floor lacquer. "Probably not?" It's too early, and my heart's hammering too loud, to indulge in nostalgia for a time we're still enduring. I zip my backpack swiftly. "By this time next year, we'll be begging for graduation."

He blows his bangs back, looking disappointed. "Guess I can't really smell for shit."

"*Cain't?*" I poke his nose. "You are sick." That Georgia boy accent only sneaks up when he's compromised by illness, exhaustion, or necessity—FaceTiming his cousins in Savannah. I give my lock one last twist, about to head off, when he catches my sleeve.

"About last night."

"Oh. Uh . . ." His cold germs have been percolating in my throat since I woke up. Now I swallow hard, my spit rasping. "It's fine. You said so yourself: we didn't break our rules." I mean, he didn't communicate that—not in words—and I got a little turned on and could tell he did, too, but no way would we have gone further. Even if my dad hadn't called.

"Exactly." Henry nods vigorously. "That's exactly what I— So we're on the same page, then?"

"Same page," I confirm.

Gradually the commotion around us thins. In a room across the hall, jazz band warm-ups are underway, a piano bleating. The bell rings.

Cautiously I say, "Need to make a stop?"

"Nah, we'll be late. I'll look off you for history."

Locker selection: a senior privilege. The rest of us make do with assignments by last name, which—since Henry and I are continually thwarted by the alphabet—places his locker as far as geographically possible from mine while remaining on school property. But instead of setting off, I flip my locker shut and we lean our temples against it, facing each other. Just like sharing a pillow, except for all the cold metal. I can almost feel the pull of his lips, the safety our kiss wrapped me in.

"Actually," I blurt, "I'm going to see if Winn's in his office."

He straightens. A shadow swoops across his face. "Now?"

"Why not? If the late bell rings, I'll wrangle a pass from him. I'm self-starting! Motivated!" My smile pressed on. "Like the Purdy Creed says."

"Sure . . ." Henry starts flipping the cap to the travel mug his mom handed him through the car window. "Yeah. Okay. Save you a seat."

I want to say something encouraging. Like *Wish me luck* or *We've got this*. But my heart's crawled up to my tonsils, so I can barely get out, "Thanks."

He leaves, and I press my forehead against my locker for so long that a hall monitor asks if I'm okay.

"Great," I mumble, hefting my backpack. "Sorry." I wait until she's gone, too, the piano approaching its frazzled crescendo.

Then I head for the art wing.

WHEN I REACH THE END of the hall, snot's crackling in my nostrils. The classroom lights are off, door shut—distressingly unlike yesterday. I squint through the fire-resistant glass panel.

Okay. No guarantee Carla even *has* art this period, and school policy says no entering classrooms without a teacher present during school hours, but I figure I've earned an exception, since teachers trust me. I wear sweaters with animals on them. Except . . . I lied to Henry. To his *face*. Nearby a teacher drones about acrylic-paint techniques while I consult my mental rulebook.

Lying to Henry about visiting guidance isn't the same as running. It's not forsaking Purdy, or fighting with him, or—my chest squeezes—sex.

It's just a first.

And I'm not about to compound that first with another—a detention slip. I slide numbly down the wall, cradling my backpack, every cell in my body demanding, *NOW WHAT?* Do-overs are so not me.

Only this time, I'm not *completely* unprepared. If Carla does show up—if she asks what I'm doing—I'll slip her the excuse I thought up on the bus. *Are those pastels still available?* Plausible. She doesn't need to know my drawing skills are nonexistent.

Or what else I've never done.

Then I look up, and she's standing over me. "Hello?"

"Hi!" Scrambling overturns my backpack. My trig textbook splatters out, and my notebooks and pencil case. Carla's eyes snap to the pencil case instantly. "Sorry . . ." I pile everything into my bag and wrench myself up, coughing wetly into my elbow. "I was . . . I forgot those pastels yesterday and . . . what's up? Wasn't expecting to see you!"

"Are you into Michelangelo?"

"What?" I wheeze.

She points. It takes me a second to realize where—my pencil case, jammed into the water bottle holster on the side of my bag. It depicts that famous scene from the Sistine Chapel, where God zaps life into Adam or whatever. I'm not religious. Or admitting my dad bought the case for me. But Carla's intensity is infectious. I pull the case out for a better look. The image blown up so only their straining hands are visible. "He's . . . cool," I say.

"*So* cool." Carla wears a baggy sweater flecked with paint, torn gray jeans. Her eyes are grayish, too, like photographs developed the old-fashioned way. Her lashes are clogged with mascara. "You know how he got his figures to look so realistic? Their fingertips? Their wrists?" She taps the case. "He dissected bodies. It was dangerous during the Renaissance, mad illegal, because of the church. He could've been executed if he got caught."

"That's—"

"The Sistine Chapel nearly blinded him. He worked on scaffolding sixty feet up in the air, on his back, with his face smashed against the ceiling, paint dripping into his eyes. For four years he did that." She pushes her portfolio onto her shoulder—the same floppy one she usually carries. "The pastels should be in there. I've got free period now, so. Extra studio time."

My muscles are zinging. I file after her into the classroom, resisting the urge to bolt.

The pastels aren't here. And the light coming through the windows isn't nearly as wondrous as yesterday—this sad dribble, like too many colors mixed together. I don't have time to act disappointed, because Carla's already examining the blank canvases propped in the corner, sizing them up. Now she crouches to retrieve a rectangular sheet of glass from her desk, its surface crusted with paint. Her palette? She reaches deeper, and her jeans slip low. Dimples wink from the small of her back. I try not to stare, feeling like I'm the one stretched out and gutted on a table.

"I like your painting," I venture.

Carla grins. Her tongue sneaks between her teeth. "Which one?"

"In the hallway. With all the reds that overlap like—like a blood puddle. Or"—I press on, registering her cringe—"maybe not blood. But there's a lot of red in the middle of the canvas. And splotches, and the background's white, so I thought . . ." My face prickles. I'm making her masterpiece sound like my maxi pad after six hours of service.

"Red's powerful," Carla says. "It can mean a lot of different things depending on who's looking."

It's something a teacher would say. Like when you can't tell whether they actually understand what you're getting at or are just pretending so you can all move on with dignity. I make myself smile. Steering my latex-y cold breath out of my mouth. "Totally."

She tucks her hair behind her ears. "You find Winn?"

"No," I murmur. But guidance appointments can run long, so even though the bell went off eons ago and Henry's got to be wondering where I am, my story remains the perfect cover. If Carla could just give me some sort of signal—make it safe to go. If she could prove some lies are worth the regret.

She squirts blue paint onto her palette, and the heater hisses. I smell Band-Aids. Burnt air.

"Believe it or not," she says, "he's been helpful with my

Yale application. We have an appointment later—during first lunch. You free then? I'll ask if he can fit you in."

"That would be . . . that'd be really helpful, actually. Should we . . ." I grope around my pockets. "My school email is—"

"Text okay? I've got your number."

"You . . . do?"

"From the gym." Carla addresses the paint she's been mixing, not me. She selects a thicker brush and holds it—not as delicately as her reds had me believe, but with purpose. Like a conductor. "When my sister signed up for class, we got a flyer with a list of volunteers in case we had any questions about what equipment to buy and stuff. You were on it." She moves the brush briskly across the palette, churning blue. "Your boyfriend's too."

My heart drops. "He's not—"

"He is your boyfriend, right? The Asian kid who barfed in your hands last semester?"

"His name's Henry," I say stiffly.

"Cool."

"No, seriously, from one white girl to another: His name is Henry Yoo, and he's been in our class for the past five years, so it's pretty messed up that after all this time his race is the only thing you've bothered to notice about him."

Incredibly, Carla lowers her brush. "Permission to redeem myself?"

I nod.

"Your boyfriend—is he the kid whose wardrobe consists entirely of Nintendo hoodies and jock headbands?"

A smile bites at my lips. "Fair." There's the smell of the heater, the slip of paint. And then I say, "We're actually . . . He's not my boyfriend. Not anymore."

I haven't acknowledged this to anybody but him, and the effort is kind of breathtaking. With four teeny words, our breakup just became that much more final. That much more real. Like with every person we tell, we're only admitting out loud that we'll never again be what we were. . . .

Minus his hips against me. The press of our mouths. This brutally rational part of me that reviews this evidence and wonders, *Is it technically moving on if we're still kissing?*

And yet telling Carla we broke up has got to be better than telling Carla nothing. The more I get to know her, the less wanting her but clinging to Henry will feel like breathing out of my mouth and nose at the same time.

"Sucks," Carla says. "I got dumped recently, too."

I figured as much, given what I overheard at the library. Even so, getting the news from her directly makes my pulse leap. "He didn't dump me per se. We . . ." But the reality of us has always been too big to explain. It's a relief to realize she's not asking me to try. At least just yet. "It was mutual. I'm sorry about you and your girlfriend, though."

"Yeah. Me too." She paints a streak.

Sensing she'd rather not talk about that, I say, "How can we text? The content blockers."

"Huh? Just swap your phone on and off airplane mode a bunch of times." She stops, a glob of blue wobbling on her brush. "Were you not aware?"

"No." My cheeks flare. "No. I completely was." So much for *everybody* knowing the workaround, Henry. Carla turns back to her canvas. A necklace clasp pokes out the collar of her shirt. Plain silver.

Nothing he would wear.

13.

WE HAVE TO DODGE my mom to get upstairs Friday night. Her hugs last slightly too long.

"Minjun," she gushes, "it's so good to see you, sweetie. Jilly still hasn't given me the full story about prom—"

"Prom was great!" Henry calls. "Thanks!"

"Your mom didn't say anything about the photos I texted her. Did she get them?"

Henry halts on the stair landing, one step below me. I tug his sweatshirt hood—*Let's go*—but he ignores me, forever more concerned with his parental approval rating than a successful getaway. "I'm not sure. She's been busy with exams and stuff."

"That's right! She's finishing up her first semester, isn't she? You must be so proud."

He smiles. "Second. She did a program over the winter to brush up on her English. But, yeah, I'll ask her about the pictures. . . ." His phone's been in his hand since he kicked his shoes off, buzzing and buzzing. He blinks briefly at the screen before swiping the alerts away.

"Yuna again?" I ask, so not prying.

"Terrific," Mom says from the bottom of the stairs. Looking at her, it's hard to see how any of my genes could've come from Dad. Mom and I have the same hair—a bouquet of frizzy curls. The same oval faces and five-foot-five-ishness, and that's just the beginning. Dad works out—for cardiovascular reasons—but my athleticism's all Mom, too. The reason sleeves pinch my arms and the nonexistence of jeans that fit both my thighs and waist is practically scientific principle. Prom dress shopping was likewise an ordeal. But convincing her not to give Henry's mom a photo of him and me was even more harrowing. *You can't give Ms. Yoo a Mother's Day present,* I said. *That's weird.* She asked why. She said, *We did last year.* I bolted to my room and slammed the door, bit down on my pillow until the howling in me went still.

That's the danger of sharing. Exactly what my parents don't get.

Feeling is an abyss you fall into. A bleed that never stops.

Also, Henry and I agreed not to tell our parents we broke up yet.

Now Mom says, "By the way, Jillian's father and I have been wondering . . . how do you pronounce 'Pyongyang'? You know, the capital of North Korea? We were watching CNN the other day, and— Hey! Whatever you two end up doing, wash your hands afterward—"

I slam my door, shouting, "*Google it!* Sorry," I add to Henry, his throat splotchy red. Normally I'd wait for his signal. This system we devised for whether Henry wants me to stick up for him. One tap on the inside of my wrist for *I got this,* two for *Destroy them.* Zero means *Don't bother*—like when some ancient teacher introduces a unit on Confucianism or Pearl Harbor while looking directly at him. Tactical silence. They'll be dead or retired soon. "I don't know why my parents can't keep their shit together around you. Should I talk to them again?"

Sprinting dislodged Henry's glasses. He rights them carefully. "It's okay."

"It's not okay—"

"Jillian, seriously, don't. If you talk to them, it's going to become A Thing. I'm exhausted just thinking about it." My bed's unmade. Henry plops onto it anyway, producing his Nintendo Switch controller. Hot pink, to avoid getting it mixed up with mine. "Ready for *Smash*? Allow me to remind you that you did swear not to be Jigglypuff every round again. Rematch rules apply."

"In a sec." I sit on the rug beneath him and open my laptop to the website I was puzzling over before he got here. Blankets rustle as Henry readjusts, resting his chin on my shoulder.

"Why are you on A-Triple-C's website?"

"Research," I explain. "I thought I should figure out who our Mandarin teacher will be, now that I'm wait-listed."

Henry wasn't as ecstatic about the news as I'd anticipated—even though Winn swore I'd be first up, and college students swap in and out of electives constantly. My spot's guaranteed.

When Henry doesn't respond, I turn to find his mouth practically on top of mine. I smile weakly, my throat killing me.

I haven't confessed to bumping into Carla in the art room. Or how the credit for getting me wait-listed is partially hers.

He frowns. "Isn't it kind of early for that? Maybe we should wait until—"

"Yeah, until we know I'm in for sure. You said." And for once, I kind of get that. Despite our most ferocious efforts, we've already screwed up Purdy once. Not to mention this mess we've made of our other big commitment—this no-fooling-around, normal-friends pledge we blurred two days after making it. So. How can I ever get to know Carla, become part of her life, when my own defies categorization? This confusion with Henry is just the start. I still can't tell what Carla thinks of me or how she feels, *really* feels, about breaking up with Bea. I threw everything away for a chance to date a girl.

For an *if*.

"That doesn't mean we shouldn't prepare ourselves," I insist. "Mandarin is hard, and our entire scholarship is on the line. A C-minus/seventy percent is the lowest you can get at A-Triple-C and still pass, just like at Elm-High. Are *you* comfortable with a C-minus on your transcript? Because I'm—"

"Then do a club sport! They count the same toward well-roundedness, and Elm-High offers tons during the summer. Vincent showed me."

I twist to stare at him. "Why didn't you take one?"

He looks startled. "What?"

"If club sports were an option Vincent offered, why didn't you go with any of them? Why did you pick the *one* class I couldn't join, too?"

"That's . . . that's not what happened. I climb, yeah, and we run together sometimes, but—what about racquetball? Or tennis? Rowing? Come on, Jilly. You're so ripped from the gym, you'd dominate all of those." He fidgets. "Can we play *Smash* now?"

Frankly, this is too much like video games already: Henry homing in on the hardest quest of all, lip pinned beneath his teeth. That's what drew us to games in the first place; seeing how determined he was to be good at them made me want to be better, too. Henry and me gripping our controllers, throwing ourselves at level after level until we'd perfected their rhythms and our thumbs blistered. Knowing, even without speaking, that we were saying the exact same thing. I hunker back over my laptop. My eyes meld with the whiteness of the screen.

"Promise you'll at least consider it," he says.

No. Absolutely not. Henry and I have never taken separate classes, and we won't now. Won't ever. Having to adjust course after our initial mishap was unexpected enough, and that requires retaliation. I will wage war against the unexpected. I will make this work. "I'm taking Mandarin," I tell him. "Winn said . . ." When I reached his office on Wednesday, Carla was just leaving, more hair covering her eyes than wound in her bun. "He said the odds are in my favor."

I raise my pencil, tracing up Henry's jaw. Then I press the blunted tip between his eyes, which widen hilariously.

He swats me away. "*Smash*. Immediately. Prepare to weep." He reaches over my shoulder, minimizing my browser, only to reveal the window I forgot I'd tucked behind it. Bent wrists and knotty arms and exquisitely shaded rib cages. Close-ups from the Sistine Chapel. My breath skips.

"Um," Henry says.

"More research." It comes out garbled with snot. "We could make a game about—"

"Michelangelo?"

"I . . ." Probably the one drawback of having every class together is there's no fibbing about where you learned what.

It's just that at school, there's the constant threat of bells to contend with or a teacher barging in to ask where I'm supposed to be, so my interactions with Carla—all two of them—have been brief. But tomorrow is Garrett's climbing class. Beginner Fundamentals, which lasts two hours. Carla will be there. If she sees me . . . if she wants to talk . . .

I'll need a plan.

"I—I was only . . ."

"Let me see." He lifts my laptop over my head. Protesting will only make him more suspicious, but I heave myself onto the bed, the springs squawking. He taps the first image. A shadowy rib cage, with text beneath that Henry reads aloud, ghosting a fingertip over the screen. " 'To Michelangelo, the male form represented the height of human beauty.' " Henry grins. "No argument there."

When I flinch, he looks down and slightly to the left, and I know he knows he's hurt me.

"It's fine. I mean, I get it." I grind the pencil eraser against my calf, hating myself for feeling rejected when he's been equally rejected by me and that's so not the point anyway.

Henry takes my hand, swirling his thumb over my palm. He says, "This is, quite possibly, the most random fucking thing you have ever brought to my attention. I love it. Our games are going to be wild as hell once we start making them. All thanks to you."

"Ha ha." Tears creep into my eyes.

I lied to Henry about Carla to keep things from getting weird, and now that lie's practically embedded. An ingrown lie. All it's done is make things weird differently. I pull away, wiping discreetly at my cheeks.

"Hey—" Henry says.

"Do you *want* to take class alone?" The accusation launches out of nowhere. But I need to know. I need to know because he hurt my feelings, and I deserve a preview of what other hurts are coming, how hard they'll hit and where.

Besides.

There's no way.

Henry guides my face around so I'm looking at him, our hand-holding no more thanks to me—fingertips barely touching. His throat clicks.

"Let me guess," I say. "Another 'happy accident' lecture?"

He shakes his head. Something's off about him now. His eyes shimmer behind his glasses, tracking my gaze as it wanders across his silky bangs and chewed-up hoodie strings. I remember being thirteen. His hair on my cheek. Our heads bent over the knot he was fashioning to safely belay me, my feet stuffed into his old climbing shoes that felt like stubbing all ten toes at once. I'd never climbed before. The wall he'd picked for me towered over us, so tall it fused with the ceiling. *Make a ghost,* he said, kinking the rope into one of the bedsheet variety—no arms, a big round head, same as his dad had taught him. *Slay the ghost, poke him in the eye* . . . until the knot was ready, and I was shaking. Henry smiled. He shuffled closer. Maybe all our whispers and cuddling over the past couple of months had made this slightly inevitable. But when our mouths met, it felt like the answer to a question we'd both been asking.

Our first kiss. His lips pressed so delicately over mine.

Four years later, which has shifted more? Us, or the answer? My face in Henry's hands. His nostrils flaking from what could be the last cold we ever give each other.

"It'll be okay," Henry says.

His knuckles brush my mouth.

WHEN WE NUDGE my door open, my parents are watching *Spirited Away* with Garrett. Dad hits pause when he hears us on the stairs.

"Hey there," he says as we crowd the den entrance, all smiles. "Heading out already, kids?"

Henry steers his gaze surreptitiously toward the TV, making it my job to formulate a coherent response despite the hair licking up the back of his head, my swollen mouth. "It's almost Henry's curfew," I say, "but I'll drive him. No need to interrupt your movie."

Dad replies, "That's fine," and Mom jokes, "*Straight home, Jilly Bean*," and they share one of their looks. I whirl toward the hall and grab my keys and jacket, my parents' eagerness drowning me.

"Good night," Henry croaks.

Under the driveway floodlights, he touches my hip. I face him, saying, "We've got to be stricter with ourselves, Henry. I mean it. No more kissing. No more slipping up."

"Slipping up?" he says, immediately pink. "We were only . . . But we both wanted . . ." He pinches his lip. "You don't have to take those rules *so* literally."

"Excuse me, the entire point is to be literal. If we aren't following the rules seriously, then how . . ." *How is this going to work?* The thought's not worth finishing. Like I'd risk downgrading our success as friends from fact to hypothetical when we've got this, undoubtedly. I fumble to unlock the car.

"Making out feels nice," Henry says, and I cringe, praying my parents won't hear. "When we're scared o-or upset. Like when my parents used to scream and stuff, and I'd come over and— A little kissing hardly counts as getting each other off—"

"What if it sort of does, though? Remember when Ms. Narine had all that coffee during bio and told us a sneeze is technically one-tenth of an orgasm? What if a kiss is, I don't know, a third of one?" Kissing Henry only makes me want him more. Exactly how I *shouldn't* feel if I'm supposed to be exploring girls. "We drew a line, okay? Now we're blurring it, mixing ourselves up. It's messy." I wrench the door open, sink into the driver's seat. Henry doesn't move, his expression lost in the tar that counts for night around here. "Whatever that was just now, that's *it*. The last time."

My speech seems to convince him. "Okay." He inhales. "Yeah, sure. The last time."

"Thank you." Our rules will hold us when we can't. All we've got to do is keep fine-tuning.

It's not until Henry joins me in the car and we're backing onto the road that his comment about kissing when we're scared starts crawling through me.

"Are you saying you're worried about something else now?" I ask.

Henry's head hangs low, his hands fisted in his hoodie pocket. *No,* I wait for him to say. *Of course not.*

"I'm saying," he answers tightly, "that I love you. I guess I'm just trying to figure out what that's going to look like moving forward."

"Good. Great. Me too." I turn back to the road, desperate for him to say more, to make it make *sense*. Henry's doubting Purdy and then he isn't. We say no messing around, then can't stop kissing. All I want is help making it fit. Between us, we share one nonnegotiable dream and two working nostrils. We can do anything.

Henry sniffs hard. "Okay," he says.

"Okay."

14.

I'M SO LATE GETTING Garrett to climbing class the next morning that he makes me drop him off at the entrance, shouldering his gear with a sarcastic, "Hooray." I watch to make sure he gets inside okay, then scavenge for a spot, finally scoring one at the strip mall a block away, where service is nonexistent despite my most valiant contortions.

Texting Henry will have to wait.

Outside the car, asphalt glimmers. A breeze slaps like wet towels. This is how summer hits upstate. You wake up every morning to frost etching the leaves until suddenly it's eighty.

At least my cold's dried up.

I cross toward the gym's back entrance—less risk of getting pasted by cars exiting the Starbucks drive-thru. Hedges are shaggier here, the parking spaces more crowded together. Flies boil from a dumpster. Beside it is a muddy blue Camry.

Carla's car.

My steps slow.

Through the broad glass of the back doors, the whole

gym's visible. Tall walls to simulate cliffs, others low and scooped out for caves, lagoons of blue safety nets waiting at the bottom. My arms twinge longingly. Henry and I promised each other we'd get back into climbing this summer, but we'll never get enough volunteer hours for free passes if we're stuck in Mandarin class. I rise on tiptoe, scoping out the guest lounge, a haphazard collection of chalk-streaked sofas in the middle of the gym.

No Carla.

I hightail it back to the car.

My bag's huddled behind the driver's seat—I'm used to churning through homework while Garrett climbs, but today's different. My motives definitely "ulterior." I yank my laptop out at a curbside table. Hello, Starbucks Wi-Fi.

In retrospect, I regret going to bed instead of pounding Michelangelo facts after dropping Henry off last night. As soon as the browser loads, I bang out *Michelangelo top five things to know.*

It's tricky, though. My head so gummed up from Henry that the words on the site where I left off—*sketches, nudes, Chapel*—only lose meaning the harder I bore into them, like food that's been chewed too many times. When I catch a swipe of blondish hair inside Starbucks, the significance eludes me.

Until she crashes outside.

". . . literally the laziest excuse I've ever heard, so don't blame me . . ." Carla strides to the curb, followed by Bea Nabarro, who's dressed in a purple polo with HOUSE OF

WOOF stamped across the chest, tucked into belted kha-kis. Carla, on the other hand, is wearing *the* most distressed jeans imaginable. An actual one-to-two ratio of denim to bare thigh.

"My reaction to your bullshit is not my problem!" Carla shrieks. She starts to walk away, but Bea stops her, palm to chest.

"Wait up," Bea says. "*Your* reaction isn't your problem? Do you not hear how that sounds?"

Carla thumps her Frappuccino onto a nearby table and rakes her hair back with both hands. "You're the instigator, okay? So you do something fucked up, and I respond—all right, I 'react' . . ." She might've just sprained her fingers doing air quotes. "But if it weren't for your crappy priori-tizing, your inability to wait, like, five minutes for me to text you back, then guess what? We wouldn't be having this argument in the first place. That's like . . . like blaming the kid who gets picked on every day for finally snapping and punching the bully in the face. We all know who gets deten-tion in that situation."

Bea slurps her iced coffee. "First of all . . ."

Carla veers around her.

"Your analogy is flawed."

And it seems impossible that neither has noticed me at a table less than five feet away, where I've been poring over an excruciatingly detailed sketch of a peasant farmer's ass cheeks (*Standing male nude from the rear*, Michelangelo, circa 1501–1504). But.

They haven't?

"I'm not a bully," Bea goes on. "And for an artist, you can be depressingly oblivious. The entire reason I assumed you didn't want to go out yesterday was because you said you had work to do, and stopped answering my messages, and—do you seriously not realize how many times you've chosen staring at a blank piece of paper all weekend over me, a person you claim to be in love with? But, sure, Carla. Go ahead. Accuse *me* of shitty prioritizing."

Carla chomps her straw—this defiant grimace. Her lower lip ripples.

"Whatever," Bea says. "I'm late for work." She stomps to her Jeep.

Just when Carla seems to have accepted defeat, she cups her hand to her mouth and roars, *Fuck you, Beatriz!*

"Fuck *you*, Carla," Bea screams back. "And fuck your painting. Fuck your crew bullshit and Yale and your fucking-ass everything. Fall into a poisoned well!" She flicks her off. A woman leaving Starbucks with three little kids in soccer jerseys can't decide who to shield first.

Only after Bea's driven off and Carla has snatched her drink up does she spot me. Her face slips a million ways.

"S-sorry," I stammer.

This scraping sound. Metal on concrete. Carla drops into the chair across from me. "Everybody eavesdrops."

"No"—I flush—"sorry she upset you."

"They." She draws her knees up.

"Oh—"

"Bea's nonbinary. They use *they/them* pronouns—I didn't correct you before because they haven't been out at school. Recently they've been feeling ready to change that, but it's also kind of overwhelming having to tell everybody." Carla hugs her knees, squeaking her straw in and out of her cup with her free hand. "So, yeah," she mumbles. "With their permission, I'm helping fill in some of the gaps. But just so we're clear, their gender identity has nothing to do with why we're not together anymore."

That's . . . evident. I nod. "I'm sorry they upset you."

Carla shrugs, still playing with her straw. Having me witness that argument must've embarrassed her. I'm about to ask if she's okay—truly okay—when she says, "You in breakup hell, too?"

Last night. Henry's insistence on taking Mandarin, and the little gasp he made when we started kissing. "Henry and I are—"

"Crap?" She holds the straw up, dripping Frappuccino slush onto her tongue with surgical precision.

"No way. We're doing . . ." *Better than you,* I could say. Our confusion over messing around beyond patched up. "We're awesome. Just, you know, taking it day by day. How's your painting coming? The blue one?" I quickly shut my laptop.

She plunks that straw back into her cup. "I trashed it."

"You *what*?" I gasp. "But it was so—"

"Promising? I hoped so." Carla shrugs her jacket off, the same shiny purple one from the other day, and I try not to gape at her shoulders, so much broader and stronger than they seem under clothes, her biceps clean scoops of muscle. She runs her palm over the shaved part of her head, choosing her words carefully. "Putting a portfolio together for Yale is a huge deal. *Good enough* isn't an option."

"Is it ever?"

She laughs. Not so loud, but enough to drip a tiny thrill through me. When Carla discusses her work, all her blurry edges snap into focus. Her hand drifts to her knee. "What're you working on?"

"What?"

She gestures at my computer.

"Oh. Um . . ." I'm smothering it. Practically spread myself across the table in my desperation to get as physically close to her as possible. Launching upright, I say, "Nothing. A lab report. I'm in AP—did you know Michelangelo considered men the pinnacle of human beauty?" A leathery taste swells into my mouth. Carla regards me quizzically.

After all that scrambling around at home, I forgot to brush my teeth.

"I mean . . ." Carla grins. "He was, like, the gayest?"

I grin back. So *not* thinking about Henry thinking about boys.

Only Carla and the musky scent wafting from her hair, like my pillow when I'm falling asleep. She slides an arm back into her jacket. Gold letters flash.

ELMERVILLE CREW.

"What's crew?" I ask. Bea flung the word at her.

"Huh? Oh." Carla twists the jacket around, like she's

just discovering what it says. "You know. Rowing." She pulls her glorious shoulders back.

Rowing.

One of the club sports Henry mentioned.

"The school hosts a coed team, but it's intramural and only runs during the summer, so basically nobody knows about it. Why?" Her grin widens. "You interested?"

"Um—"

"Some of our most dedicated members graduated last year, so we're, like, desperate for new people."

She unfurls, her legs so long I almost trip in my haste to pack up and follow her. Clouds part, dumping buckets of sunlight as we cross the parking lot. My head pounds. Crew means rowing. If I joined, I'd see Carla every day. In a *boat*. Birds singing. Sunshine skimming our arms, my hands on her waist as I help her onto the . . . dock or whatever. No difference anymore between fantasizing and doing, each breath an opportunity to ask her out.

Heroically I keep all this to myself. By silent agreement we seem to be migrating back to the gym, though I'm not sure why or when we decided to do that, and now it's too late to intervene.

Garrett *can't* see me with her. For a seventh grader, he's upsettingly intuitive.

Carla says, "I'd just thrown that painting away when you saw me coming out of Winn's office. In case you were wondering why I looked like a wreck. How'd your appointment go? You applying to an Ivy, too?"

"No—"

"Hmm. Do you, like, not have the grades or something?"

Which is a fairly wild accusation coming from a student who's not Honors track. Before I can defend myself, she smiles innocently around her straw, and . . .

Oh.

Is this . . . ?

Are we . . . ?

I've never flirted with a girl on purpose before. Never flirted with anybody besides Henry—and we were friends first, so for all I know, that doesn't count. My heart goes arrhythmic. This is *happening*. But I can also feel my face mushing up, stiff and hot like it always gets when I'm being teased.

"It's just that we have other plans for college. We do. Henry and I." The second the words are out, I want to dive into the mulch on the strip-mall median. Slumber there forever with the toads and seeds so that when I reemerge centuries later, neither of us will remember this. One shot. I had *one shot,* and I brought up my ex.

But when I summon the courage to glance at Carla, wincing through my hair, she just says, "Can I ask you a question? It's okay if not. It's kind of personal, and we don't know each other very well yet."

Personal? *Yet?* We're on the median now, alone save for Starbucks seagulls and a little tree with a sign looped around it that reads HI, I'M YOUR NEW TREE. I squeeze my lips together, too nervous to speak, blood howling like *Ask me ask me ask me ask me ask me.* Oh God, this might get awkward, but what else could she be about to ask? How many other types of *personal* can there be? She's going to ask if I like girls. I'll ask what gave her that impression, and she'll be happy to inform me. That's a conversation two girls who're into girls would totally have with each other.

Right?

Carla shifts uneasily, thumbs turtled in her sleeves. "I guess I was just wondering how you and Henry do it."

Wait.

I scrape up a laugh. "What?"

"Stay close," she whispers. "I've watched you around school all week. Nobody would ever think you two just broke up. And you're still planning on going to the same college? I would give anything to have that sort of connection with Bea. *Anything*. It's . . ."

So hard, she says.

"I love them so much."

And now it's time for my input. Me and the Jupiter-size hole I've chewed in my cheek. I don't know, I tell her. I'm positive that's what I say. I tell her, Henry and I just aren't like other couples . . . and then I mumble about ambition and Purdy and the necessity of us. At the gym doors, we part amicably.

"Thanks." Carla's blushing, too. This smear of red across her cheeks. "I really—I owe you coffee sometime. Or ice cream. Do you like mochi? Some people don't. It's, like, a textural thing."

I pry on a smile. "Sounds great." I say I forgot to drop my bag off, then lock myself in the car, my eyes burning.

I get that Carla's wrapped up in Bea. I get that just

because she has feelings for them doesn't mean she'll never have feelings for me. But I was hoping that if I asked how she knew I liked girls, she'd giggle around her straw and say, *There's just something about you. . . .*

Then I'd know what, too.

15.

HENRY CAN'T TALK BECAUSE he's late for youth group.

"It's Saturday night."

"I know," he says, propping his phone on his desk, the video quality not exactly enhanced by the dingy hues of his bedroom. "There's this lady at church who lives alone and has trouble getting around by herself, so a bunch of members went over to help spring-clean her basement. I had work," he goes on, twisting out of his I Love's polo, "but we're see-ing a movie at the mall afterward. I already told everybody I'd meet them there."

"Oh," I say. He tosses his shirt to the floor. "Want me to pick you up? I'm, like, ninety percent positive my parents will give me the car." The mall isn't far, useful only for its movie theater and proximity to Sonic. All the good stores are at Crossgates, in Albany.

"I— Hold on." He calls out the door in Korean. "My mom's driving. She's— Almost ready, Umma!" Back to me:

"She's meeting up with some friends from her nursing program for dinner."

My temples thump. Youth group on a Saturday isn't unprecedented, even if Henry would be the first to argue that believing in God doesn't automatically make him, quote, religious. But on this night . . . *this* Saturday . . .

It wouldn't be so urgent if we'd gotten to exchange more than a couple of texts before his break ended, or if I were the teeniest bit more ignorant, so I could ask to join him. Here's the deal, though: There aren't many Korean Methodists in the Hudson Valley—or Korean people, period. Narrow that down to kids our age worth tolerating, and the number's practically nonexistent. As hard as it is to understand how alone that can make him feel, I'd never interfere with his time with them.

So I say, "Are you in a bad mood or something?"

"Bad mood?"

"You're being grumpy." Granted, grumpiness is a core part of Henry's personality. World's Best Grandpa, etc. But this feels different, and it's a little baffling.

He bites his lip.

Yeah. When he gets *this* grouchy, there's a zero-point-nothing chance it doesn't involve his family. "Did your dad call?"

"I mean . . ." Henry roots around in the dresser, his back to me. "Not recently, that I know of. I think he's still kind of pissed at me for deciding not to keep my dual citizenship. He actually thought I was going to serve in the Korean military, when I was born in Savannah and haven't been to

Korea since I was, like, seven. Sometimes he calls my mom when we're at school, but Yuna would've given me her take if he had."

"I know. Hence why I don't think talking to her is always a good idea."

"She's my sister."

Half sister. Her mom is Mr. Yoo's first wife, and Yuna was practically in high school when he met Henry's mom, but I swallow the reminder—it's the one area where Henry resents specifics. "Okay, but remember the last time she came for Christmas and spent the whole visit dropping hints that maybe her job would move her back to New York soon, when none of that was true? I get that she doesn't want you to feel all lonely and sad on the other side of the world, but sometimes—"

"For your information, she was really supportive when I came out to her in April."

"Oh. I didn't . . ." I didn't realize he'd told Yuna. "Okay. That's . . . that's awesome. April meaning . . . April." As in, before May. Before he told me. Which kind of throws that text she sent after prom into an entirely different context. Did she *know* he'd been wanting to tell me? I shouldn't mind, but the thought pinches hard.

"That must've been difficult," I rally. Unlike my parents, who literally cannot shut up about dating and sex, his don't talk about that stuff at all. Until now I hadn't considered where Yuna might fall on that spectrum.

"Yeah," Henry says. "Like, she finished high school in Georgia after she moved to the U.S. with my dad and went to college there, but she's still spent most of her life in Korea, and people there tend to not be as accepting, so I was definitely nervous. She was cool about it, though. Actually, she said she's friends with some gay guys in Daegu who are out." He smiles a little. "It felt good telling her."

"I'm happy for you," I say. Then, "Who else knows?" Not that he has to justify this or anything. He can be out to whoever he wants. Whenever he wants. Just like me.

But.

"Nobody. Well." He reddens. "My mom knows we broke up."

"What?"

"Wait, have you *not* told your parents?"

"Of course I haven't. We agreed—"

"Sorry, but what was I supposed to do, indefinitely maintain a fake relationship? My bad." He grabs one of his nicer holographic Pokémon shirts and shoves his arms through the sleeves. "If I hadn't said anything, my mom would've figured it out anyway. She's been suspicious ever since I ditched our prom sleepover. Don't be mad."

"I'm not." I guess. . . .

I don't know. I did tell Carla.

Still, it feels like he's taken a pretty big step without me.

"How'd she react?" I make myself ask.

He groans, like, *How do you think?* "Now she'll be even more on my ass about bringing home a nice Korean church girl. Believe me, this has in no way improved my quality of life. But I figured . . ." He hesitates, smoothing his shirt over his hips. "I mean, I do want to be out to my parents someday. Eventually. So I figured I'd start with my mom, and our breakup, then keep dropping hints here and there until we're both ready. Seriously, she cannot handle surprises. My dad's going to be harder, but he makes everything hard. I'm not going to let myself stress about it too much yet. You're telling your parents soon, aren't you?"

I twist my ponytail over my shoulder, so nonchalant, when all I'm thinking about is Carla's shoulders, and bringing up rowing club without Henry scrutinizing my miraculous change of heart, and how I kind of want to masturbate but also desperately need to cry.

"I wish you'd warned me," I say as he finger-combs his hair.

"Huh?"

"About your mom. And Yuna. I wasn't prepared."

Henry's quiet while he finishes dressing. He tosses something into the trash by his desk, and I wait for him to pump his fist and go, *Kobe!*

"Okay," he mutters. "I mean, I literally just told my mom today, so you've basically known as long as she has, but whatever."

"Why today?"

Henry stops, looking indecisive. "It just . . . felt like the right moment, I guess. But next time I get the urge to share my personal business with somebody I trust, I'll be sure to run it by you."

"Listen." I bend over my phone, so he'll get every word. "It's not *your* personal business. It's ours. There's no going rogue."

His jaw squirms. "Here's an idea: Why don't we make a list of everything we haven't thought of? That way, nothing will surprise us ever again."

"Perfect."

Only when he raises his phone to capture the full majesty of his eye roll do I realize he wasn't serious.

After we say goodbye, I open my laptop back up to Purdy's list of suitably well-rounded activities. *Rowing* is right there, nested between *Religious missions* and *Sanskrit*. Two clicks and I'm on the Elmerville Crew website, where an array of kids in matching purple-and-gold jackets beam back at me, posed with oars that could've propelled the *Titanic*. Carla's easy to pick out. Baseball cap and bike shorts, her legs as long as the Hudson itself.

None of our rules would forbid my participation. In fact, one gives me a pass: *Purdy first.*

Except if I mention rowing to my parents, they'll ask how much it costs. They'll interrogate the coach about what gear I'll *actually* need versus what's recommended, and shriek that it's just so great, *so wonderful,* that I've decided to be a joiner for once. *This is a bold new step for you, Jilly!* Yeah. That's me. Signing up for a sport I'd never heard of until, like, seven hours ago. Seeing Van Gogh moons and stars in Carla's hair, but nothing to say.

I smack my laptop shut.

16.

SCHOOL ENDS JUST WHEN it seems determined not to, and in the two weeks that follow, there's no distinction between summer and waiting. This drizzle of days.

No, Winn emails after the Fourth of July. No Mandarin updates. Sorry.

By Friday, I'm wearing my mouth guard full-time. Classes at ACCC start Monday.

Tactics must evolve.

Henry's scattered dispatches aren't helping us strategize. He's picked up as many extra shifts as possible before schoolwork takes over his vacation, which wouldn't be *so* awful if my parents weren't making me volunteer at the clinic, thus rendering talking to him at any point during the day virtually impossible. Every afternoon, Mom drags me on rounds through downtown Albany, convincing any IV drug users we spot to exchange dirty needles for free clean ones. Thankfully, my role excludes needles. That's Mom's job, cheerfully directing each client to plunk their wares in a biohazard container labeled SHARPS. Mainly I offer brochures with titles like *You Can Break Free from Addiction* and *How Methadone Can Help,* a concept that's almost interesting. Both heroin and methadone are opioids, but heroin is illegal and harmful, methadone legal and less so. Take methadone every day and your cells get tricked into thinking you're high when you're not. Then—well, it's not so different from Henry and me getting all that kissing out of our system. Gradually taper the dose until, voilà, dependent no more.

When the sun's at its most incinerating, we offer bottled water and Snapple, too. Mom and I loop through block after block, sweating in the giant clinic van while I refresh my inbox at two-minute intervals.

Luckily, the van's at the shop this afternoon, needle exchange canceled, so Mom has no problem being persuaded to let me leave early. Heat hits like a blast of bad breath as I rush down the clinic ramp. Today is ACCC's New Student Orientation, and Henry won't be so anxious if I'm there to surprise him.

Our car's AC has miraculously resurrected itself, so I crank it, reveling in the freeze. Google Maps urges me past Albany's Catholic high schools and the university that half our classmates will attend. On Lark Street, rainbow flags drape smoke shops and restaurants, left over from Pride Weekend in June. Driving by, I force down memories of all the links Henry sent that I still haven't looked at, thoughts of how comfortable he seems identifying as gay, like slipping his arms into a sweater he knew would fit. The same label I've stretched over the sum of me.

Uptown, Albany reverts to gray scale. Banks, lawyers' offices, pharmacies . . . low effort for a state capital. I accidentally pass campus twice. In my defense, I've never visited—my knowledge of it is limited to emails about elementary school science camps and Elm-High's hockey teams routinely getting housed here. Buildings huddle around a square courtyard, stacks of blank concrete, the overall effect so *less* than extraordinary that even when I confirm the address on my phone and realize that the silver-embossed sign to the left of the intersection does indeed say ALBANY COUNTY COMMUNITY COLLEGE—GROW YOUR MIND HERE, it doesn't seem real.

Maybe it's like a video game, where a new area loads only as fast as the graphics can render. Every moment that passes escalates this Mandarin situation from non-problem to very much of one. It's reduced my processing speed.

I take the first side street that isn't a left turn, then park parallel-ish to a hydrant, flip the hazards on. Totally legal.

I'm not sure which building hosts orientation. Henry never did send pictures, but I've got half an hour to do my own sleuthing. Seeking shade, I plant myself beneath a tree at the edge of the courtyard, brushing AC goose bumps from my arms as students pass in small groups, pixelated through the leaves. I try not to stare at them too obviously. Or at the concrete buildings that are actually more stately than decrepit when viewed close-up, this first taste of college

Henry's gotten without me. Branches overhead bulge with anonymous fruits. I pick one and sniff—ew. Smells like puke. I drop it just as Henry crosses the courtyard.

Adidas bag slung over his shoulder, glasses glinting in the sunlight. I push through the crush of backpacks and iced-coffee cups to reach him. "Henry!" I call.

He's in a patch of shade now.

"Henry, hey!"

Laughing with a stranger.

He pushes his glasses up on his nose. Our whole relationship, we've had this special sense for when the other is nearby.

Which is why it's kind of weird that the other boy notices me first. He touches Henry's shoulder.

"Surprise!" I say as Henry spins around.

"Jilly." His mouth flops. "What are you doing here?"

"Why? Is this not allowed?"

"Of course it is. I just— Wow. I'm kind of overwhelmed, sorry. This is amazing." He crams a piece of paper into his pocket—a campus map, it looks like—and goes for a hug, squashing me to him.

I barely hear the other boy say hi.

"So. Um," Henry says nervously, "Jill, this is—it's Stevie. Stevie, Jill."

I saw the insides of my cheeks, awaiting the necessary qualifier. Not *my girlfriend,* obviously, and *ex* would be harsh, but . . . best friend? Naturally, we never did work out how to introduce ourselves to new people. Probably there are a million more things we've forgotten—invisible swarms of oversights liable to strike at any time.

Henry wiggles.

I realize it's getting awkward that I haven't said anything.

"Nice to meet you," I manage.

"Same," Stevie says. He's skyscraper tall. East Asian. Shredded jeans and a pink T-shirt, a caramelized glint to his hair.

I ask, "Are you taking Mandarin, too?"

"Um." The grin vanishes. "No?" He slides Henry a look.

"Sorry." I flush. "I didn't assume that because you're— It's just that, it kind of seems like you two know each other—"

"Our moms are tight," Stevie answers. "I'm only here because my sister Bekah's in the cosmetology program. She's actually studying to be a makeup artist, but the aesthetician classes always need guinea pigs. Just doing my part." He has a twangy accent that I can't place but that definitely could not have originated anywhere in New York, let alone the entire Eastern Seaboard. "Y'all should come sometime. Free facials."

"Huh." I pretend to consider it, so nicely. Beaming major *Let's go* vibes at Henry, who's turned a spectacular shade of hot dog.

Seriously, if orientation sucked that hard, he can tell me about it in the car. Windows down, highway air frothing in our faces. Once we're home, he'll be ready to explore new options. The lack of characters to memorize makes racquetball mighty enticing.

Henry says, "I had no idea Stevie would be here. We bumped into each other, like, right before you showed up. It was so—"

"Random," Stevie interrupts.

"Totally," Henry says. "It totally was."

I sort of laugh, too.

And then Henry wipes the sweat off his lip. Stevie palms back his hair.

Now's my chance. "So. Ready?"

Henry hesitates. They look at each other. "Actually—"

"We were going to get bibimbap on Madison," Stevie says.

Henry sucks his lip.

My teeth crunch together. Is Henry hanging out with this kid because their moms are friends not charitable enough?

Now he steps closer, taking me gently by the arm.

"Can't you go later?" I whisper in a rush. "We have to go home and start planning—"

"Jill," he says.

"I shared you on a list of all our best alternatives this morning. You haven't made, like, any changes to the Google Doc—"

Henry shushes me. A finger to my lips. "*Jillian*. I can't."

My eyes almost cross. Stevie turns away, flicking politely through his phone. "Why?" I say.

He lowers his gaze.

"Henry?"

When he meets my eye again—another buffering error. Henry's lashes glisten like he's holding back tears, and Stevie taller than Wilson Longchamps but roughly as tall as Parker

Evans. And when I got here—his casual brush of Henry's shoulder . . .

Henry wobbles into focus. He's rambling about lunch, and I care, except I don't. Our Google Doc— But when I grab for my phone, it clatters to the asphalt. Stevie jumps.

"Your screen broke," Henry says.

He says we'll fix it.

He starts to cry.

It's not that bad a crack, Jilly.

No big deal.

17.

WHEN WE CLIMB INTO THE CAR, we still haven't spoken. Henry fumbles with his seat belt as we lurch downtown.

Finally he tells me, "That wasn't how I wanted you to meet."

I stare at the Subaru inches ahead of us. Bike rack and DOG MOM stickers. My mouth guard sucking my teeth. "Hate to see a plan get ruined."

"It's not that dramatic. Stevie's . . . Our moms met at church, and we've been texting awhile, but other than that we've only been hanging out on our own for the past few days. Since school got out."

School? Our last final was two and a half weeks ago. All those times I assumed Henry was busy working . . .

"Look," he continues. "I get that this is kind of a lot, but it is for me, too, to be honest, and we've both got to process—"

"Really? It's pretty clear to me. One"—I count on my fingers—"your unprecedented demand in taking a class we're both terrible at. A class at another school. With one remaining seat! Two—"

"Are you serious?"

"Pressuring me to do a completely different activity so we'd be apart for the whole summer. All that talk about happy accidents, like we can just leave our lives up to the whims of the universe and be fine? You've been scheming behind my back this entire time! Coming up with your own plan. Without me. Just to put the moves on some college boy."

"Oh my God, fact check. *One*"—he grapples with my clenched fist, forcing my finger back down even though I'm driving—"that accusation? It's wild. Literally the hardest you have ever Jillian-ed. Two, Stevie isn't in college. He's sixteen."

I slam the brakes, almost pasting a squirrel that can't decide which side of the street to be on. "Sixteen?"

"Did you not hear him say he's helping his sister?"

I did. Just.

No way.

No way that giant's younger than us.

I glance at Henry, who gives his glasses a righteous shove. "You think I've been against you all along. Orchestrating this grand deception. Did it ever occur to you that by encouraging you to enroll in something else, I was just trying to nudge you out of your comfort zone for once? You know, being your *friend*. Like how you're completely failing to be mine right now?"

"You think I'm being a bad friend? On what grounds, drawing a perfectly reasonable conclusion?"

"Okay, well, for your information, I didn't know Mandarin was almost full when I enrolled. I thought . . ." He slumps against the window, hugging himself. "The more I thought about it, the more it seemed like a blessing in disguise. A step in the right direction, so we'd both get space to explore our identities, meet new people, exactly like we wanted. And then I found out Stevie was going to be on campus all summer anyway."

"So you lied," I say. "You didn't just randomly bump into each other. Cool. Thanks for clarifying."

"No, I didn't! He said he might be around, but we didn't make any specific plans until, like, right before you showed up. And . . . look, until recently I didn't even know what was going on between us, if anything. Stevie Lim is, like, the quietest kid in youth group. He hardly speaks."

It's hypocritical. I know that, considering I've told him nothing about Carla. But I can't stop my mouth from cracking open as Henry's gaze tugs toward me, sensing my comeback before I do: *If you met him at youth group, then why didn't you mention meeting him at youth group?* "Did he go the other weekend?" I ask instead. "To the movie? Is that why you told your mom about us? Why you didn't want me driving you?"

He rubs his tongue over his teeth, avoiding my eyes.

"Henry."

"So what if it was? Up until now youth group was practically the only space you and I got from each other, and now we . . . have a little more. Isn't that why—" His voice teeters. "Isn't that why we broke up?"

"Space?" I scoff. "No, not why we broke up. You use that word so much. What do you think it means? Freedom? Pretty sure it's the opposite, based on these past couple weeks. Sporadic texts plus no hanging-out equals, like, no oxygen." A black hole licking its lips.

"You think I haven't realized that now?" he wails.

Frankly, no. If I've out-Jillian-ed myself, I don't know what that means for Henry and this new bug in his programming. One that turns him into the exact inverse of the good, dependable boy we both know and need. I only hid my talking to Carla to protect his feelings. Because he got so freaking ornery every time she came up, and I hated doing that to him, but now he just . . . expects me to accept his own infatuation? His own lies? As our silence hardens, I look over to see him clutching my mangled phone.

Hoarsely, I say, "You should've told me. About Mandarin."

"Like you would've heard," he snaps back.

Five minutes later, trapped at the longest red on Lark with my jaw still seething, I say, "I'm a good listener."

Henry's tiptoeing his fingers up my arm. "Sometimes."

"When your family upsets you, which is constantly, I don't listen out of duty. I listen because I love you and you don't deserve their bullshit—"

He snorts. "That's different. Do you not know how you get once you set your mind to something? Take it from me, an expert: you're impossible. Like, it's worse than arguing with my mom. From day one, you were maniacally insistent about taking Mandarin together. Even if I'd had the wherewithal to explain what I was doing, you were so ir-rational, you wouldn't have given me the chance—"

Irrational? "I am *so* not irrational. If I was, how would we have gotten this far with Purdy? It's a miracle we didn't fuck up worse."

Henry goes silent again.

AC snarls through the vents.

Obviously, we're not fighting. There's a difference be-tween a fight and an impassioned discussion about a topic of critical importance.

We both understand that.

"I asked you," I whisper, digging my thumbs against the steering wheel's ragged stitching. So I won't want the words back. So I won't scream. "I asked you point-blank if you wanted to take that class alone, and you didn't say . . ." Bringing this up tumbles me back to that night. Henry's knuckles on my lips.

I don't remember what he said.

That conversation ended with us kissing.

Henry must be reliving it, too. He quickly pushes his glasses up, scrubbing his eyes with his fist. "I told you I was scared! It was like . . . constipation. Verbal constipation. The words were there, but I couldn't get them out."

Red light. Again. The steering wheel judders, moist from my palms.

". . . hope you understand I wasn't hiding Stevie," Henry's saying. "You have no idea how badly I wanted to tell you about him. Seriously. Another gay Korean American kid from the South? In *Albany*? I've been losing my shit over here. And, okay, maybe he's way more into Jesus than I am, and winces a little every time I swear, but he's so cute and pure, and he already knows all about you, but—I don't know. Things escalated so quickly after the movie night. It's been confusing. But so good. But confusing—"

"Yeah," I cut him off.

At the next light, I take my phone from him, assessing the damage. Ordinarily downtown is our favorite part of Albany. When we were younger, before we got our licenses, Ms. Yoo would drop us off for dates here, and we'd poke around the cafés and vintage record stores, sipping hot chocolate, brownstone houses on either side of us, packed tight as books. Now those memories feel like somebody else's. A tabby cat perches on the nearest stoop, licking her butthole.

"I'm sorry," Henry says.

I drop my phone into the cup holder. "It's old anyway."

"No, I mean, I wasn't as forthcoming about Mandarin as I could've been, or Stevie. You're right. Point conceded."

While he gnaws a hangnail, I flip back to my first impression of Stevie. Towering beside Henry in his ripped jeans, friendly, but at the same time sort of not. And yet after my phone detonated, when Henry turned to him and whispered he was sorry but lunch wouldn't work today after all, Stevie nodded and dug out a tissue for Henry from a little pack tucked in his pocket. His concern so inconvenient that *I* could've sobbed. If he'd had the decency to be less understanding, just one-tenth more of an asshole, my observations might add up to something. As they are, they're worthless. Indicative of—what? A handsome boy with an indeterminate place in our perfectly crafted plan.

At the thought, tears file into my eyes.

My war against the unexpected made me overlook what should've been the most painfully obvious, expected thing.

Of course Henry would eventually develop feelings for a boy.

Of course he'd want to date somebody else.

"I'm sorry, too," I say.

We're pulling into his driveway, with the strip of turf sprouting inexplicably down the middle, when Henry says, "Wait." He cups my face in his hands once I've finished parking—"Here"—and reaches into my mouth, gently unhooking my mouth guard with his finger. "So you won't sound stoned for the rest of this."

"How would you know how stoned sounds?"

He shrugs, sheepish.

Like either of us would do a drug.

My keys dangle from the ignition. I yank them out, wishing just this once we could exit a vehicle without twenty-five minutes of soul-baring. I'm sick of confessions. Sick of tasting rubber and futile, prickly truths. But neither of us moves. The AC keeps blasting as quiet pools around us, making the car feel extra hermetic.

Henry pops my mouth guard in and smacks his lips. "Mmm. Tastes like retainer grime and your anal-retentive nature."

"Henry." Now I'm holding his face. A countergrip, forcing him to look at me. "We need to be honest with each other from now on. Full-court press, no holds barred, violently honest, or else this isn't going to work. Can you do that? Can you be totally honest?"

"Can you?"

Aquamarine smearing my shirt.

Carla crunching her straw at me.

"Of course," I bark.

"Then me too." He nods once, his glasses skidding halfway down his nose. "For real. Absolutely."

"Okay, so tell me where you're at with Mandarin, because I spent a lot of time compiling that list, and if you're going to date—" The notion's strangling. "What I mean is, there's no law saying you have to be on campus to hang out with Stevie. You already have been anyway, so . . . Onward. Personally, I'm leaning toward racquetball. Nett is a jerk, but we've got sick hand-eye coordination, and Mandarin is so freaking difficult—"

"Jillian," Henry says. A prayer, sigh, and spray of mouth guard spit all in one. "Listen to me. I speak Korean. And, yeah, maybe I'm not as fluent as my parents would prefer, and my accent sucks, but unlike you, I've already learned one language that doesn't stick to English speaking patterns. It helps, even if Korean and Mandarin don't have anything to do with each other otherwise. I will destroy this class. Or—maybe 'destroy' is too strong a word. But I'll get by. Trust me."

The guard's special. Made by my dentist, for me. When Henry opens his mouth, it slides from his teeth and plops I-don't-want-to-know-where.

"Awesome," I say.

He smiles guiltily.

"So you're just going to go off without me, then. You're dead set on . . . on . . ." We're still holding each other's faces. Henry tucks my hair behind my ears, and, God, I love how he does that. I love how, no matter what, he keeps all my pieces in exactly their right place.

I can't be mad at him.

I can't.

Our rules don't allow it.

I wobble from the car. Henry shoves his seat back to dig for my mouth guard. "Racquetball would be a great fit for you," he says. "You'll . . . Shit, almost had it. . . . You're so freaking competitive, and either way, we just need to knock out these extra credits or whatever. What'd we say—Purdy above all, right?"

Henry's in serious danger of getting sucked under the seat himself, his whole lower back exposed, easily twice as pale as the rest of him. I think of Carla's dimples that day in the art room.

"Jill?"

"Purdy first," I correct him quietly. "The wording is, 'Purdy first.' Rule four." Which I'd like to take back now. Or edit. Add a disclaimer: *Together, or not at all.*

"There's still time," I say. "You're right—you *are* better at Mandarin, but enrollment doesn't close until after the first two weeks. You could help me. . . ." My knees crumple. I plop into the driver's seat, and he flicks my mouth guard, furry with lint, at me. "Somebody might drop."

"Taking separate classes is the right step for us," he answers, pushing himself up. "Regardless of how we got here. I know you know that."

Okay, but what if I'm already sick of thinking about how we got here? Or where we're going? What if by the end of this, Carla's nobody, and all I'll want is to hold him and cry into his neck that smells like everything good?

"We can't," I say.

Henry rounds the car and taps the windshield, glaring at me through the grime and bug splats. "Hello. Extrapolate. If when you say Mandarin is hard, you mean it's hard for you, then maybe that's applicable to other situations. Maybe when you say *we* can't, you just mean *you* can't. Has that never occurred to you?"

No, I could shout.

I could tell him, *There never was any difference until literally just now.*

But.

"Not racquetball," I tell him.

If this is what we're doing. If we're really going to say screw it and open ourselves up to all this not-knowing, and peril, and being apart . . . a little bit of that has to be okay with me. It's got to be on my terms.

"Sure," Henry says encouragingly. "Of course. What, then?"

Unlike where I live, surrounded by woods, there's hardly

any distinction between which parts of the enormous field by Henry's house are his and what belongs to the orchard. Unless you're paying attention, that is. I listen for the fizz of electric wire.

"Jillian?"

A sob pinches my throat.

18.

Greetings, Elmerville Rowers!

Coach Johnson here. As you know, THE SUMMER SESSION WILL BE STARTING MONDAY, JULY 10! It even seems we have a NEW MEMBER joining us, which is GREAT! Please be aware that all rowers are required to pay a fee of $200 prior to our first meeting, and should expect to complete a swim test if they missed the previous season. In addition, rowers must bring their own gear, regardless of whether we'll be practicing on land or water. This includes:

Spandex shorts (*Loose-fitting clothes NOT PERMITTED*)
Short-sleeve athletic tee
Change of clothes
RAINCOAT*
<u>Reusable</u> water bottle to respect our beautiful planet
Hat

Sunscreen

Sunglasses

Nutritious snacks

YES, we row IN ALL WEATHER, except high winds, thunder, or lightning!

On Monday, we will have land practice at the Elmerville High weight room starting at 6 a.m. Water practices will be Wednesday, Thursday, and Friday, with a bus leaving from the Elmerville High senior parking lot at promptly 5:00 a.m. to reach the Canning Preserve boathouse by 5:30. NO, we will not be waiting for you for ANY reason, so *PLAN ACCORDINGLY.* Arriving late means YOU MISS THE BOAT. PUN INTENDED.

That's all for now. Please feel free to email me with any questions or concerns you might have (especially NEW MEMBER!).

See you there!

19.

I HAVEN'T HEARD FROM Henry about getting a ride home from the clinic the night before crew starts, so when Big Purp rolls up alongside me on my way to the bus stop, I nearly sob with relief.

"Oh my God." I hug him through the driver's-side window. "You're lucky I didn't Mace you, creeper. How was class? I thought you'd be home by now."

"We just finished up," he says into my neck.

We?

I pull away.

Stevie Lim waves from the passenger seat. "Sup."

I wave back limply.

"We're hanging out at my place tonight," Henry rushes to explain. "My mom's making dinner and everything. I was going to call, but this is perfect. Hop in?"

I shift positions, going for noncommittal, only to accidentally snap a wet bra strap against my clavicle. The five blocks between the clinic and the Madison Avenue stop might as well be ninety in this heat. "My first practice is tomorrow," I say. "I thought we'd . . . I was trying to see if you wanted to help with my night-before ritual, since we didn't get to do one for you." First we'll arrange clothes. Blue spandex shorts and a crumply gray T-shirt I bought at Marshalls. Barely one step up from Elm-High's dorky gym uniforms. We'll chant the Purdy Creed as candles weep wax all over my carpet. "Did you not get my texts?"

"We'll do it after," Henry says. "Stevie's got to be home by ten." He turns to him. "You don't mind if Jilly joins, do you?"

Stevie's been courteous this whole time, ducking—all six foot hundred of him—to see me across Henry. Now his smile slips.

"No prob," he says.

Henry twists around. It takes me a second to realize he's manually unlocking the back door. *Click*, and the back seat looms mustily before me.

An uncharted expanse.

"Jill?" Henry says.

Obviously, rules of shotgun dictate that Stevie remain seated. He got there first, but if seniority, sheer rank, doesn't entitle me to overthrow him, what does? I'm pulling my brains apart for an excuse, when Henry says my name again: *Jilly*.

So much for space.

Only the middle seat belt works. I don't figure this out until we're moving, and have to ride thrust forward, my prickly knees jutting over the console that Stevie's mistaken

146

for his personal elbow rest. The song they were listening to—that they must have turned down when they spotted me—murmurs through the speakers. As Big Purp picks up speed, I text my parents what's happening, then swipe to my thread with Carla. The text I poured hours into composing crouches unanswered, mocking me.

Three hours, twenty-eight minutes, and counting.

We've texted only one other time, and not since vacation started. For all I know, she forgot my number.

My backpack's at my feet. Reflexively, I check to make sure the bathing suit I bought on my lunch break is still inside—like I was *so* successful at hiding it from my parents all afternoon that it might've dematerialized. I haven't ventured past my ankles in a body of water since Henry taught me about the kappa, so none of my old bathing suits fit me.

"What'd you do during class?" I ask Henry.

"Not much," he answers.

Which could be real, or code for *dry heave over the bathroom sink*. I examine Stevie for clues. His hair's the same summery brown it was when we met the other day, the top half knotted into a bun that pokes over his seat. The closeness of the car forces me to notice more against my will. Diamond studs in both earlobes. Freckles on his nose. Brutally adorable. The corner of Henry's textbook peeks out of his bag. Desperate for a distraction, I yank it out. *Integrated Mandarin for Beginners*.

Inspiring.

I crack the book open. The pages are yellow at the edges,

like an old person's fingernails. Undeterred, I churn through them, fighting to make sense of what he's in for. Notes in blue ballpoint flood the margins.

I must make a noise. Henry looks back at me. "What?" he asks.

"Somebody wrote in this. They gave away half the answers to the homework for unit six—more than half." I flip the book around to show him.

"I got my textbooks used, remember?"

"What if the teacher accuses you of copying? Or gets mad in general?"

"So get this: Dr. Lin-Claros doesn't collect homework or really care whether we do it at all as long as we show up on time and participate. My final grade's all about the test at the end of the quarter." He chugs from his Nalgene and burps before slotting it back into the cup holder. "College is nothing like high school."

"Can confirm," Stevie says. "Well. That's what my sister tells me."

"Yeah, thanks." Like I wasn't rapidly coming to that conclusion myself. Elm-High's textbooks predate Henry and me by centuries, but make one mark in them and teachers act like you spit on their firstborn. I study the page again, my vision strobing slightly.

Doctor. How can the teacher's title make *Henry* seem so much more important? Elevated, in this way that makes me feel incredibly not—clammy and five, like I can't wipe my nose by myself.

Henry has a professor.

An almost-boyfriend.

And tomorrow I'll be at my first crew practice, with Carla. Everything about me screaming *starter.*

Since I joined crew, I've been devising methods for coming clean to Henry about Carla's involvement. Only, he's been so excited about Stevie—and soft-serve ice cream machines on campus, and this book he found in the library from the 1880s—that the timing never feels right. Tonight would've been ideal. I cram the textbook back into Henry's bag and watch Stevie scratch at a tiny scar on his elbow.

All we've got to do is survive one night of this kid. *One night* hanging out with Henry's crush, everything normal and supportive between us and not like our whole fucking everything is falling apart. What better way to prove our rules work? I'll just tell him about Carla afterward. *Violently honest,* we said. And if the choice is between seeing Henry with Stevie or not seeing Henry at all . . .

Up front, Henry white-knuckles the steering wheel. Back straight, hair carefully mussed. Stevie smiles at him, and Henry smiles back an alarmingly long time for somebody who's driving.

I dip back to my phone.

"Sorry. Um. Jilly?"

My name in Stevie's mouth.

His loose, easy limbs jutting from my seat.

"Are you excited about tomorrow? For—what was it, rowing practice?" The question creaks out, like Stevie's not so confident about making conversation with me. Like he wants to get it right.

"I—"

"Jilly's strong as hell," Henry brags. "I couldn't sleep the other night, and so I watched some rowing clips on YouTube? People taking oars to the face, getting knocked off boats. Ain't going to be easy. If anybody can do it, you can, though."

The *ain't* throws me so badly that I almost don't realize Henry's talking to me. I didn't pick up on it at first, but his Southern accent has poked through more the longer we've been in the car.

"Sort of," I say. "I mean, I'll get through it. I guess. But this is really for—"

Carla.

I clear my throat. "It's—it's about—"

"Your scholarship," Stevie cuts in. "Henry told me about that, too."

"Oh. Yeah."

Abruptly, Henry turns the music back up. The song is hysterically bubbly, a sugar enema. K-pop, which he despises. I push my phone between my sticky thighs and lean as far back from them and the panting AC as I can, ridiculously conscious of how much room I'm taking up, my stench and soggy clothes. Come on, Carla. Answer. I'd put the phone away, end this torture, if it wouldn't undermine my tactical approach. You can't reply *haha sorry! just seeing this!!* if it's true.

We're close to Henry's. The landscape out the window draws together, shapes familiar as the insides of my own eyelids in the fuzzy half-dark. Antonelli's produce stand—closed most times of the year except now—and apple orchards, though the trees aren't doing much but being green. The standard Elmerville jumble of forest and farmland.

My parents don't know about Carla, either. Only crew, once my cover story about taking early-morning volunteer shifts at the climbing gym got blown up by a permission slip. Which my parents signed. Most of their commentary revolved around the practices' heinously early start times, plus the program's cost, which I had to pay by raiding my stockpile of birthday money. Naturally, my mom couldn't resist asking how it felt for Henry and me to be beyond each other's reach most of the summer, but I mumbled my way out of it.

Purdy first, I told her.

"But, yeah," I croak over the music, "tomorrow's going to be great. I'm pumped." The Purdy people already emailed me, anyway. All I've got to do is submit a letter from my coach confirming that I completed the season. That I was, quote, *a crew teammate in good standing.* Until then, my eligibility will be marked *pending.* I brace for Stevie's follow-up . . .

. . . only to realize he's telling Henry a joke with an incomprehensible punch line. I guess because I missed the beginning.

"Wait," I say. "What—"

They bust up.

We're home before they manage to compose themselves. Henry noses Big Purp under the basketball hoop and we all get out. Henry opens my door from the outside this time, but still giggling, wiping his eyes. Stevie throws his hood up and leaps onto the porch. *Thud*. He could've walked . . . ?

At least Henry and I have the driveway to ourselves.

"I'm really glad you could come." He squeezes my hands. "You are, too, right? This is okay?"

My sweat's beginning to dry, and I'm shivering in my tank top. Henry's glasses are edged in gold.

"All good," I promise.

He looks relieved.

I check my texts as I follow him inside, slithering my thumb up and down the crack in my screen.

WE GO STRAIGHT TO Henry's room. In all the years I've been coming here, we've rarely hung out anywhere else. Tonight, though, I kind of wish we were downstairs, propped at the kitchen table or in the silvery-carpeted TV room. Somewhere random, that's not so covered in Henry.

Stevie pulls off his hoodie, which Henry instructs him to toss wherever.

"Wherever?" Stevie responds, all mischievous, and I'm about to say, *Wow, what a clever innuendo,* when I realize the Nintendo logo on his white T-shirt actually says NINTEN-HO.

That is objectively hilarious.

Flowery music wafts down the hall—Ms. Yoo must be watching TV in her room. Henry goes to tell her we're home.

"Too much food," I hear him saying. He switches to Korean as my phone hums.

Omg! You're serious???

Carla wrote back. I swipe to reply, almost slicing my thumb off.

Yup. New member = me lol.

Wooooooo!!!!

hah so cool you changed your mind.

Tomorrow is gonna be r o u g h

But i'm so ready

I nibble my lip, vaguely aware Stevie's on the move. He revolves slowly, not touching anything, like you can learn all there is to know about somebody through a self-guided tour of their room.

Hah.

Stevie knows nothing about Henry. He doesn't know how we came down with swine flu on our eighth-grade overnight to Manhattan and basically had to be evacuated back upstate, or how terrified he is of spiders—even video-game ones. Stevie hasn't spent sufficient time with Henry—not nearly enough time—to master his array of grandpa sweaters or sense when to jump in if his glasses start to teeter. To do that, he'll have to be with Henry as long as I have. Every second of every day.

Which even I can't do now.

I tap a reply out to Carla, so casual, then slip my phone into my waistband. Stevie approaches the dresser, unwinding his bun so hair tumbles past his shoulders, longer than

Henry's and lusciously curly. I watch him scoop it back with both hands.

Then he rolls something out from behind Henry's hamper. A basketball.

"Henry doesn't play anymore," I inform him. "Basketball . . ." *It reminds him too much of his dad.* But since I'm not here to catch Stevie up on the intricacies of Henry's abandonment, I don't say so.

Stevie spins the ball on his finger, smiling at me. "You sure about that?"

"Uh. Yeah?"

Henry returns. Or tries to. He's barely through the door before the ball's hurtling for his head. He catches it. I duck and scream.

"Ohhhhh shit." Stevie howls as Henry advances, crossing the ball through his legs. "Watch out, dawg!"

Dawg.

He lunges after the ball and they tussle, laughing even when Henry's glasses go skittering across the floor.

I look at my phone.

Ok so tell me

How're you spending your last night alive

The ball dongs off Henry's headboard. "Wait." He giggles. "Hold on, my mom's going to kill us. . . ."

You first

154

> Ugh I was thinking I'd check out this party

> interested?

Stevie has Henry in a headlock now, their arms flailing. I almost trip over them on my way out.

After Mr. Yoo left and Henry's mom reclaimed the bathroom off their room for herself, the extra one upstairs became all Henry's, the shower tiled pink and wallpaper flaking, saturated with boy. I toe the toilet seat down and sit.

> party?

> wellll not like a PARTY party

> just some cool kids from the pride center

> taking slight advantage of Pauline Pappas

> whose parents are outta town

Pride Center?

The words shimmer like mirages on my battered screen. I worm my toes into the bath mat, my heart pounding.

Carla Kaminski invited me to a queer party.

> And sure

> pregaming crew isn't a SMART choice

> but what are parties for if not to ease our woes

> come onnnnnnnnn

> better than mochi, right???

I don't know. I don't know I don't know I don't know. I want to support Henry. Be the best friend I need to be, even though he should've asked ahead of time whether I'd be okay with hanging out with Stevie. He could've considered, for one fucking second, how just seeing him in the car might pulverize me.

haha yeah

so that's a yes???

Bea's going for sure

And Libby's dad won't let her go out

I really don't wanna face them alone.

Down the hall, the boys won't quit. Ms. Yoo thuds from her room, shouting at them to cut it out. I wait until she's left, then creep back, relieved to find Henry lounging on his bed alone.

"Hey," he says shyly. He takes my hand and rests it on his stomach.

"Where's Stevie?"

"You hear my mom light us up? He evaporated." He grins, upside down. "For real, though, you were taking forever—it was either bring him downstairs or wait and see how long you were going to blow the pee window."

I thump him—"Asshole"—and trace under his shirt, his skin flushed and warm from wrestling. "I wasn't pooping."

"Maybe not yet, but my mom made yuringi. RIP your stomach lining."

"Right."

Dinner.

He crushes my hand to his belly. "I can't eat."

I kneel beside him. "You mix up hunger with nausea when you're nervous." Which sucks and all.

But.

"Do you blame me? He's so cute. And muscly and sweet and, ugh, exactly our type of nerdy." Henry smiles faintly. I move my hand, not pulling back, just . . . Doesn't he see how excruciating it is for me to be here? How hard I'm trying to make this work? Google's already coughed up plenty of info on Steven Jaewoo Lim. A varsity athlete in basketball and baseball. Captain of his old school's intramural pickleball team.

I'm done hearing about him.

"He's from Dallas," Henry goes on. "Did I tell you that? His family moved here back in January, and he goes to Albany High, but I don't think he's made many friends yet. Did you see how he tried to block me once I got the ball?" He sits up. "When have I ever laughed that hard?"

He hasn't. Not even when I discovered you can tickle his hips just by looking at them. Does Stevie know that? When he figures it out, will Henry say, *Jillian knew that first*? I could ask him.

I could ask how this kid, a *junior,* is already so important Henry's pretending to be all about basketball again, when we both know he isn't.

But I don't know. I circle his thigh with my fingertip, like he hasn't already felt me trembling.

"You okay?" Henry asks.

Maybe I am Carla's second choice. . . .

"Hey. Are you scared about tomorrow?"

But I'll take that. I'll take anything that doesn't hurt as bad as this.

I yank free and shove past Stevie as he's coming upstairs, dodging Henry's shouts and the screen door snapping at my heels, Ms. Henderson's gutters blinking with Christmas lights she leaves up twenty-four seven for the world to see. Humidity cocoons me. Fireflies fritz over the lawn. I break into a jog.

It's not running if Henry doesn't see.

#1—NO FIGHTING

#2—NO MESSING AROUND????????

~~#3—NO MORE RUNNING~~

#4—PURDY FIRST

20.

THERE'S NO INDICATION WHEN we pull up to the big white house three streets from Henry's that a party is going on. I wait on the curb, subtly coaxing fresh air into my pits, while Carla reverses and parks farther down the road.

"Sorry," she says, hurrying to meet me. "Performance anxiety."

"No prob." I attempt a smile. She's dressed in a gauzy crop top with high-waisted shorts, exposing a flaky temporary pizza tattoo and a glimmer of stomach, like I wasn't sufficiently light-headed. While we navigate the driveway, currently a Tetris game of bad parking decisions, I consider my own ensemble. The same baggy running clothes I wore to the clinic.

"I'm glad you could come," Carla says.

She's sweaty, too. Her arm slides against mine while she feels for the doorbell, regret and hope and soggy air sporing mold in my lungs.

"Same," I get out.

Between here and Carla picking me up at the end of Henry's street, I've thought up twice as many ways of apologizing to him than of telling her *You look incredible.*

The doorbell trills. I whip out my phone and toggle to Do Not Disturb, canceling one billion missed texts from Henry. "So," I say. Carla looks to me expectantly. Her septum piercing twinkles in the porch light. "H-how was your Fourth of July?"

"Okay, I guess. Yours?"

A scratchy blanket over my shoulders. Watching fireworks spit and fizzle over the trees with Henry on his screened-in porch. My face flames.

The night warbles around us.

Literal crickets.

Okay. Not-Henry. Not-Henry. Say whatever, as long as it's Not-Henry: "It—it was . . . um . . ."

Pauline Pappas kicks the door open and tackles us with cheek kisses. I shrink from the warm press of her mouth.

"Oops," I mumble, afraid Pauline will mistake me for a prude or something when I just would've appreciated a warning? She's shorter than I remember from elementary school, stocky, with twisty hair, the skin of her chest flushed and sticky-looking. I wonder if she's drawn many stick figures with pubes since switching to Catholic school. When I whisper this to Carla, she giggles.

"Oh my God, right?"

We're headed for what must be a basement, descending

lushly carpeted steps that narrow like my windpipe the closer we get to the bottom. Pauline's squeal filters down behind us as she welcomes more newcomers.

Carla's saying, "Pauline's still kind of A Lot, but she's made a surprisingly adequate president of the Pride Center's teen club so far." She places a hand on my arm, and I promptly liquefy. Even if she is just steadying herself to ensure that Pauline's out of earshot. Turning back around, she adds conspiratorially, "Not that I voted for her."

My own laugh gets gulped down when I see the door up close, ajar and molting rainbow stickers. A handwritten sign taped to it that reads ALL ARE WELCOME HERE! Which . . . should be reassuring, a promise of an actual "safe space" instead of the one my parents insist they've created, but it's because of this promise that the message feels kind of threatening. These kids go to the Pride Center, don't they? This place I only learned about because Carla explained it to me five minutes ago, on the drive over? *I'm gay, too,* I practice telling them in my head. *I'm. Gay.* Repetition will make me more convincing.

Forcing my attention back to Carla, I say, "I literally forgot she existed until just now. Henry's going to . . ." and Carla looks at me, like, *going to what?*

My lips press shut. Pauline Pappas transferred to Mount St. Mary's in sixth grade.

He never met her.

Music throbs from behind the door, not as loud as prom but enough to upend me, and Carla's nipples are visible—

aggressively visible—through the thin fabric of her crop top. Mine tighten and tingle.

Pauline rams between us. "Shit, it's not locked, is it?" She bumps the door wider with her butt, tendrils of hair shellacked to her glistening face. "Enter!" Her arms flail wide. "Enjoy responsibly!" And it hits me:

She's drunk.

The only truly drunk person I've ever been around besides at prom, and my mom at that one Christmas party. With the door open, the music's inescapable, a song I know I've heard, popular a few summers ago, the kind that encodes itself into your DNA even though you'll never remember a word. Laughter shrieks down a whitewashed hallway, and there's an area with a table pushed against the wall where people are dancing. I expected a finished basement, but there's basically an entire extra house down here. I turn to Carla, who says, "Surprised you didn't invite him."

It takes too long to realize the *him* she means. Henry shouting after me. His hips grazing Stevie's as they rolled on the floor. "Oh," I say. "He's actually . . . busy. Tonight."

"Too bad. Everybody's welcome." She wipes a thread of hair from her lips.

My nipples are hard. That's now irrefutable. My nipples are hard, and I forsook Henry to be with this girl I barely know, who I'd let do anything to me. I wait for her to say more. Something like, *But it's better with just us.*

Carla links arms with Pauline. "Be right back!" she shouts at me, already merging with the dancers, a jubilant mass of flannel and undercuts even more daring than Carla's. "Go ahead and make friends—everybody's cool here. . . ."

Stranded, I look around.

Okay. The basement is full of faces, only a handful school-related. Where are these kids *from*? This is my first party. My first time I'm not where I told my parents I would be. Panic crashes over me. I back into somebody, and they go, "Whoa!," slopping beer onto the carpet.

If Henry were here, he'd assure me we're not the terminally pathetic ones in this situation. What's so cool about guzzling booze and blacking out and barfing? He'd remind me to stick to my objective: impressing Carla. He'd say, *You've never bombed anything in your life besides Mandarin, Jillian Bortles. Not a test, or a fitness assessment, or the most diabolically sprung pop quiz. Failure is alien to you. Your very essence rejects it.* Except Henry's not here, because I just up and bombed the biggest test of our lives.

I push toward what seems like a living room only to find it more packed, the sofa heaped with strangers smoking weed and playing *Mario Kart*. I do a quick scan, noting pronoun name tags—*she/her, they/he, they/them*—feeling lost without my own. Like everybody here's batting varsity gay while I'm stuck in JV.

A kid on the sofa arm to my right offers up their controller—*Want to play?*—and I squeeze my arms across my chest and say, "No thanks," even though I could spank all of them as long as they let me be orange Yoshi.

They shrug. "Okay, let me know if you change your mind."

Then I look closer and realize this person is Bea Nabarro. Only, a way more dressed-up version of the Bea I'm used to seeing around school. More dressed up than prom, even. Their plump mouth dark like a cherry and black braid tied with a velvet scrunchie. I smile. They smile back—probably wondering what's wrong with me. My stomach pill-bugs.

"Nice blazer," I say, because it's true. Stiff-shouldered and open, a gold leaf pattern stitched over the pocket.

They seem to relax—"Thanks, my cousin's"—and hold up their sleeve, showing off more gold—a row of buttons, winking in the TV's light. "From Colombia. He bought it last time we were there, but I forced him to give it to me. . . ." I bend closer, straining to listen despite the slamming music and the fact that I now officially have no reason to be here, because how could Carla ever want me when she could have dazzlingly gay, confident Bea Nabarro?

Still, as we pull apart, my eyes catch at the navy fabric again, so intrigued by how it might stretch over my own shoulders that I start to ask, "Can I . . ." *try it on?* But Bea's busy with *Mario Kart,* lips pursed at the character selection screen.

I watch them and their friends race for a while, soothed by the dips and turns of tracks I've bested millions of times, and when I glance at the sofa people again, they're completely reconfigured, Bea nowhere among them. A boy with braces tries to pass me another controller, but I lurch away from him, heading—where? Stretched across the wall behind the sofa is a giant Greek flag, its white stripes taped over with multicolored construction paper to make them gayer.

Nearby there's an entryway to a small kitchen—a *kitchen,* in a basement—and as I edge closer, I pick out Carla's husky voice, then a person who might be Bea saying, "Okay, okay, okay." And I want to snatch Carla away but don't want to, either. There's got to be a bathroom down here. Somewhere to hide. I ask the sofa people, who answer, "For sure, down that way, to the left." I thank them, then don't move. Introduce myself? I could.

They wait. A mosaic of smiles. Visions of Henry and Stevie bloom behind my eyes.

The bathroom is cramped but mercifully empty. I huddle with my back against the tub, refusing to cry.

I am a college-bound rising senior and resident of New York State.

A self-starter.

Motivated.

Ambitious—

Somebody knocks.

"Oh. Um. One sec . . ." I start to haul myself up.

The door creaks.

"Lock's broken," Carla informs me.

"I"—mash my palms into my eyelids as she comes closer—"yeah, of course. How'd you know where to find me?"

"Some of the kids playing video games thought you'd been in here awhile, so one of them came and got me. Apparently, they saw us arrive together."

I blink up at her. "That's . . . really nice of them?"

She shrugs. "Queer party."

My jaw aches. I'm clenching my teeth again, but Carla's back is to me as she examines herself in the mirror. She doesn't notice. Won't, unless I want her to. *Oblivious,* Bea called her.

"Are *you* okay?" I ask.

"Ugh." She gathers her hair, lets it drip back into place. Flannel sleeves droop around her waist, her movements smudgy. Overly deliberate. "You heard that?"

Technically no, but according to the SAT, inference-making is my superpower. I nod, and the back of my head brushes the plasticky shower curtain behind me. It has seahorses on it. The decorative soap on the sink is a seahorse too, the tiles lullaby blue.

"We weren't *fighting* fighting," Carla says quickly. "Just having a louder-than-average conversation. I'd say you know what that's like, but you and your ex are perfect, and it's disgusting, so . . ." She tilts her head, and the shaggy bob Henry once accused of resembling a lampshade tilts with her. "You good?"

"Of course."

A reflex.

My raw, tear-soaked face.

"I—I just . . ." Think, goddammit. I'm resourceful. Motivated. Ambitious . . . "It's just all the smoke out there. The pot smoke. It irritates my eyes." I cough feebly.

Carla crouches close, her breath spiked with whatever she drank, smelling like something my parents would store in the garage. "Aww. Poor baby . . ." She fumbles to push my hair off my forehead, the spark of her skin on mine so electric I don't care whether she's truly concerned or just sober enough to want to seem like it.

I can't let her know what happened. Can't allow her to think for one second that my and Henry's titanium bond might be disintegrating. Until tonight, when she texted me, our rules always came through for us. I'm not blaming her, but that's the heart of it. The shameful, sloppy truth. Henry was with Stevie, and her name popped onto my screen. I decided: break one rule, or let them shatter me.

With a sigh, Carla slumps beside me, our backs to the shiny porcelain tub. "Ten bucks says Bea's fingering Rachelle McNutt on the stove right now. Nine o'clock and they're already scoring— What?" She grins. "Are you blushing because I said 'fingering'?"

"No!"

She pokes my thigh. "Hah, that's totally it. People are always hooking up at these things. You get used to it. It just, you know, sucks to be left out." She lets her head fall back, unfurling a smile. "Don't you think?"

My sense blurs. I fasten my hands between my knees, so wet it's petrifying. *Careful,* that ache says. It says, *Go for it.*

It says, *You misunderstood her before.*

Only, nine o'clock means Henry's mom will be getting ready for bed soon. After that, he won't have long to wait. Ten minutes and she'll be out and he can kiss a boy like he's dreamed of all this time. And I'll . . .

Tears roar up all over again. My composure this too-full

cup I'm forever stuck holding. I can't tell if Carla sees. She moistens her lips.

"I . . ." I begin. "I—I think . . ."

I've got to make this mess I made worth it.

Whatever it takes.

21.

CARLA'S BEDROOM IS SMALL, and her furniture doesn't match, the walls cluttered with art I don't understand. Some of it is her own—swipes of charcoal, a series of randomly overlapping cubes—but most are printouts or are torn from books. She flops onto her bed and gathers a comforter off the carpet, swaddling herself so only her eyes and nose are visible. Offering me no clue about where to sit, what to say. Her house isn't what I expected. Squat and square and agonizingly quiet, her parents and little sister probably asleep. On her comforter, tabby kittens float through a galaxy of stars.

She says, "Thanks for driving. This is cool, right? You can stay until I sober up? If it's too risky, you could always drive my car home and pick me up for practice in the morning. Like, if your parents are the 'nuclear option' sort."

I haven't checked my phone, scared of seeing for myself how many more texts Henry's sent—or worse, if he's given up. But the dashboard clock read 9:35 when I pulled into Carla's. Not exactly late. "I can wait. As long as you're okay with it."

She grins. "Totally."

"Great. I mean . . . cool." I peer at the wall over her head. More cubes. "I think my parents might be the opposite of the nuclear-option sort, actually." I'm more concerned about explaining to Carla why the street she's dropping me off at is on the other side of town from where she picked me up.

"Lucky." A slurry giggle. "Can I vent to you for a sec? I just, like, so need to vent."

"Sure." Her desk chair is loaded with what must be crew equipment—a Nike duffel bag and sneakers, a stopwatch— why?—and an unopened box of PowerBars. One by one, I move everything to the floor. The chair makes a fart sound as I lower myself onto it.

"It's like," she begins, "like Bea enjoys messing with me. Sometimes I swear they do. Sometimes I think making me feel bad is their only way to experience joy. All because I prioritize my art? Am I not supposed to do that? If I don't get into Yale, I'll die. Also, Bea doesn't even like Rachelle McNutt. I know for a fact. They just want to make me jealous." She snorts. "Like I care."

"That's tough." Even I, with my ricocheting nerves, hear how hopelessly unsupportive this sounds. I can do better. But it's hard with wisps of hair pulling from her bun, her face framed by stars.

The desk is shoved close to her bed, our knees inches apart. When Carla knocks hers against mine, all her breath goes out. "What's your ex like in bed?" She smirks. "Is he big?"

"I'm not telling you about Henry's penis." That's completely private—she should know better than to ask.

Carla roars *"Penis!"* and shakes her head, wisps swirling. "I cannot believe you just said that."

"That's the correct term," I say helplessly. "The anatomical one."

Carla pours herself backward, this sloppy slow-motion collapse across her bed. "No, I totally get it. Next time somebody says 'dick' around me, I'm going to correct them. I'm going to be like, 'Excuse me, don't you mean "penis"?' And when they ask why I care, I'll just say, 'Jillian Bortles told me.'"

"You should," I say, smiling.

She's not as funny as Henry.

"Is he talking to any new girls?"

"They're not"—*a girl,* I'm about to say. But then, outing him wouldn't be right, either. "No," I finish. A little awed that Carla Kaminski, of all people, would make that assumption.

She yawns against the back of her hand. "You know, texting you is different from talking in person. In person you're much more . . . Do you suffer from a lot of neck and shoulder tension? My mom's a licensed massage therapist and sees clients in our spare room. I know the type."

Wow. If I'm uptight enough for her to worry, that must make me the epicenter of tension itself, a human fault line. I laugh for real. "You think I can't loosen up?"

"Hmm, well, my parents would say, 'Can't is for quitters.' Sooooo . . ."

"I'm not that, either." In my head this sounded bold, but out loud it's defensive and flat, literally everything flirting isn't. I squeeze my hands between my knees, commanding myself to relax. Clearly, Carla doesn't understand the torment that goes into texting her. Every word a mini Purdy essay, calibrated to make her want me.

I guess I've got to prove this Jillian is worth it, too.

"That's better," Carla says as I clamber onto the bed beside her. "It's so cold in here with the air-conditioning." She giggles into the mattress. "Thermal charitttyyyy . . ."

"Definitely." Except we're not touching. I hug my knees and stare at her messy walls, my crotch thumping.

But just acknowledging the chilliness makes closing the distance that much easier. I lie back, and she rolls closer, her hot, boozy breath sloshing over me. My fingertips move across her cheeks. The unfamiliar contours of her jaw and cheekbones, that braided gold septum ring.

She says, "Do you want to kiss me?"

And I really almost lose it. I've fantasized about kissing a girl for so long. Kissing *her*. But now . . . the reality feels even huger than I counted on. My answer a side door to slip out, right into what being Henry-less makes me.

"Yes," I say.

Her lips are thin and hard, demanding in a way five months of staring didn't help me anticipate. I caress her bony hip, and she tugs the hem of my shirt, slides her hand beneath it once I nod permission. I can't help the noise that comes out of me.

"Shhh." She laughs into my mouth. "My sister's across the hall." Her hand wavers at my sports bra. "Tell me what you like?"

"Oh . . ." Her openness unbalances me. Like I needed further confirmation this wasn't going to go down like it does in books and movies—two people who magically know how to make each other feel good just because we were born with the same parts. Carla's body couldn't be more different from mine. Angles and swerves as baffling as the sketches on her wall. Hesitantly, I guide her hand under my bra, hoping that she won't feel me shaking. That I guessed right.

Add my body to the list of things I know only because Henry explored them with me.

We kiss more. Harder this time, until she pants and writhes against me. Her thumb brushes my nipple, and I gasp.

"Sorry," she says. "I should've asked."

"Don't be. It was . . . it was . . ." Not a Henry-feeling at all. A cataclysm.

A wrecking ball.

Carla says we can go further if I want. "I'm down. Your call."

I want to go further. I want *this*, her hand under my bra

and her mouth tasting like sour cherries, but my lips won't move, my jaw's locked. *The ideal candidate possesses these and other immutable characteristics consistent with domination of college and life . . .*

We lie in the dark until it's safe for her to drive me home.

22.

"BUT WHY, JILLIAN?" Dad demands. "Why would you lie?"

Mom sets a glass of orange juice in front of me. "Minjun called—"

"I *was* with Henry."

"No. That's not good enough. You might've been with him at first. But when he called us in a panic, saying you weren't answering your phone, that you'd disappeared . . ."

The juice stings my lips. I sip slowly, glaring at Garrett, who's crouched on the stairs. I'm going to murder him. And Henry. I'll kill anybody who won't let me finish my Golden Grahams in peace. My parents loom over the table, one on either side of me. Mom crosses her arms like, *Well?*

"I'm sorry." But sorry isn't enough. Same as the first and fifteenth and millionth times I said it. So I try a simpler version of the explanation I gave when they ambushed me on the driveway at midnight, after Carla patted my arm and drove away. "The party was loud, and I couldn't hear my phone going off. . . ." My voice thins.

Rain thumps against the house.

"I just don't understand," Mom says.

Honestly? Same. "Let me get this straight," I say. "*You're* the ones who were so excited about me drinking at prom, which I didn't even do, but now that I actually have fucked up, I'm in trouble for fucking up *too* much?"

My parents exchange glances.

Calmly, Dad says, "You're not in trouble for going to a party."

"Then why are you yelling at me?"

"Nobody's yelling!" Mom says. "We're trying to wrap our heads around—"

"Oh, you want all the juicy details, right? A play-by-play?" I tip closer. "Want to smell my breath?" I'm sure they'd be thrilled to hear I wasn't drunk—just kissing a girl who was. They'd assure me, *Oh, honey, you have every right to back out of a sexual encounter, anytime, for any reason. . . .*

Mom doesn't bite. "Come on, Jillian. You're a responsible kid. Why not tell Minjun where you were going?"

"Hah! This is so about details. You're just dying to find out why my and Henry's exact coordinates weren't known to each other this one freaking time?" I grind the glass against my lips, catching myself.

If I say any more, it'll be the whole thing.

My parents soften. "Jilly," Mom says. "It's obvious something's going on between you—"

I push up from the table. "I'm going to miss the bus."

"It's five-thirty in the morning," Dad tells me. "Practice

can't start this early. Don't you think you should double-check the email?"

In fact, I think this is all pretty hilarious. My own father suggesting *I* didn't check an email. As if my whole existence, for the entirety of high school, has not been devoted to checking email, preventing catastrophes. Meanwhile, practice starts in thirty minutes, and I slept probably a fraction of that. My eyelids feel like wadded-up paper.

Mom follows me into the hall. I cram my feet into my sneakers, shoulder my duffel. "Phone," she says.

I bristle. "What?"

"You heard right." She sticks her hand out. "Breaking boundaries isn't consequence-free."

My phone's already packed. But I dig it out and slap it into her palm, and if she registers the broken screen, her puffy morning face doesn't say so. I watch helplessly as she pockets my phone in her robe, and with it any hope of apologizing to Henry for the next half century. "When do I get it back?" I demand, already knowing the answer:

When Your Father and I Decide.

I shouldn't have gone straight to bed after Carla dropped me off. I could've called him. But I was escaping my parents . . . practice was in a few hours . . . I had to sleep. . . . How was I supposed to know my parents would wake up with my alarm, prolong this lecture to infinity?

". . . take the bus straight to the clinic when you're finished," Dad instructs from the kitchen. "We mean it, Jillian Leigh. No pit stops. If you're running late, call us from the gym office."

Fine, I mumble.

No phone. No Henry. Only half of a first time with a girl who now, after I froze up on her, probably hates me. Awesome. Exactly what I planned for summer.

I don't even slam the door as I leave.

THE WEIGHT ROOM IS in the school basement, at the end of a long, murky hallway that smells like the town lake's bathrooms. I stand at the back, vaguely absorbing instructions.

". . . wrists *flat,* hands on the outside . . ." Coach Johnson, a white lady my mom's age, wearing sunglasses indoors, straddles a machine that could be a video game weapon if it were mounted on a mutant's shoulder instead of the floor. Some kind of elongated buzz saw with pulleys and a handle at one end, a seat set far back at the other. Even the name sounds video game–ish. Not *rowing machine,* as it so obviously should be called, but *erg.* ". . . no *T. rex* arms . . ."

Altogether, about fifteen of us have assembled around the cruddy exercise machines and racks of dumbbells—mostly kids my age and a smattering of underclassmen I only sort of recognize. Among the seniors I note Libby Joseph, Victor Castellini, and Tyler Stands, whose name sounds like a sentence. Tucked in the corner, Carla murmurs intently with Angel Pagan, a junior. She hasn't looked at me once.

". . . to minimize vomiting . . ."

My curls slump over my shoulders. I wrangle them while Coach distributes packets, and since I'm farthest back, the sound of fluttering papers goes on painfully long while I wait for one to get to me. I count three, four, *five* pages stapled together—a list of rowing exercises with accompanying illustrations. Trap bar deadlifts. Elevated split squats. Batwing rows.

These words are made up.

"Questions?" Coach asks.

Tyler pokes up her hand. She's small for her age, and in the very intense competition for which of the white kids' legs have seen the least sunlight this far into vacation, she might beat Carla, Victor, and me. Her calves are so milky pale they're painful to behold. The tips of her blond hair are dyed blue-green, like they were dipped in algae. "Who's keeping time, Coach Johnson?"

Coach Johnson—*Coach J,* as she reminds Tyler to call her—motions at Angel, but instead of stepping forward like she clearly wants, he uncurls his fist to reveal . . .

A red stopwatch.

The one I moved off Carla's chair.

"Kaminski let me borrow it," he says.

"I could—" Tyler protests.

Coach J claps. "All right, stations . . ." and the groups disperse, shuffling groggily toward various pieces of equipment. I try to catch Carla's eye, but she ducks her head and sidles with Angel to the erg Coach J was straddling. I should talk to her—I *have* to talk to her, explain myself—but I also can't be the only one standing around. Desperate, I page through Coach's handout, but I've never actually lifted weights before, and there are so many options. Beneath my feet a yellowish stain's splashed across the cement floor.

While everybody but me gets situated, I narrow my eyes at the stain in increments. Measuring the blur.

Technically this is not my first time at school alone.

Sometimes Henry is absent. Or his mom has to work, so she'll drop him off to meet me at first period, but every time that's happened—really only a handful of times—I knew not to worry, knew the frantic ache of *Oh God, where is he?* would subside the moment he slid into the desk next to me. Now there are no desks, and the chances of Henry materializing are as minuscule as the chances of winning his forgiveness. Of course. Of *course* he called my parents. After what I did to him, that's the least I deserve—

"Excuse me?"

My head snaps up.

Coach J consults her clipboard. Carla, slicking her hair off her forehead, loiters behind her. My heart starts to race. "Jillian, is it . . . Bortles?"

"Present," I choke out.

"Welcome. Ready to go?"

"Uh . . . yeah. I was just about to do some . . ." The packet's flopped open to a random page. "One-arm overhead . . . presses . . ."

"Not so fast."

"What?" I glance around. On the erg, Angel, tan and monstrously fit, despite being, like, fifteen, wrenches the pulley so hard that the mechanism squeals. *Whoa,* somebody says, *easy* . . . "I—I know what I'm doing. I mean, I haven't ever worked out like *this,* but I run a lot, and I'm a really good climber, so"—I flex, showing her the weird, not-*un*obscene bulge of my forearm, courtesy of many tough ascents—"I've got it covered."

"That's very exciting. But we need you to pass your swim test first."

Swim test—

Shit.

My bathing suit.

I left it in my backpack.

In Big Purp.

"Today?" I say.

"Safety first." Coach J shrugs.

"But I'm . . . I forgot my . . ." I gesture at my tee and spandex shorts.

Coach J insists they'll be sufficient. "Water practices start Wednesday. We've got to make sure you can tread water, swim submerged, execute some sort of backstroke—it's all in the email."

Email.

Right.

Out of excuses, I proceed numbly to the hall.

Carla falls into step behind me.

"So, Bortles," Coach J says, "what brings you to crew?"

I'm dimly aware I should've anticipated this question, and there are answers, but when I open my mouth, all the good ones skitter away. My head aches, and I woke up wet, and I can feel my hair fizzing around from the drooling summer rain.

Carla says quietly, "We don't get new people too often."

Wait. Does Coach J think I'm *new* new? Like, to the

school? That's a common misconception among teachers who aren't in the Honors program. In ninth grade, Mr. Lopez made me stand up and tell our entire health class where I was from, which would rank as my most traumatic classroom incident if not for the video he showed us later on of a person having a baby.

"I guess I'm just . . . expanding my horizons," I answer, deciding this isn't the best moment to ask for my letter. I've got to prove I'm worth it first. And I'm slightly preoccupied by Carla, who I'd hoped to both make up with and avoid.

"Exciting," Coach J repeats.

I look over my shoulder, feigning interest in the receding weight room. Carla walks with her arms tight around her middle, the husks of her sweatshirt sleeves hanging at her sides.

She was already talking to Angel when I arrived. *Whispering*, really. Heads bent, eyelashes lowered, completely locked into each other. No way could I have interrupted. Not even to say *Good morning*, totally calm and unconcerned, like I practiced the whole way over. That was twenty minutes ago. Fifteen, at least. We've had plenty of opportunities to acknowledge each other since. I've got to say something.

"How do you know Angel?" I ask. Which is immediately awkward, since she's rowed before, and he must have, too— their acquaintance isn't exactly a mystery. It's just . . . the way they were whispering . . .

I can't tell whether she's squinting at me from the overhead lights, whose rays are like scalpels this early in the morning. "He's Bea's cousin."

"Oh—"

Coach J shoves open a door marked POOL. "Let's go, ladies. We're short Assistant Coach Eugene for today, and Stands can't be trusted not to go after that stopwatch."

Elm-High doesn't offer swimming as a gym elective every semester, and it's not coed, so my knowledge of the pool is based solely on rumor. One time some guys broke in for a senior prank and jerked off into the filters. Pregnancies were reported.

"When you're ready." Coach J flips a page on her clipboard.

I turn to Carla, holding my breath against the smack of chlorine, only to see she's already taken off her sweatshirt and the tank top underneath it, exposing creamy bare stomach again, and the pizza tattoo, her breasts cupped by a neon-orange sports bra. More naked in front of me than when she stroked my nipple.

"Easier to get it over with," she says simply.

"Definitely." I edge with her to the ledge, trying not to stare or think of those breasts pressed against my arm. It's a small pool, with lanes roped off by buoys, the water primordial green.

No way would sperm survive here.

"Is this . . . safe? Wait." My gaze jerks back to Carla. "Why are *you* taking the swim test?"

"I broke my wrist hiking and had to sit out all last summer. Hard to row in a cast."

"Really? I don't remember that." Realizing as soon as I say it that of course I wouldn't. A year ago, we didn't know each other. We weren't anything.

After last night, how will we ever be?

"*Ladies,*" Coach J barks.

She says she needs to see us swim. Down and back once, and if we can do that without drowning, she'll time us while we tread water, and if *that* goes well . . . It's irrelevant, because I'm standing beside Carla with a blistering headache and spandex shorts clawing my ass. The email mentioned a swim test. Fine. It didn't mention squats, or machines called ergs, or Angel Pagan being Bea's cousin. They don't look related. Bea short, with their soft round face, and Angel tall and pointy, freckled everywhere. Is he the cousin who gave Bea that blazer? What were he and Carla just talking about? I back against the clammy tile wall, hands squeezed under my armpits. Pull it together. Get *one* thing right.

"Hey," I say to Carla.

Coach J blows her whistle.

Carla offers a hesitant smile.

"I wanted to . . . a-about last night—"

"Oh God, let's do ourselves a favor and forget that ever happened." A shrill giggle. "I was so drunk!" She jumps, walloping me with a tsunami-grade splash.

"Bortles!" Coach J raps out. "On the count of three, or you're out of here. *One.*"

Okay.

"Two—"

OKAY.

"*Three!*"

Water shoots up my nose.

23.

WHEN I DRIVE GARRETT home from the clinic, my back-pack's on our porch. Inside is my bathing suit and a note that looks like it was written on the bus.

Jilly,

I tried to drop this off before but your dad was here and I had class. Please please PLEASE text me back. EVERYTHING IS SO MESSED UP!!!

By the time I've called my parents on the house phone to tell them we're home safe—*yes,* I know they've got that big grant proposal to finalize, I *know* they'll need me to pick them up late—Garrett's ready with Henry's number.

"You owe me," he says.

"Correct." My fingers stumble over the rubbery house phone buttons.

"If Mom and Dad find out—"

"Gar, tell me what you want, and I'll get on it. But I need some privacy first, okay?"

He nods. At the very least we both relish a mission. I wait, the phone tucked against my shoulder, until I'm sure he's not snooping on the stairs again. Then I hit call.

"Hello?" Henry says breathlessly. "Jillian, oh my God—" A hiccup cuts him off. "Where have you been? Why are you on your house phone—"

I'm grounded, I inform him. And he hiccups louder and says, "I'm sorry, Jilly. I'm so sorry. You must hate me."

It's a pretty night now that it finally stopped raining. The sky more blue than dusky. I squeeze up onto the counter, resting my cheek on my knee. "You hate me."

"Never," Henry says.

"But I broke a rule. We said no running."

His hiccup comes out ragged this time, a half burp. "It's not about that, Jillian, Jesus! Could you forget our rules for one fucking second?"

"What are you talking about? The rules are the entire point!" I broke one, *one,* aside from our blurry kissing saga, and look what happened to us.

"No, *listen.* I'm not mad at you, and I didn't *mean* to put you in a tough position, but you also didn't have to come with me and Stevie if it was going to be such a problem. Where did you *go?* You scared the shit out of me. I thought you were dead. You could've— You—"

"Henry."

He's hyperventilating.

"Henry!"

His breathing jumbles, grating in my ear at first, then slackening as he calms down, like our car when it overheats. Out the window, the tent glimmers. My fingers stink from chlorine.

Tentatively, Henry says, "Jilly? A-are you there?"

What do you think? I almost scream.

He hasn't asked how my night went. Or the first day of crew. He doesn't know I spent a whole three-hour practice doing dumbbell curls in waterlogged spandex, wondering how to take it all back.

But I need him to know. Without Henry, who will make sense of me?

"Come over," I say.

WE SNEAK UPSTAIRS. Henry sinks onto my bed, and I lock all the doors, then sit beside him, our thighs skimming briefly through my pajama shorts.

He says, "You don't have to explain why you left. I get it. Stevie told me."

"Stevie?"

"After you ran off, I went ballistic. I called your parents and called you. I probably would've called the freaking FBI if Stevie hadn't said he wanted to go home. He said . . . he said it wasn't fair for me to invite you on our date without running it by him first, and that you were obviously super uncomfortable with it, too. So, yeah, *I'm* the one who messed up. Not you." He swallows. I see the spit lurch down his throat. "Maybe that didn't come through on the phone."

Not exactly.

But.

"What'd you do? Drive him home?"

"His sister came and got him." He plucks at a thread on my bedspread, flopping back with a groan. "That's what I meant by my note. But we're okay now. We were talking right before you called, actually."

"Oh." My face smolders.

I've got to get my priorities straight.

Figure out how to survive this club sport Henry still hasn't asked about. Get away from him before I start sobbing. Turn myself back into who I was before all this happened—so sure about so much. Maybe then I can decide what to make of Carla blowing me off at the pool like nothing happened in her room, when something absolutely *did,* even if it wasn't how I'd imagined. I could forgive Henry for not putting together how furious and sad being around him and Stevie made me, until Stevie said so. Because he's some fucking expert on me.

Whatever.

Stevie might as well be.

I might as well put out a call for the job the second I get my phone back: *One girl in need of a best friend, since the boy who is no longer cares to be.* The thought's obliterating. There is no replacement Henry. But no reason, either, to explain how selfish he's being. I fold my knees to my chest and stare at my backpack, shimmery wet from where he left it on my porch. "I don't need it anymore," I say.

Henry glances at me, diligently ChapSticking. He caps

the tube and puts it in his sweatshirt pocket, all without sitting up. "Need what?"

"The bathing suit. I only bought it for the swim test. It was today. And I crushed it. So thanks. A lot." I wedge my chin between my knees to keep from looking at his fingers knotted in my bedspread, his lips waxy with ChapStick. Strawberry, like his mom always buys him. When he reaches for my hip, he's already licked half of it off.

"Jilly—"

"Sorry," I say, unable to rub the nastiness from my voice, "but do you, like, not care where I went last night at all?"

"Of course I do," Henry replies. "I'm just . . ." He sighs. "Worried about Stevie. I mean, he said we're cool now, and I believe him, but I also don't really know him well enough to read him yet, you know?"

He hiccups, and I funnel all the stinging, every throb of my body, into my narrowed eyes. If he's determined to fixate on Stevie, I can at least let him know how crushing that feels. So.

I tell him all about the party. I tell him Carla picked me up from the end of his road and we went home together, kissed and got to second base beneath her starry comforter. "We stopped," I admit, even though it kills me. "She could've done more, and I wanted to, but then . . ." I trail off, hoping he'll force me to reveal more, so I can give these wild, gnashing feelings somewhere to go that isn't my responsibility, but he doesn't, which hurts worst of all. He knows I never quit. He *knows* how desperately Carla matters to me.

Henry might be tearing up, but it's hard to tell behind his

plastic lenses. His hand falls from my hip. "Wow. That's . . . a lot."

"It wasn't," I shoot back, grinding my teeth against my lips. "You're not *listening*. She—I don't know what happened. I froze up. I—I was so into her. I *am* so into her, so what's wrong with me? I'm not inexperienced with sex. You and I have done . . . But she's . . ." *What?* And what am I? My gayness over now? Failed? My own eyes start to sting, but I'm not going to cry. I refuse. Tears are futile.

I deserve to scream.

"She's incredible! Literally the only reason I joined crew! Not that it really matters, now that I've gone and fucked that up, too."

When I lift my head, Henry's glasses have slipped off. I should find them before they get crushed, but at the same time it's been so long since I've seen his whole face, I can't help letting them stay gone a little more. Even if he is just blinking furiously at me. As startled as I am by what I've revealed.

"Oh," he says.

And I really could sob, because I know I said it first, but *oh* doesn't count. *Oh* is what you say when a teacher corrects you. Or you realize you've been attempting to solve a puzzle in a video game wrong for, like, ten minutes and just discovered the real solution. *Oh* isn't empathy, or understanding, or rage.

It's nothing at all.

"What's wrong with me?" I whisper. "Henry, what's wrong . . ." until he hooks my waist, hauling me on top of him, and I want to push him away—I *should* push him away, but his warmth blankets me, his belly molten against mine where his hoodie's bunched up, so necessary and familiar compared to my flailing with Carla that I suddenly can't remember what's dangerous about this. I surf his breathing, the rise and fall. My cheek in that scoop between his neck and shoulder.

"I get it." His lips at my ear.

"No—"

"*No*, listen. Why do you think I didn't tell you about Stevie? He scares the hell out of me. I'm terrified he won't be you!" We're supposed to be sneaking, but he practically screams this. I slap a hand over his mouth, and instead of squirming away, he pokes his tongue at my fingers. *Terrified*, he said.

I'm terrified he won't be you. . . .

Lying in Carla's bed after we stopped kissing. My fists bolted to my sides, wanting her like I've never wanted anybody.

Five years with Henry. Ten semesters. One thousand eight hundred twenty-five days.

And the brush of a girl's thumb blew every single one apart.

I pull myself up. Not one to one anymore. But my hands still climber's hands as I push under his shirt. He twists so I can take it off the rest of the way, and we press our wet faces together.

The condom is in my dresser, untouched since prom. I

open it carefully, and we laugh at the diagrams that show us how to roll it on. Then I help him inside me.

It's exactly like I imagined and literally everything but. All slipperiness and noise, stifling our cries in each other's shoulders and the smack of my headboard. Neither of us knows quite what we're doing, but I don't care. I kiss him. Kiss him hard. And it's not like it was with Carla.

But it's something.

#1—NO FIGHTING

~~#2—NO MESSING AROUND?????????~~

~~#3—NO MORE RUNNING~~

#4—PURDY FIRST

24.

AT HOME THE FOLLOWING evening I boot up *Super Smash Bros.*, but I'm useless, can't play for shit. I selflessly volunteer to bring Garrett to the orthodontist, then go straight to I Love's, scattering pigeons as I whip into the tiny employee lot around back. Garrett sighs theatrically while I load him up with quarters.

"Wow. Next-level subterfuge. You realize you're not actually grounded, right? You don't have to use me to do it with your boyfriend."

"Do—what?" Garrett's twelve. I don't know what he understands about sex, let alone what he might've heard coming from my room last night.

I don't want to find out.

"Shut up," I say. "I am too grounded. When's the last time Mom and Dad confiscated anything of yours? And where did you learn the word 'subterfuge'?"

"Video games." He frowns at his bounty. "Is this your snack money?"

"Enough for ten mini packs of Goldfish and, like, twenty failed rounds of *Mortal Kombat,* so knock yourself out." I Love's—in addition to serving the thinnest crust this far up the Hudson River—boasts a glorious array of arcade cabinets. Most are older than our parents, and the graphics look like cats drew them, but the difficulty curves are so diabolical that even Garrett's hooked on the challenge. He scampers off, leaving his door open. I shut it and wait a beat, my back pressed to the scalding car.

Henry's where I figured he'd be. Sticky break-room table. Book open, cheek propped on his fist. But as I draw closer, I realize he's not reviewing vocabulary or sentence constructions.

He's texting.

"Henry?" A ceiling fan whacks hot air over our heads. Dust coats lockers where each employee's name is scribbled in duct tape. H YOOOOOOOOOOO, Henry's reads, not in his handwriting. Waiting for him to look up, I try to plot out what I might say, but the words that crowd my head are only ones video games have taught me. *Phalanx, rout, faction.* Words for war.

"Henry."

I drop into the chair beside him.

"Henry."

He claps the textbook shut on his phone, and my chest snags, and then we just look at each other. "Jilly . . . ," he begins.

"How are you?"

"Great," he says.

I let my backpack slither to the cement, unable to decide if he means that—how *could* he mean that—or just wants to seem brave. I can see him kind of wondering about me, too. "Same," I say. "So great."

He swipes a nervous glance at the office across the hall. "Listen, you can't just—"

"Sorry, since when is visiting you a fireable offense? Your boss couldn't care less." The man's too lazy to copy keys, which is why I'm able to sneak back here at all, the rear entrance marked EMPLOYEES ONLY permanently unlocked during business hours. Besides, the restaurant's blessedly dead on weeknights. I bend to unzip my backpack, rooting for the diagrams I printed out at the clinic. Coach J sent them at 4:25 this morning. *Subject: TOMORROW.* "This isn't even an official break room. It's a closet with a microwave. You've literally fing—" *Fingered me in here,* I'm about to say, stopping myself as Henry turns a thousand shades of crimson. I double over my backpack, whipping through folders I forgot were in there, muttering, "What'd you want me to do, text instead? My parents aren't giving my phone back anytime soon."

"Okay, first, way to misconstrue facts to your advantage. You'll recall my boss had a family emergency that day—"

"And left you in charge because of how much he trusts you!" I meant to be funny, but the words chafe and strain. My cheeks heat up. Henry gets redder, too.

My one day off crew, and the torment of using my

shoulders after endless sets in the weight room matches the soreness between my legs exactly. I fumble to get Coach J's handout onto the table.

"What's this?" Henry asks.

"Boat parts. Tomorrow's our first day out on the water, and Coach won't let me join if I don't know them."

"Your coach said that?"

"No, but—I wouldn't put it past her. She's tough. Just quiz me, okay?" Once I've got them memorized, and my success is secured, our friendship reestablished, we'll be ready to talk.

He pulls the paper closer. "Um. Starboard?"

"Right side of the shell when you're facing the bow. 'Shell' is the technical term for the boat. And the bow's the front."

"Port."

"Left side."

"Gunwale."

"That's the bottom of . . . No wait, the top . . ." It's no good. My sense of what I'm doing as fragmented and scattered as in the moments that followed googling how to properly dispose of a condom. Henry leaving. Pressing myself against the covers after the door shut. Sobs plugging my mouth like river mud.

" 'The top edge of the side of the boat,' " Henry reads. "That's . . . specific." He sets the paper aside, his gaze sliding everywhere but my face.

Okay. Having him quiz me was a bad idea. Tactical error. No problem—I just wasn't counting on his being so distracted. Should we focus on him instead? Is that the best plan?

I force myself to ask, "How's Mandarin?" Class started last week, and we've hardly talked about it.

"Well, my decision to *not* expose myself as a high school student lasted the whole five seconds it took for the professor to introduce me as a Purdy candidate, and I blanked on the word for video games, so the entire class thinks I'm super into water polo now, but other than that . . ." He's talking too fast, and I'm staring at the diagram, the arrows indicating each part of the boat absolutely unquestionable. Bow. Stern. Blade. Penis-in-vagina straightforward.

Henry awaits my reaction.

"Cool." My teeth sink into my lip.

His looks like a chewed eraser.

I can't hold back any longer. "Do you regret it? Having"—my voice pinches to a whisper—"sex?"

He taps his fingers on my handout. "Do you?"

"I'm not sure," I admit, which, like all our truths, only makes the situation even more fantastically complicated. We said no messing around and blew that twice by kissing, which confused us enough. Sex feels stratospheres beyond that. "*Regret* isn't the right word. It's just I . . . What I'm getting at is . . ." But I don't know. I don't know how to explain why what felt so good in my body felt wrong everywhere else. It's my fault. If I'd just stayed at his house like he expected of me, found a way to *deal* instead of running to that party where I didn't belong anyway . . . "We can't take it back."

"I know," he says helplessly. "But—"

"Dude." Henry's coworker stomps into the break room. Patrick Young, star football person and fellow newly minted senior, eyeing us like, *The fuck?* "We're getting slammed. What are you doing?"

"Nothing," Henry says. "Is my break over?"

Patrick crosses his arms. "Listen, Yoo, I like you. We cover for each other when one of us has to poop, and I'm sure your girlfriend's cool, but I've dealt with you guys slobbering all over each other at my locker since seventh grade, and not once have I complained. Not once! The least you could do is not contaminate our job."

"We weren't—" I start to say.

"I can't work under these conditions." Patrick retreats backward, pointing wildly at us. "I don't feel safe!"

We get up stiltedly, like our legs are asleep even though we weren't sitting that long. Henry's apron is green like a car air freshener. He ties it on, and I stuff Coach J's diagram into my bag and follow him up front, down a passageway that reeks of mildew and burnt marinara. The dining area isn't much better. Virtually empty, despite Patrick's pleas, minus some old people gumming macaroni salad and Garrett menacing the candy machines.

Henry reads my face out loud. "Pat's a little dramatic."

"He's an asshole," I mumble.

Can Henry and I not have a conversation, one *single interaction*, without everybody assuming we're only there to inhale each other? Because if others decided to get a fucking clue and noticed Henry and I are changing, I wouldn't mind copying off their notes for once. Nothing about this visit has gone like I needed. Stiff, and awkward, and wrong.

"Henry!" Garrett calls, his braces smeared with M&M's particles. "I set a guy on fire and ripped his whole spinal cord out!"

"Oh, hell yeah," Henry replies. "Me too, you just missed it. Easy on the machines, all right? They jam." He plucks a pencil stub from the mug by the register and scribbles in his waiter's notepad, oblivious to me waiting patiently for him to finish the sentence that Patrick interrupted. *I know. But . . .*

When he doesn't, I say, "You're taking orders telepathically now? You've really leveled up."

"It's for me," Henry replies. "Well, Stevie and me." My jaw tightens. He fiddles with his apron strings. "Stevie's never really had New York–style pizza. Isn't that wild? I'm— Oh, hold on." He edges past me to check on one of his tables. An old lady incapable of googling what a calzone is. I linger long enough to hear him be like, "Uh, so it's like pizza, but with a roof on it . . . ," then peek at the notepad he left on the counter. Nothing objectionable about what Henry wrote: banana peppers and spicy sausage. Extra olives. π for pie. Of course he did. I skip to the next line:

1 moss sticks xtra berry

I don't realize Henry's returned until he touches the back of my hand, his fingertips shiny with pencil grit.

"Raspberry sauce?" I say.

"Stevie didn't believe me that that's considered a viable combo up here. I'm proving otherwise. Part of his upstate initiation process. Then we're going to the . . ." He carefully places some menus he collected by the register. "Why? Is that problematic or something?"

"No," I say, though the spark in my chest would like to report otherwise.

"I wasn't . . ." He fumbles with his apron strings again. "I wasn't planning on telling him about . . . what we did yesterday. Do you think I should? I don't want him—I mean, he and I aren't dating officially, not yet, so it doesn't qualify as cheating, I don't think, but I should still probably tell him, right? It feels dishonest not to. I'm just kind of nervous about his reaction, given the other night."

"*His* reaction?" Hurt soars through me. "But, Henry . . ." What about us? How will we ever succeed as friends if trying only makes us more tangled—when we just gave each other one more part of ourselves we'll hold on to forever, one more feeling too huge to name? And if he refuses to talk about us having sex . . . if he can't even call it sex . . .

What am I doing here?

I push his notepad at him, wanting to smash it in my fist. "Here's some advice. Maybe your precious time with Stevie would work out better if you quit trying so hard to impress him. Watching you show off your basketball skills was painful enough."

His forehead creases. "I wasn't showing off. Stevie's the one who can dunk."

"Pretty sure it doesn't count as dunking if your feet never

leave the earth. In case you haven't noticed, that kid is inappropriately tall."

"I like tall guys. I—I like basketball." He smiles weakly. "I've actually been—"

"Well, when you have that nightmare where you pack yourself in your dad's suitcase and end up suffocating—"

"I haven't had that dream in months!"

"Yeah, since you gave up basketball." I bring my teeth together so hard they click. Henry cradles his notepad like a wounded paw. "I'm sorry," I whisper. I've never used his dad against him. We've never—

He slips the notepad into his apron. "No problem."

When I squish the skin of his elbow, he doesn't pull away. "It's so flexible," I say. He squishes mine back, retaliating.

"If you do have that dream," I go on, "just call my house. Like always."

"You know I will. It's okay."

Right. I exhale. We *are* okay. Just.

Staggeringly.

"I should get back to work now, though," he says.

"For sure," I tell him. "Me too. The boat parts." I turn away and shout for Garrett, my fingernails buried in my sides.

25.

"JOSEPH."

"Here."

Fluorescent light sears my eyes.

"Pagan."

"Here."

The black, bottomless sky.

"Bortles."

Redundant.

"Bortles?"

Everybody—literally *everybody*—witnessed me fling my-self onto the bus at 4:58, seconds before it pulled away.

"Here," I mumble.

Coach J moves on. "Castellini."

"Here."

"Stands—"

"Present and *ready*!" Tyler screams.

The Canning Preserve is on the Hudson River, just east of downtown Albany, this network of wooded hiking, biking,

204

and jogging trails where people occasionally find bodies. Not my first choice of destination for a five a.m. workout, the bus's bumping and exhaust fumes already making me regret breakfast.

"Kaminski," Coach J says.

No answer.

I twist slightly in my seat.

Carla's two rows behind and opposite me, one knee poking into the aisle and a sketchbook resting on top, giving no sign that she's even fractionally more well rested or excited about our first water practice than I am. Her hand moves deftly, gangrenous with charcoal.

Focus on Purdy. If I just focus on Purdy . . .

"Kaminski?" Coach J repeats.

Carla looks up. Our eyes catch through her hair.

"Here," she rasps.

My heart grinds out this extra beat.

Once she resumes sketching, I slump back around. I'm sitting alone—a minor blessing—but the bus window rattles nonstop, making it hard not to gnash my teeth. I've never been mobile, let alone conscious, this early in the morning. The world so deathly silent as I tripped down my porch, no birds singing, no headlights carving up my street, *nothing*. Nobody greeted me when I boarded the bus. My path to the nearest empty seat littered with hushed giggles, a side-eye or three, for the sloppy new girl. Now, from my vantage point in the almost-back, I scan juniors with workbooks open, prepping for the August SAT, and some smaller girls who must've just finished eighth grade swiping on mascara.

Tyler Stands is up front, directly behind the driver, a whistle pinched between her lips so it wheezes when she breathes. Between us, Angel Pagan plays on his phone, and Libby Joseph sits apart from Carla, which is interesting. Aren't they, like, best friends? Fed up, I lean my head on the window to stop its rattling, but the vibrations ripple through me instead, a secret transmission only I can hear:

Go the fuck back to bed.

True to Coach J's email, we disembark at the Canning Preserve parking lot at promptly five-thirty, the sky stained pink. I leave my duffel with Assistant Coach Eugene, a Mr. Nett clone in charge of transporting our gear, and then line up with everybody at the mouth of a wide gravel trail, where Coach J announces we'll jog to the boathouse. Amid the groans, I can't quite hide my smile.

"Remember," she cautions us, standing wide-legged in her spandex shorts, "it's a mile and a half, and this is our first warm-up before we stretch. The key is to go slow, pace yourself . . ."

I whup them all.

Except the boathouse—or what I deduce to be the boathouse, this long, dark green shed structure just off the riverbank, with a dock nearby, a sign out front that says HUDSON VALLEY CREW—is padlocked. I wait for the others to catch up, listening to the water slosh. It's weird, because I've lived here my whole life, but to me the Hudson River's basically a creepy uncle. Always just *there*. And sure, the water's mostly clear and sometimes freezes solid in winter, which is cool, but it also smells like stewed leaves, and I'm pretty sure our bio teacher found a two-headed frog here.

Coach J mentioned stretching, so that's what I do, pulling my foot behind my butt and balancing against the shaggy wood of the boathouse, so motivated, the Purdy-est girl imaginable. What's a little uncertainty between Henry and me when I've never met a wall I couldn't climb, a runner I couldn't beat? Water practice conquered.

The crunch of gravel alerts me to Angel Pagan's arrival. More sophomores trickle in behind me, followed by Carla taking lazy, loping strides. I drop my stretch and proceed to the start of the dock, which must be a gathering point. As the stragglers arrive, they press in quickly, forcing me forward, until I'm only two people behind Carla. Coach J, her eyes on me, asks if we thought that was easy.

I laugh. "Yes?"

Nobody else answers.

"Right," Coach J says. She blows her whistle and screams, *"To the big oak, down and back!"* And I don't know where that is so I take off after everybody, clawing through a pack of elbows and flying gravel until I reach the lead, then realize I've overshot it—I passed the big oak—and the others are already looping back. So I run harder. I *lap* them, and when we've done that ten times and I'm sort of getting winded, another whistle blast pierces the air. *"Jumpies!"* They're essentially squats except while leaping straight into the air, arms thrust back in a rowing motion.

For five minutes.

"Push-ups!" Coach J calls. "Two hundred!"

By the thirty-fifth, the whimpers start, and I'm floating above my body.

"Thirty-six!"

"Thirty-seven!"

"She'll send us to Jesus," Victor wails, and I drag myself up onto my crumbling wrists to see that *Tyler Stands*, tiny Tyler Stands in plastic wraparound sport goggles, is responsible for setting our rhythm. I take five breaks and barely make two hundred without barfing Golden Grahams all over myself. By then, the shriek of Coach J's whistle lives in my gray matter. Casualties are innumerable. But while I flatline in the dirt, the others are already scraping themselves up and heading for the boathouse, where, Coach J insists, we're all in charge of getting our shells. Still, seems like everybody else's got that covered. I toddle over to Coach J.

"When's the quiz?" I ask.

"Quiz?" she says.

"For . . ." I gesture at the improbably skinny boats being brought toward the docks, lifted high overhead. "You gave me that handout to study, remember? About the boat— *shell,*" I correct myself. Henry would be proud.

She points at the shell Carla's setting down with the help of Libby and some other girl with sleek black pigtails who might be a year younger than us, Tyler hovering nearby. "You're with them. Bow side. Stands will get you situated."

Dismissed, I proceed to the dock, rubbery and oxygen-deprived. My assignment to Carla's boat either miraculous or some cruel, cosmic joke. Possibly both. Oars have been brought out, too, tall and fiberglass-slim, just like on the website. Dutifully, Carla passes me one, and I try not to clutch too hard while she rights her Yankees cap, her lips glimmering with SPF, smelling like coconut. Whatever was bothering her on the bus, she seems to have put it behind her.

"Guess I'm in your group," I manage.

"Yeah, bow side?"

"How did—"

"You know Rayna Prokopi? You took her seat. She graduated last year."

"Oh," I say.

"We row coxed four," Carla continues. "Know what that means?"

"Um. Coach gave me a handout. . . ." Which I very inconveniently left on the bus, but even then, it didn't explain what actually *happens* in the shell, did it? Embarrassed, I say, "But yeah, I think I've got a pretty good—"

"It means there are four of us in charge of rowing—me, you, Libby, and Pris"—she points to the girl whose name I didn't know, whose pigtails drape her broad shoulders—"and Tyler. She's coxswain."

"Cox-in?"

"Coxswain. She steers and keeps us on rhythm but doesn't actually row. It's a good position for somebody on the smaller side, because she might interfere with our speed otherwise."

"Deadweight!" Tyler calls proudly, triple-knotting her All Stars.

"What's bow side do?"

Carla grins. "Row, obviously. And you're middle of the

boat, which will probably work out, seeing as you're ripped, but I wouldn't sweat the particulars—Coach assigns you where she needs you."

Ripped? My ears buzz. Possibly from gnats. "What about you?"

"I'm stroke. You're behind me."

Joke, then.

Noted.

There's a whole checklist of safety precautions to overcome before we're actually ready, which I mostly follow, though my spirits take a serious dip when Coach J hands Tyler a megaphone. Assistant Coach Eugene appears to help Tyler steady the boat. "Girls one," he says. "Bow side. You're up."

Pris—I think that's her name—steps forward, nodding at me. "That's us. We board first." As in, get into the boat, as she readily demonstrates. Just, *step off the dock* and get in, the motion treacherous and seats slithery on their runners, prime for pinching fingers. Now I get Coach J's ban on loose-fitting clothes. I've barely gotten settled, thanks to plenty of coaxing and help rigging my oar from Eugene, when I identify an entirely new complication: the oar is on my left.

I'm right-handed.

But I can't say shit, because Coach puts you where she needs you, Carla said, and the pinkish glow of the back of her neck is making me dizzy and I need this. *I need it.* Purdy first. Libby's behind me, and Pris is last. Finally, Tyler steps into the front. Her megaphone crackles.

"Oars across," she calls.

I jerk my oar.

"Ready? *All row!*"

We push off, and the seat slips with the heave of my shoulders, launching me backward. "Fuck!" I yelp, more surprised than hurt, and as the other shells—all coxed fours, like ours—maneuver forward, Coach J and Eugene putter after us in a motorboat, which is heinously unfair. Haltingly, we row to the middle of the river, my muscles gasping as my seat slides and I match—*try* to match—Carla's gliding strokes, which would be fine except the front of the boat is actually the back and we're all facing the wrong way, opposite the direction of travel. Only Tyler faces forward.

"On the feather!" she cries.

I glance over my shoulder, startled by Libby scowling at me in a gray BLACK GIRL MAGIC T-shirt she's already sweated through. The other shells—two crews of boys, and another of girls—bob ahead of us, oars loose. Waiting for us. "Feather . . . ?" I say.

"Like this," Carla answers. On the next stroke, she rotates the oar handle with a flick of her wrist, just as the oar paddle—*the blade,* I remember—emerges, keeping it parallel to the surface of the water. I copy the movement exactly, only to push us farther left. Behind me, Libby Joseph huffs in frustration.

"I'm *going,*" I insist. We start wobbling closer to the group.

"Easy on port," Tyler says.

I sense the girl called Pris make some sort of adjustment, two rowers down. "What?" I say.

"Easy on—"

The oar slips from my trembling hand and I catch it at the last second, smashing the blade down into the water, propelling us even more off course. Which is great. I've totally got us. I totally— But Tyler's screaming, and I have never hated anything more than this. I roar. I jam the oar back down—fuck feathering—I'll get us there myself, the crash of megaphone static and my thrashing drowning out Tyler's panicked squeaks. The boat judders, stops completely. Libby pitches against me. My jaw cracks down hard on Carla's shoulder.

Silence.

"We're stuck," Tyler says.

"Stuck?" Libby repeats.

"Mud flat," Pris calls.

Carla gapes back at me. "Are you okay? You're—"

Bleeding.

My mouth full of dirty pennies. I twist away from her, spitting a jet of crimson into the river.

"Oh shit," somebody says.

Overhead, the sky's become recognizable again. Delicate blue. And everywhere, chirping. Megaphone-loud over the grumble of Coach J's motorboat.

The birds are out.

I'M AT THE BUS stop near the school, debating whether four hours of stapling or inventory checks would be better for concealing bloody gums from my parents, when Carla drops beside me, squawking as her thighs hit hot metal. I guess I could've warned her. Mostly I'm glad she can't see whatever my face is doing through my billows of hair.

"Morning," Carla says, pummeling a hunk of black clay.

"Morning."

We just completed a decade's worth of physical activity in three hours, and yet it's still early enough to justify this greeting. Above us, the sun sizzles, an overcooked egg. Carla shapes her clay with determination, shaded by her Yankees cap. Her hair's pulled back, her Converses crisp white. My mouth throbs. If I'd known she was taking the city bus, too, I would've hitchhiked back to Albany.

"Did you sneak out or something?" she asks. "I didn't see you leave."

If *waiting until everybody's left the locker room to scurry in and change* counts as sneaking, then okay. Before that, I was in Coach J's office—which is really the wrestling coach's office during the school year—getting a fresh ice pack for my mouth and getting chewed out. Lacerations, she'd cheerily pronounced, once the motorboat caught up to our shell. In private, she was blunter. *That was extremely reckless, what you did out there. You could've tipped the boat over. Drowned!* Like it's my fault life vests would tangle our strokes.

I force a shrug. Ants spray from a crack in the sidewalk.

"Listen," Carla says. "The first water practice is tough. Don't beat yourself up—"

"Thanks."

"By August you'll be—"

"It's cool," I tell her.

Carla pauses, then mashes the clay faster. "My first time out on the water, I threw up on Tyler."

I process the visual. She and Tyler are the only two teammates in our shell who face each other. "No."

"Yup. Luckily Ty was cool about it." Carla smirks. "She doesn't have your reflexes, though."

I laugh, and the tension between us—if that's what it was—unwrinkles. A hopeful development. Carla's not exactly bursting with reasons to be nice to me. "That was literally almost a year ago." I get it, though. To our peers, the image of me cupping Henry's puke must be indelible—a Henry word that means *cannot be erased or removed*. Evidently the only move I'm capable of lately.

Breeze slithers, damp and mosquitoey.

"Why do you do this?" I mean, why would anybody subject themselves to waking up at the ass crack of dawn only to get screamed at, row in circles, bust capillaries, if the threat weren't Purdy-level? "What about Yale? Your portfolio?"

"Hah, Yale and my portfolio are *exactly* why I do crew. It's easy for me to get swallowed up in my head, especially when stakes feel high. I guess rowing helps get me out of it. As for you . . . let me think." She narrows an eye, almost imperceptibly. "*Expanding your horizons,* you said?"

I suck my lips, pulling loose a fresh thread of blood.

Expand or nuke them after today. If I don't claw myself off Coach J's shit list, and soon, I'll never get that letter.

But I don't have the fortitude to get into Purdy, or Carla's incompatible pursuits. "I get it. I fucked up. But I'll do better. I'll— It's not like everybody else was totally on point, either. Other than you and Tyler"—whose role still feels extremely adversarial, for a team sport. "Libby was a mess." I could hear her blades slapping behind me the whole time, off beat. And she had the audacity to blast *me* with dirty looks on our trek back to the bus, after we'd properly atoned for my sins by rowing another two hours and lugged the shells back to the boathouse.

"Can't say much about Pris, but Libby's . . . Libby. If it helps, she's not really thrilled with me at the moment, either. Bea and I have been texting. She thinks it's a mistake."

"Oh," I say. "That's . . ."

Great.

She nibbles more clay off with her fingers. "I've actually— I have kind of been meaning to talk to you. About last weekend. Is now okay?"

My shoulders tense. That's why she's here. Are there no restrictions on how many times a person can be humiliated before noon? This is the first time either of us has invoked the party since our swim test two days ago. I'm not sure I'm ready. But if I answer no, who's to say she'll offer the opportunity again? It's not like I don't know what she'll say. "It was just a hookup," I babble, "and I ruined it—"

Her mouth bends. "Jill—"

"I— I'd never been with a girl before. I panicked, I froze, I—"

"*Jillian,* wait. That was your first time with another girl?"

I nod miserably, prepared for her to make fun of me again. Push me away from her. Call me a fraud, a loser, sad

for deluding myself with Henry all these years, for not realizing sooner. "I should've told you. I'm sorry—"

Clay gets in my hair, and her clavicle practically decapi-
tates me, but it's a hug just the same. I put my arms around
her, stunned.

"Please, you have nothing to apologize for. I only said
that stuff about being drunk and forgetting it ever happened
because I was embarrassed and thought— It doesn't matter
what I thought. But damn. First time." Her giggle brushes
my ear. "I'm honored. Truly."

We stay hugging, the stickiest parts of her body slowly
adhering to mine. Her coconutty sunscreen smell distinctly
un-Henry. Then again, this whole conversation's nothing
like how he's been since crew started. Open. Easy.

Our arms slide away, and Carla tucks the clay into a
Ziploc. I should thank her for understanding, but relief
blurs me.

"I wanted to go further," I admit.

"Oh, same, so bad. I masturbated after I got back from
dropping you off."

Wow.

That's direct.

Also, blushing activates my sunburn. "I would've, too,
but—"

"You passed out?"

"I wish. My parents were screaming at me."

"Shit, that's right. They were waiting for you on your
driveway, weren't they? Hard to be horny under those circumstances. My condolences." Her tongue pokes between

her teeth. "You know, when we kissed . . . it did feel heavy, and I wasn't sure why. So. Thanks. I appreciate the context." She stands up and stretches like a cat, scooping her duffel off the sidewalk, and I think—I could sit forever like this. I could stay on this bench for the rest of my life and watch sunlight play off her unshaved legs. "For what it's worth, I totally thought there might be something going on between us before the party. Something casual and fun. I'm glad we could talk."

My laugh comes out sharp. "Nobody's ever used that word to describe me."

"Fun?"

"What? Casual." I shove her. A tiny shove, not hard at all. She grabs my wrist in her slippery hands to avoid toppling over.

"You'll do better tomorrow," Carla says. "See you around, okay?"

I jab my toe at ants as she saunters across the parking lot.

Casual is Henry pretending we didn't have sex. It's putting up with his Stevie obsession and spending an entire summer in a boat with this girl, when I can't handle one night in her bed—nothing I know how to do or be. And yet I have no choice. Not if I want to get that letter. Not if the okayness Henry and I established is going to stay that way.

"See you," I whisper.

My tongue feels like her wet black clay.

26.

"**OVER HEADS, READY!**" Tyler bellows.

I hoist my end of the boat up, my forearms twinging. Our shell isn't heavy, but after rowing for hours after my mishap yesterday, and virtually zero sleep, my stamina's tanking. Henry didn't call last night. Not that he said he would. But I lay in bed with an ice pack numbing my cheek and the house phone propped on my pillow, imagining what I'd say if he did. *My first water practice was awesome.*

So fun.

Pris is ahead of me, supporting the shell over her own head, so close that one wrong step and I'll collide with those formidable shoulders. Behind me, Carla squirms, whimpering about horseflies. Libby tells her to calm down. "I can't!" Carla says. "They're attracted to our sweat, Libs. They feast on our pain— Ow! Shit!" The air between us feels different somehow. Like the molecules are zipping faster, carrying more charge. I don't know if she senses it.

But I want to.

"Heads *up*!"

We march the boat down the dock. Trash clots the oily water, the clouds bulging heavy and black, like my exhausted muscles. It was an ordeal getting the boat off its rack without gouging or dropping it, and I'm certain half of Tyler's calls are unnecessary, but after lots of huffing and coordinated sidesteps, we lower the boat into the water while the other teams are still squabbling up at the boathouse. My first victory.

"Nice," Tyler says. She prides herself on efficiency. I'm not sure about her yet, but she's a good cox, Carla says, and I appreciate her need for order. Even if it's not on my terms.

My second time boarding the shell, and I pull it off with minimal flailing. Coach J paces the riverbank, barking instructions she gave, like, five minutes ago. Once we've all climbed aboard and completed safety checks, we're supposed to practice reversing—twisting our oars 180 degrees and paddling backward. The shell rocks as Carla and Libby get settled, destabilized by the heave of too many bodies. Libby fastens her oar, mumbling, "Go easy on us, Bortles."

The back of my neck tightens. I'd give her a nasty look if swinging around wouldn't capsize us.

Pris sighs. "Libs."

"Sorry, was that an inappropriate request?"

"I know, but come on, she's new." Pris—whose full name is Priscila, or so I might've overheard on the bus, when she and Angel were joking in Spanish—has a quiet voice, soft and curled like a rose. I don't know if sticking up for seniors is a habit of hers, but I crack my wrists and triple-check my own oar, mouthing *thank you*, even though she can't see.

Tyler gets in last, taking her position in front of Carla, and we wait an eternity while the other teams board their shells one by one. Then Tyler says, "Hand is up!" Which means . . . what, exactly?

Oars creak.

We're starting.

I hurriedly tighten my grip on the oar shaft, copying Carla's motion. Fortunately, backing the shell *does* turn out to be easy, with less reliance on feathering. We end up parallel to Angel Pagan in the middle of the river, his bonfire of reddish curls pushed back with a yellow headband. I notice we row the same position, though his crew's populated by boys who look more sleep-deprived than I do. "Yo," he says. As we bob next to each other, he sticks his thumb out at me—"Meat Wagon"—then points to his chest and nods approvingly. "Meat Wagon."

Meat . . . what?

"Yo," I answer, not convinced he's lucid.

He jabs his oar at Carla. "You stopped answering last night. Don't tell me—my cousin came over?"

I go still.

"No comment," Carla replies.

"Wowwwwwwww."

"Oh my God." She plunges her fist into the water, splashing all three of us. "Angel, way to make assumptions . . ." But the smug arc of her mouth—or what I can make of it from my vantage point inches behind her—tells me all I need to know. My raincoat clings to my shoulders, the creases of my arms, like half-molted skin.

"Bea's off work tonight," Angel teases.

"I'm aware."

"Hold up—aren't you going to thank me for reuniting you?"

Carla gags, which I interpret as part of their routine until she picks something off her tongue and examines it in the grayish light—a straggly looping hair that's got to be mine.

Oops.

She flicks it into the river. "You're a disgrace to your namesake. We're about to get poured on because the real angels in heaven are crying right now."

"Excuse you, I have no control over my name. It's a burden, but also very popular with my family in Colombia— which, by the way, *you* constantly disgrace by mispronouncing with a 'u.' Bea told me. And when you two get married, I demand—"

Coach J and Eugene putter up in the motorboat, and as Carla and Angel snap to attention, I can't decide whether it'd be better or worse for me to hear the end of that sentence. "Our upper bodies must be feeling pretty fatigued after our first day out here," Coach J begins, seated in her boat. A chorus of weak *yup*s go up in acknowledgment, but I don't contribute, to show how game I am for what's next. My stomach not at all churning from the shell and my newfound connection with Carla already combusted. "We're going to start with drills that emphasize our glutes and quads," Coach

J says. "Bigger muscle groups that we forget if we think of rowing only with our arms." She demonstrates with the oar draped across her boat. "Straight arms. No bent elbows," to engage our thighs or whatever. Once she's satisfied that we've got the technique down, she sends us off, pointing to an industrial-looking building across the river that I guess we'll be rowing to. "Winner leads tomorrow's warm-up."

I perk up.

A race?

"Ready? All row!" Tyler's command goes up with the other coxes'. I dig my blade into the water. The effort of keeping my elbows straight ripples through my core, to the root of my tailbone. I chomp down, fighting through it. It doesn't matter that Henry didn't call and probably isn't awake yet. Or that he's probably meeting up with Stevie after Mandarin again, for ice cream or bibimbap or just to stroke locks of hair from each other's eyes. I can do this. I *have* to do this.

Purdy first, or nothing.

Four strokes in, and the sky darkens exponentially.

"Well," Pris says, "good thing we brought our raincoats."

Just as I'm asking, "Is it really supposed to—"

The sky cracks.

Rain thrashes my eyelids. Thrashes my nose. The boat heaves like we're under attack from some million-tentacled kraken, slapping at us from all directions. Tyler's command gets lost over the pounding. My sunscreen liquefies. I try to wipe it, and my oar slips, fucks us up, because of course it does. A gust scoops Carla's Yankees cap off her head, and she wails in despair but doesn't break her rhythm.

"Bortles!" Coach J screams from her motorboat, and I tingle with shame to know she's singling me out. "You're bending your wrists and letting your elbows go. Remember what I said about *T. rex* arms?" I scramble to make the correction. "Better." She tucks her clipboard in her raincoat, and I can keep this up, I know I can, even if bending my elbows took the pressure off my butt muscles, which are blazing. We press on. I struggle to match Carla's strokes, eyes scrunched against the whipping rain. Breakfast stings my throat.

We lose.

The last boat to arrive back at our starting place, crushed even by the second crew of boys, coxed by Victor Castellini, whose teammates consist of noodle-y freshmen. "Took you long enough," he calls to Tyler, grinning. Tyler flicks him off. Or seems to. I smear sweat and Banana Boat from my eyes with the heel of my hand, but it's useless. The rain so thick it's like peering through a shower curtain.

"Again!" Coach J shouts. "For Friday's warm-up!"

"Ready?" Tyler says. *"All row!"*

"DON'T GET TOO COMFY," Coach warns as we shamble onto the bus. "Soon as those winds die down, we'll be back out there." I'm among the last to board, my shoes squirting Hudson with every step, fully prepared to sit and grow mold while the non-grounded burrow into their phones.

Except then I pass Carla, and she slides over to the window, making room for me. Like we planned it.

"I'm soaked," I say, plopping onto the seat.

Strings of hair drip down her cheeks, her pink lips dewy with rain. "Welcome to your first crappy-weather practice. I recommend embracing it as part of the experience."

Which, yeah, might work for her, and that's great and all, but so far this crew venture has been nothing but miseries. Still, I smile to show I'm willing. Carla has that effect. "I'll try."

"Soooo," she says.

Despite myself, my smile widens. "So?"

"Bea and I hooked up last night. What's new with you?"

My face does, like, three different things at once, and I can tell Carla notices all of them. God. She basically gave Angel the same info—it's not this massive revelation. I swallow as she leans in, whispering sleepover-style.

"Not really sure how I'm feeling about it, honestly. Obviously, it felt good. But the more I think about it, the more I wonder if it maybe wasn't the best move." She searches my face. "Know what I mean?"

It could be Henry not calling or the closeness of the air. The humidity like a hand over my mouth I want to push off. But I say, "I think so."

Then I say, "Henry and I . . . we had sex too. Recently. A-after the party." It feels like unzipping my skin in front of her. Letting her peer into the whole entire mess of me. *I don't know what I am*, I just told her. *Only what I want.*

And half the time I can't even get that right.

"What was it like?" she asks.

"I. Um. Well. We definitely—we did pretty much everything back when we were together. Hands and oral and all that. But, yeah, that was technically our first time—"

"With his penis in your vagina?"

I scream. Carla laughs and bumps her shoulder into me, redder than I've ever seen.

"Oh, so it's cool for *you* to give me this big lecture about using the proper terms—"

"That was *so uncalled for*!"

"—and now you can't handle when the tables are turned? I see how it is. Little Miss Bortles and her double standards over here." She grins.

Pris whips around. I had no clue she was in front of us. Her pigtails sprang loose in the wind, and the black curls frizz wildly, electric against her dark brown skin. "Somebody say 'penis'?"

Just when I figured my cheeks couldn't get any hotter.

"Jill did," Carla says. "She—" Then, inclining her head a little, "Can I tell her?"

No, is my immediate reaction, but then, I just told Carla, who now knows I slept with Henry after failing to sleep with her, and what could be more exposing than that? Plus, Pris had my back out in the shell. Remembering that, I unclench. Incrementally. "It's cool."

"Jillian had sex with her ex-boyfriend," Carla reports.

Pris's eyes widen. "Damn."

To my horror, Angel pops up, too. He drapes his arms over the back of the seat, initiating a scuffle for elbow room with Pris that she wins easily. "You're in good company," he says. "Carla here—"

She slaps at him. "Ow!"

Pris looks to me. "You want to talk about it?"

"This is a safe space," Angel insists. "Ask Kaminski—ow!"

"I don't know," I answer Pris truthfully.

"Can I ask questions, and you tell me when to stop?"

Sounds reasonable. I nod.

"You used protection?" she asks.

"Yeah, of course."

"Did you come?"

Um. "Well . . ."

Angel breaks free from Carla to pat my shoulder. "Better luck next time, buddy."

"It wasn't like that," I say. "I could've if . . ." *If he'd lasted longer, we hadn't been sneaking, our plans weren't disintegrating before our eyes . . .* "It's just, we're broken up, and . . ."

"Wait." Carla squints at Angel. "Is an orgasm, like, required to have a good time? You don't have one, so what, that's it? The experience is void?" She says this with such conviction, I push down my retort about Henry getting me off countless times. I mean. He has. But.

She's right.

"Wow, okay, Socrates, want to give me a heads-up next time you decide to get philosophical at"—he taps his Apple Watch—"six-forty-seven in the morning? I'm taking a nap. Goodbye."

He slinks back around as Pris says, "Grown-ups are

speaking, Angel, thank you." She smiles encouragingly at me. "Sorry, back to you. Does it matter that you're techni- cally broken up?"

"Exactly," Carla chips in. "As long as you both enjoyed yourselves and got consent and were safe—"

"It did feel good," I whisper. Everybody says it's sup- posed to hurt your first time, and maybe it did a little, but not the hurt I'd always privately prepared for. Just at the edge of pain. And then . . .

"Wow wow wow," Carla says.

That sliver in her smile.

"It's just that we said we'd be friends."

"Friends with benefits." She shrugs.

"*Regular* friends."

Not to mention I said I was gay. *Henry* said he was gay. And for him maybe that still works, but enjoying sex with him even a little only makes my relationship to the term that much more scrambled. It reminds me of the bootleg Poké- mon stickers we covered our folders with one school year. The sides curling up on their own. How we used to sit on the floor of his room and pick and pick.

If *gay* won't stick to me, what label will?

A soft laugh from Pris. "When you find out what a 'regular' friend is, be sure to tell me, okay?" She turns back around, tucking in AirPods.

Carla nudges me. I look at her, and we laugh a little, too, but I'm not sure why, and all I can think of is how if sleeping with a boy could be that good, sex with a girl—whenever I have it—might destroy me.

Meaning, the opposite of destroy. Which makes me think of Carla's hand under my bra, and how her sigh flushed across my lips when I kissed her, like that's helpful.

Only, the atmosphere of the bus is sort of pushing my thoughts there, anyway. Almost as dark as when we boarded at five this morning, quiet and, despite Coach J's warning, *cozy,* my arms and Carla's face a scatterplot of rain shadows. Grazing her palm over her stubbly undercut, she says how nice it is to be able to talk about her relationship problems with me. "Angel is a child, and clearly biased, and Libby . . . Don't get me wrong—we're still best friends. It's just that in the past she's gotten too wrapped up in the drama between me and Bea. You've seen for yourself how intense they and I can get. So, it sucks, but I respect Libby's need to tap out."

"Anytime," I say, excruciatingly flattered. I don't care that feeling safe with her has nudged me to reveal more about Henry than I ordinarily would've. Or if she draws the wrong conclusion and thinks we're doomed, like her and Bea.

I say, "I know what you mean about the intensity. It feels like as soon as Henry and I figure out where we stand, the ground shifts under our feet. Having sex is just the start. He's so different with—the new person he's into, and I thought I could handle that. But it's so hard. We're supposed to be the same." It's not moving on if he gets there without me.

Music squirts out Pris's AirPods. Funky instrumental stuff. She nods to the beat as she refastens her pigtails.

Teammates or not, she and I are practically strangers, and it's been easier, just so much less stressful, talking to her and Carla about this stuff than Henry. He's the only person I've *ever* confided in. I never counted on that shifting. Or feeling so right.

After a second, Carla says, "Is this new person Stevie Lim?"

I jolt. *"How?"*

"They stopped by Teen Night at the Pride Center on Tuesday. Stevie's been attending on and off for a few months. His sister usually brings him, but I'd never seen Henry there before . . ." She does that thing where she narrows one eye, studying me like I'm a painting she's not sure about, a color she can't quite perceive. "They were holding hands. It was sweet."

I want to tell her how, when Henry and I started dating in seventh grade, after we kissed for that first time, when we realized there could be so much more to us than what we'd been . . . Stevie Lim hadn't been part of that. It seems so fucking impossible that we could ever make room for him.

"Yeah," I mumble. "Guess you know why we broke up. He's gay, and I'm . . ."

She touches her lips together. "You're . . . ?"

Working on it.

27.

I'M ON MY HANDS and knees in the closet, counting supplies while Garrett mashes Switch controls. Twelve bags of plastic cups, twenty-five cases of gloves . . . thirty-seven reasons to avoid social work at all costs, or so I informed Mom when she printed the checklist. In reality?

Inventory was my idea. Clipboards soothe me.

"Crap," Garrett mumbles. He shoves the Switch at me. "Can you help?" He means with the words—a literal wall of text scrolling almost as fast as I can read out loud, but I do my best. "Thanks," he says, when I pass the game back. "Sorry I'm slow."

"Gar, for the millionth time, your learning differences aren't the problem. This is on the developers. There should be an audio option for that part. When Henry and I have our own game studio . . ." Surely not my first time starting a sentence this way, but definitely the first time I've ever paused. Garrett blinks at me. "We're going to fix that," I finish.

He taps the A button, unimpressed. "Why do you get to be good at everything?"

I think of crew—the churn in my arm muscles, the fury and panic of continuously falling behind—then skip to the next item on my clipboard. Squint at the shelves. A procession of boxes, sterile grays and blues.

Hmm.

"Mom?" Her office is across the hall. My kneecaps about to split. I sit back, groaning from the effort of using, like, eighty different muscle groups I never knew I possessed. That storm chased us off the water for more than half of practice, and I'm still suffering. "Mom, where would I find—"

She appears in the doorway. "Jilly? Everything okay?"

"Yup." I pluck up the clipboard. "What's this? You listed it on the inventory sheet, but I don't see any. 'Dolo' . . . "'Dolo-phin-e' . . ."

Mom looks where I'm pointing. "Dolophine. It's a brand name for methadone, but we recently switched to a different one. Your father was supposed to cross that out."

Meds aren't in this closet. I get to my feet.

"The nurses will handle that," Mom says.

"Okay." I try to nudge past her.

But Mom's a solid force, more wall than door. "Garrett," she says, "what would you say to pressing pause on the Nintendo for a while and helping Dad shred some files?"

Garrett says thanks, but he'd like to save that opportunity for the future.

"It wasn't an option. Come on." Ignoring his whines, she helps him off the floor and shuts the door firmly behind him. I squeeze my hands into fists behind my back, wishing the running shirt I'd changed into after practice wasn't turquoise. No way am I blending in with tongue depressors. Mom motions to the little cart beside me that nurses push sometimes. "Set that clipboard down a second?"

I set it down.

Mom holds my phone out.

"You know," she says, "as much as this thing is your lifeline, your father and I are both so impressed by how well you coped with not having it for a couple days. If he hadn't reminded me, I would've forgotten we had it at all. That's a real mark of maturity, Jillian." I nod and take it from her, surprised by the disappointment thrumming through me. My phone looks so . . . the same. Not that I expected my parents to pay for repairs during my punishment. Besides, *you break or lose this, that's on you* has been phone rule number one since eighth grade. Mostly I was hoping the crack in my screen might seal itself up, like a broken femur.

"Thanks," I say belatedly.

I prepare for a joke about how I must be dying to talk to Henry. How we spend so much time texting, what could possibly be left to say in person!

Mom smiles. "Moving forward. That's what matters."

"Yeah." I don't mean to unlock my phone. It just does when I lift it higher, revealing a cascade of Henry texts. All but two are from the night of the party.

Mom squeezes my arm as I grapple for the clipboard. "Hey," she says, "you miss your boyfriend. That's okay."

"Mom." She has no idea what she's talking about. No

idea to what depths I'm missing him, or what that means. I barely do myself. "Okay, I appreciate that, but—"

"You two have never spent any significant time apart, have you? Well, except for when he visited Korea, but even then you FaceTimed the whole trip away—"

"Mom."

"Missing somebody just means you care about them. And you two are just so busy this summer on top of being apart, so it's understandable that you might be experiencing some friction. But I'm telling you—*embrace* that friction. Let it in. If your father and I let every tiny disagreement get between us, then . . ." Well, their relationship would've imploded, and while she goes on and on about these years being crucial to me fostering vulnerability and trust as I learn to navigate relationships, and that I'm always welcome to share anything, *anything at all*, that might be bothering me, my thoughts flicker back to Carla and Pris on the bus. How freeing it felt to open up about orgasms and sex without pressure. Carla and Pris didn't pry for information. They didn't praise or reassure or congratulate me, just for having an experience. They listened.

They let my feelings exist.

"Mom!" I say. "I'm sorry, but this isn't what I need right now."

She fizzles. "Honey—"

"You asked what was bothering me, so I'm telling you. This is bothering me."

"I'm trying to help—"

"Okay, but it's not, so . . ." I pop my brows at her. "Stop?"

Mouth open, she steps back. I slip past her into the hallway.

A note above the staff bathroom toilet in Dad's handwriting asks employees to kindly wipe their tinkle off the seat. I lock the door and then review Henry's messages carefully, deleting ones from the party without reading them. Of the two that are left, the first—JILL. SERIOUSLY?!?!?!—is timestamped 7:32 Monday evening, right before I called him and we had sex. The next, sent a minute later, is a GIF of Pikachu short-circuiting.

I don't know what I expected, since we didn't talk last night, either. Maybe, just maybe, I convinced myself that he deemed calling my house too risky. But he still could've texted encouragement for practice. Blasted me with emotional support GIFs, knowing I'd get them later. Now the prospect of updating him on practice, having to define terms like *cox* and *feathering* while he listens blankly, fills me with foreboding.

I settle for a text. Elbows sucked to my sides as I type to avoid brushing the mossy mop in the corner, startled to see it's only 2:15. Swear to God, working out at dawn means having to endure two days in one.

Heyyyyyyyyyy, I write, figuring that's the best because it's neutral. A reset. Mandarin just ended, so he'll respond soon.

Four hours later, my phone buzzes. Henry informing me he's SO overjoyed I'm not grounded anymore and OMG MY CAR FEELS LIKE THE FIRES OF HELL??!?!?! Call me? I have so much to tell youuuu 🖤 🖤 🖤 I put my phone away and board the bus with Garrett to marinate in pollutants and crotch sweat, more aches in my body than words I know how to say.

28.

TEMPERATURES IN THE NINETIES. Sweat in all my crevices. After the first week of crew, the July heat bursts on us like a gooey pimple.

The days cram into each other, one ending just as I come to terms with starting another. I'm at the boathouse every weekday except Monday, reserved for weight room privileges, and Tuesday, the most random time of all to have a break. A finger in my face: *You want to think you're done, but you aren't at all.* On Tuesdays, dragging myself to the clinic, fending off my parents' concern and Garrett's nonstop requests for *Zelda* assistance, I become intimately acquainted with every nook of my body, parts that, before rowing, I did not know existed, never fathomed could ache. So it's not just me making copies and disinfecting counters. My calf bruises and I are making copies. My trapezius quakes as I get the Clorox off the shelf.

When my alarm goes off on water days, I lie in bed with limbs so heavy it's like the entirety of the Hudson River has been poured on top of me. At practice, I resort to the bare minimum—obeying Coach J and Tyler, measuring my strokes, doing whatever I need to do to keep eyes off me. Like I need any more reminders that I'm the weakest, the least experienced, the most likely to flail. No word from Coach J about my letter, though I've approached her about it twice. *Wait until August,* she said.

Henry comes over on Saturday, two weekends into the season, our first real hangout since crew started and we had sex. We sit on my bedroom floor without touching and swap updates on our ongoing well-roundedness. An oral quiz he thinks he did okay on. Some kids he's formed a study group with—college kids—who smuggle beer into the library but respect that he doesn't want any.

Henry doesn't ask about my crew IQ increasing. He doesn't ask what I've learned as I piece together each position, their duties and drawbacks and significance. But if he did, I'd tell him, *The other seats are designated in ascending order from Tyler on down:*

Seat 4—STROKE
Carla Kaminski, who conveniently neglected to inform me that stroke is the most technically competent rower, a living textbook diagram. We're all supposed to follow her timing, which I do, while also being distracted by practically everything else about her. Multitasking.

Seat 3—MIDDLE CREW
Me. The middle crew is the boat's engine. We're the

strongest rowers, and the beefiest physically—which explains Angel nicknaming us the Meat Wagon. I know Coach J only assigned me here because that other girl graduated, but I like to think she judged my biceps accordingly.

Seat 2—MIDDLE CREW
Libby Joseph, who some days does not totally despise me.

Seat 1—BOWMAN
Pris Mejia, whose dad rowed for Mexico in the Olympics. She's got the best reflexes—and stomach—since the front part of the boat rocks hardest, *and* she's just as technically proficient as Carla. It's pretty impressive.

The days seep by and I don't think I'm getting stronger. I don't think I'm succeeding, or making gains, or winning—really anything. Mostly, I miss sleep. But I don't skip practice. I show up every day, and when we leave, I'm already kind of looking forward to our next time out on the water. It's mysterious and gross and completely uncalled for.

But also, Carla.

Over two weeks have passed since we sheltered from the storm, and while I'm usually too sun-cooked to do much but mumble good morning at her at first, each practice seems to bring us a little closer. One day I try to catch her in the locker room, thinking maybe she'd want to go back downtown with me, or get lunch together, if my parents don't mind, but she leaves without changing, her portfolio swinging off one shoulder and her crew duffel on the other.

"How's rowing?" Henry asks when we meet up at his house that night.

"Rowing? Rowing is . . ."

Carla's dripping hair when I confided in her about him during the storm. Rushing out of the locker room after practice so I wouldn't drool over her back dimples—except for today. The one day I stuck around for her. Of all days for Henry to finally ask about crew. I reach up for a blanket on his bed and cocoon it over me, perilously exhausted.

"It's fine."

Henry peers at me.

"I'm serious."

"You don't sound serious. You sound . . ." He leans closer. *"Piqued."*

"Piqued? Are *you* serious?"

"Dead serious." He gets his notebook out, turning the page toward me so I can see the characters he's been copying. My eyelids droop, but I nod like, *cool,* and he makes a table with room for definitions and phonetic pronunciations, using the side of his phone for a ruler. "Stevie's taking the SAT in August," he says, starting a new line where the last ended exactly, torturously precise, "so I let him in on our vocab-pounding strategy of slipping the words into everyday conversation. Not like, *ostentatiously* or anything, of course."

Suddenly, this blanket doesn't feel so cocoon-like anymore. Just itchy. The thin one his mom installs on his bed every summer, like we weren't cuddled under goose down two months ago. "I think Carla . . ." I drill my finger into the rug, wrestling for control of myself, this conversation. "I think she wants to be casual with me. As in, hookup-casual. A friends with benefits situation."

Henry stops drawing. "What about Bea? Carla's still into her, right?"

"Them," I correct him. Then, realizing Henry might not know, "Bea's nonbinary. They go by 'they/them.' But that's what I'm worried about. I mean, Bea's cool, so it's nothing against them. It's just, today, when I went to see if Carla wanted to hang out after practice, she was rushing off somewhere."

"Where do you think she was going?"

"That's the problem. I don't know. She's never in a rush. Maybe . . ." I twist my finger deeper. "Maybe she was going to meet Bea? They're not back together, based on what she's told me. Which brings me back to the casual thing. Because, like, if that's what Carla wants . . . if . . . if she thinks we could—"

"That's not what *you* want, is it?" Henry interrupts.

I bite my lip. Could I be casual with Carla?

"Jillian."

I want to be that hair in her mouth.

Henry clicks his pencil on my arm. "When we broke up, you said you wanted a girlfriend."

"I do," I say groggily. "Well. I said I wanted to *date* a girl—"

"Right, so"—he tucks his chin, busily flipping back through his notes—"that's the type of girl you should go for instead?"

The blanket slides from my shoulders. I tuck it back, resentful that now we can't whisper about how gloriously unexpected it was getting rained out of practice with her, how turned on it made me. What's the point of having a best friend, if not to share precisely this? But then, Henry knows me best. Even if all he thinks about is Stevie now. Even if we haven't touched or talked, *really* talked, since we had sex. How's that for casual? He tosses his notebook onto the bed.

"Want to go for a walk?" he says.

We get lemonade at the farm stand, and he pays for mine.

TWO DAYS LATER, July 28, I peel myself off my sheets to discover multiple weather alerts and an email from Coach J titled HEAT WAVE.

NO, she writes, apocalyptic temperatures have no bearing on whether we'll be out on the river. I thump down my porch into Jurassic heat so smothering that on the walk to school I sweat through my bra and suck down all my water. I refill at a fountain just inside the lobby, then drag myself onto the bus.

The ride to Canning is stuporous even for a Friday. Angel Pagan slides from seat to seat, bartering for higher-SPF sunscreen, while Victor naps face-first against the window and Carla scratches at her sketch pad, fumbling to keep her packet of markers from bouncing into the aisle until I say,

"Here," and tuck them between our thighs. Then—since we do sit together every day, Bea or not—I dip my head to see what she's working on. She never tells me not to.

Most of her sketches are body parts. Hands, ankles, wrists . . . surprisingly anatomical detours from the abstract shapes that dominate her paintings. She even drew my nose once, poking my cheek this way and that with the eraser end of a pencil while I blushed and giggled. But today's sketch is completely new. A *T. rex* waving tiny rainbow flags.

"What's that for?" I ask.

"Pride Center." She uncaps a marker with her teeth. "Pauline roped me into making posters for this big dance we have coming up August twenty-fifth. We try to schedule it between prom and homecoming to support kids who might not feel safe or comfortable attending either at their schools. You been yet?"

Henry distant and flustered as he fought with his bow tie, his shoulder melding to mine as we slumped on the steps. The two of us not yet over, but ending. "I . . . yeah," I say. "I—I was at prom. I saw you—"

"Not a dance." She laughs. "The Pride Center."

"Oh."

Right.

Theoretically, I could. The Pride Center's in downtown Albany. Since the party, I've driven past it on van rounds with Mom, everything about it—from the differently striped pride flags parading over the entrance to the rainbow tulips painted on the sign—hilariously obvious once I knew to look for them. But the possibility of my parents finding out

I'd visited, or, worse, bumping into Henry and Stevie there, sucked all the curiosity out of me.

So.

Better to avoid it every time we drive by. Better to stare out the van windshield, not thinking about Henry holding Stevie's hand in a dusty old brownstone, the type of Albany house we love most.

"No," I say.

"Well, you totally should. During the school year the Teen Nights are just five to eight p.m. on Fridays, but so many kids drop by over the summer that the directors reserve the whole first floor for us to hang or do whatever. They put games and activities and stuff out, but you don't have to participate if you don't want to, and—I don't know. There's just constant chill vibes there."

"For real." Pris turns in her seat, and I jump even though her sitting in front of us is practically tradition. "Don't let the thought of just randomly showing up to a strange building with kids you've never met intimidate you. It's the safest, most low-key place imaginable."

Put like that, it is slightly tempting. After all, I went to Pauline's party with Carla when I hardly knew her and joined this baffling team, both of which seem like the definition of *dropping in*. And I'm surviving.

Partially.

"You go?" I ask.

Pris nods. "I'm bi."

"Really?" I had no idea, but also—why would I expect myself to know that? "Cool."

"So cool." She grins. "There's a Teen Talk every Friday from five to six. It's a support group. I was a mess when I first started going, but they've really helped me out."

"She's still a mess," Carla says to me.

Pris jabs her middle finger into Carla's cheek.

"Ten minutes!" Coach J calls from up front.

"Okay, yeah, I'm a mess, but I'm a mess with *confidence* now. There's a difference."

Pris's grin widens, flashing greenish glow-in-the-dark braces that Angel not incorrectly claims look like boogers. "But seriously, before I started going I was obsessed with this idea that I couldn't really call myself bi if my attractions weren't fifty-fifty. I was like, well, if I go whole months feeling like I'm more into guys, and then meet this girl I'm super into and all dudes cease to exist for me, what does that mean? By the time I started questioning this stuff, I'd only dated girls and come out as a lesbian, which was kind of also confusing." She sighs. "Anyway, Teen Talk helped me work through all that. I still haven't had a boyfriend, but I know now that doesn't make my bisexuality any less legitimate."

"So true," Carla says. And then they start talking about other stuff—Victor's painful crush on a sophomore in Girls Two that he persists in denying despite all evidence to the contrary, and an odd smell that's recently infiltrated the weight room—but I keep quiet, curled against the window. We've turned off the highway, onto residential streets seething with fog. Headlights bob through the gloom like the bulbs of anglerfish.

Bi. Could that be what I am? Parts of Pris's description of herself seemed to fit me, but there were others that didn't—like being curious about guys. No matter how much fun Henry and I had while we were together, no matter how intimate we got, how real it was, sleeping with him after almost sleeping with Carla helped me put together that our attraction wasn't super physical. Like our intensity's based more on what we do for each other emotionally than on our sexual chemistry. Because of that, I can't really see myself wanting to get with another boy. At least not in the discernible future.

But that was also sort of Henry's point when we first talked about identity stuff. He said, *I'm going with "gay" because it feels right for me. That might change someday.*

The road bunches, turns to gravel, and Pris settles back into her seat. For a while, nothing passes between Carla and me but the squeak of her marker. A question burns in my mind. One I was desperate to ask her long ago. I decide to before I lose my nerve.

"How do you identify?"

"Queer," Carla answers.

I'd been expecting some pause, or a breath—anything that would've signaled the teeniest bit of self-doubt or reflection. But Carla said this automatically, without lifting her eyes from her sketchbook.

"Do you go to Teen Talk, too?"

"In the past, yeah, but not for support sorting out my identity. Queer works for me. All it really means is 'not straight.'"

"But . . . 'not straight' could mean, like, ten million other things too." Like lesbian. Or gay. Or pan, or asexual, or bi like Pris—

"Yeaaahhhhh?" She laughs. "What can I say? Ambiguity suits me. No limits. No restrictions or questioning who I want to kiss or date or have sex with. Absolute freedom!" Her arms fling wide.

The bus hits a pothole, jouncing us to the ceiling. Carla's markers scatter. I help her pick them up, then clutch my sloshing stomach, wishing I didn't drink so much water.

WE PUSH OFF THE DOCK when the first rays of sun are poking above the trees, Tyler screeching, "Oars across!" then, "Way enough!" which means to just stop. From the banks the Hudson looked sluggish, as delirious from the heat as we are, but the current is faster now that we've rowed from the dock—faster than I've experienced yet, our shell getting lapped and tossed as we wait for the other rowers to get in their shells and join us, wind whipping thick and hot like we're stuck in a hair dryer. My stomach, which hasn't felt great since that last bounce on the bus, cramps harder. Of all days to be first on the water.

"Roooouuughhhh," Pris calls from the bow. "Feels like I'm riding a freaking bull up here."

"Riding *what*?" Libby calls back.

Pris splashes her.

In front of me, Carla sits as gracefully attentive as ever, the back of her neck radioactive pink where she always forgets sunscreen. The others get situated in their shells and paddle out to join us, the slither of their oars mingling with the constant mutter of Coach J's motorboat. The farther we row from the dock, the less I want to be out here, the more this urge to *turn around, go back* claws at me until it seems impossible to continue, impossible that my arms and shoulders could execute one more stroke, one more poorly timed feather. Whatever's pulling at me, it's not soreness. I've battled muscle fatigue, cramps, insects, all month. This is deeper. Cellular. Like I'm being forced to divide when I'm not ready, the pull of the shell in one direction, and call of the shore from the other, splitting me in two.

"Dude." Libby's voice booms at my skull. "My watch says it's ninety-six degrees out."

"Ninety-seven!" Tyler chirps.

"Child abuse," Libby says.

I lose track of what drill we're doing as soon as Coach J explains it. Megaphone static crackles as I chase Carla's rhythm, mechanically obeying Tyler. I can't tell what I'm doing right. Only, I don't care. Heat wobbles off the water. Carla's words tumble through me. *All queer really means is "not straight."*

Not straight.

The second she said it, I knew. Like how I understood when Carla first entered the gym that whatever her existence did to me marked both an end and a beginning, only I had no sense of how to untangle where each started, and what they would do to me. Like how I knew in my bedroom, even before I got the condom out, that I was going to have sex with Henry. *I knew.*

What Carla said matched me.

Only, queer's not acceptable. The squishiest, most un-definable label of them all, fine for other people, but not me. Not a *Purdy*, my entire high school existence devoted to the pursuit of this one thing. It means I could date a girl or not a girl. I could date somebody who's trans, who's nonbinary, or a boy who isn't Henry, my dating future as big a blank as this searing white sky above me.

Well-roundedness times infinity.

My breath gets short. My calves quiver. The oar jerks from my hands but instead of retrieving it I double over, gasping between my knees. I think Carla's rotating in her seat to see if I'm okay. I hear her, then Tyler, and the mega-phone's crackle but all mixed together, murky and indistinct, like I'm slipping underwater.

"Jillian?" Carla says. "What's—"

"*Whoa!*" Pris shouts.

The boat tips when I dive into the river. I feel it rock be-neath my feet as I push off, and the screams get swallowed up by splashing—mine first, then everybody else's. I don't care. I'm swimming. And the current gets its arms around me, but I wriggle out; no way will the oily suck of the Hud-son claim me. I aced the swim test. I'm strong. Meat Wagon. My shoes fill. I kick them off and thrash until my heels graze mud. I heave myself up the bank on my knees and throw up all the water I chugged before practice. And the stuff I must've sucked down getting here. More than what I ever knew was inside me.

29.

OTHER THAN TO CONFIRM that I'm breathing and didn't get any scrapes that'll turn septic from pollution, Coach J doesn't speak to me. Not even when my teammates struggle to shore with the shell, soaked and retching, and at least two of them—Libby and Tyler—in tears. Carla's hair is matted to her scalp. I get up when I see her, but she sloshes past me.

"All right," Coach J shouts from the shore. "Bring it in, everybody! Bring. It. In!"

Practice is over.

The bus ride back to school is a funeral procession. Nobody speaks, or accidentally unmutes a video on their phones, or anything. Up front, Tyler sniffles while Carla consoles her. I realize she's crying because her microphone got ruined.

Once we disembark in the senior lot, Coach J says, "Bortles? Get over here. *Now.*" The plastic shower shoes I dug out of my bag creak as I shuffle over, none of the excuses I've thought up safe to tell a coach I hardly know, who barely likes me anyway. Before I can reach her, Eugene intervenes, whispering rapidly into her ear. She listens to this fresh emergency, then says to me, "Dry off and meet me in my office. Quickly."

I'm the last in the locker room. The other girls grant me a wide, staring berth. Tyler blasts her hair under the hand dryer. Libby picks her locs gingerly with a comb, glaring at me. I don't see Carla anywhere.

Once everybody's left and I'm sure I'm alone, I change, then shovel my wet clothes into my bag. No time to dry them. *Quickly,* Coach J said. Ducking out of the locker room, into the clammy basement corridor drenched with chlorine stench, I'm nauseated all over again. My phone hums in my bag. Definitely my parents. No way has Coach J not already called them. I'm just beginning to consider how I'll explain myself—*I got sick from the heat, it's nothing, I'm much better now, really*—when I look up.

And there's Henry.

Peering through the stairwell door. "Jillian? Holy shit!" He pushes toward me. "This place is a freaking maze. Do you know how long I've been looking for the weight room?" He stops short, taking in my half-dried hair. "Are you okay? What happened? I've been calling you."

I start to answer. The moist air sticks in my throat. "I—"

"Where's your phone?"

All I can think of is how weird it is to see him here. Pool shadows wriggle over the cinder blocks behind him, across arm muscle diagrams and old spring sports schedules, a poster detailing bench presses: wide grip, close grip, tempo, like I've talked about all month. And Henry still doesn't re-member the weight room is Monday-only. When he lurches for my bag, I swing it away from him. "We can't have phones out on the water. What are you doing here?"

"Check it now," he says.

"Why?"

"Just check your phone, Jilly!"

Something about how he says it—the urgency, and anx-iousness and excitement—gets through to me, makes my pulse scrabble too. I paw through my duffel, anticipating a text from him that would've been better conveyed never: *I ASKED STEVIE OUT! He's my bf for real now!!!!* But aside from a bunch of missed calls from him, one notifica-tion dominates my screen. Caller: PURDY FOUNDATION.

I stare. Henry mashes his hands together, so much emo-tion squeezing onto his face he might actually combust. "Is this . . . ?" I say.

"You got it, too." He slumps against the poster. "Oh God. It's The Call! We did it!" I lower my phone, and his arms snap around me.

"It's July twenty-eighth," I say against his shoulder.

"Perfect, right? We've got to celebrate."

"But"—I wriggle free—"The Call's supposed to come at the end of August. Purdy said our eligibility had been de-ferred."

"Well." His brow wrinkles. "Yeah, it's a little confus-ing, and not the timeline we'd expected, but—listen to the voicemail. All you've got to do is email back and confirm you'll resubmit your junior transcript with a grade from this summer—or whatever it is you need. That letter from your coach you mentioned. That way, the Purdy people will know you're still serious about being considered. That's why I'm here. We should reply together," he announces, producing his phone. "So . . ." His eyebrows prick.

He's waiting for me to dictate.

"Um . . . um," I stammer.

His fingers poised over the keys.

"Henry, I . . ."

Wrong. It's just all wrong. Henry here and The Call coming early when my chances of completing the season are irreversibly fucked. For all I know, Coach J's going to kick me off the team, and I can't comprehend sharing any of this with Henry yet because . . . because . . .

For weeks I figured if I just focused on Purdy—if I stuck to that one rule while the others lay smoking behind me—then we'd be okay. But what I realized about myself today is bigger than the four years of college to come and the four years of high school we spent getting there. It's bigger than Purdy. Bigger than *us*. Because it's about me.

And that's choking.

"I'm queer," I tell him.

"Yeahhhh," he says. "I know?"

"No, like—that's my identity. Remember how I picked gay before? But I was talking to Carla on the bus this morning, and that's what she called herself, and it just, I don't know. It was kind of out of nowhere, because it's not like I've never heard that word before, but when she said it, it clicked. It just *clicked*. And then I . . . I jumped out of the boat."

"Wait," he says. "What? Where? In the pool?"

"The river." Pinching my eyes shut, I whisper, "Everybody's so mad. Coach is going to kill me."

"You swam *in the Hudson*?"

"I . . . it wasn't on purpose"—I grab his sleeve—"prom night, remember? Fight or flight? It was just like that."

"Jesus Christ, you have to go to a doctor. Like, right away, I'm serious, before you start glowing. And what do you mean, your coach is going to kill you? We're in. We got The Call. If she disciplines you, and you lose your good standing—"

"What if I do?" I shoot back.

Henry laughs. A nervous gurgle, like his belly during tests. "What are you talking about?"

Honestly, I'm just putting it together myself. But if I can be queer—if I can be practically *anything,* so contrary to who or what I thought I was—who's to say the future we've painstakingly designed for ourselves is also right? Maybe my last remaining defense is to just screw it all, embrace the last bit of certainty I've got: Not Henry's. Not straight.

Not Purdy.

Nothing.

"I mean," I begin, fumbling to pin some intelligibility, any sense at all, to what I'm saying, "we've hung out three times, Henry. Exactly three times, in the past three weeks, and when we're apart, we barely speak. How's that going to work when we're in college? Maybe instead of responding today we should go home and think some more. Independently."

He screws his eyes up, squinting at me. "Sorry, are . . . are you asking me for space?"

"No! I—it's—you're oversimplifying. Just a little time apart. To make sure this is what we both really want, considering . . ." I suck my lip.

He laughs harder.

This horrible cackle. "Okay, I take back what I said before. This is peak Jillian. Everything by your rules, on *your* terms—"

"Our rules!"

"I don't give a shit about rules!" Henry says. "How can I make that more clear? I want you! I want us! We promised we'd stay friends. We said we'd do whatever it takes." I've been gripping Henry's sleeve this whole time. Now he jerks free, shoving at his glasses. "What was the point of any of that if you're just going to walk away?"

"I'm the one walking away?" I cry. "When I literally just said you have, like, zero time for us anymore?"

He gnaws the inside of his cheek, looking confused. "We're both busy. I have class. You've been a zombie since crew started—you fall asleep half the time I try to talk to you. And then Stevie—"

"This isn't about Stevie! Is that all right with you? Can we talk about something else for one fucking second? You're such a hypocrite. You expect me to put up with you blabbing about Stevie, but I've mentioned Carla, like, *twice* to you, ever, and you still got pissy and changed the subject. You're jealous of her. Admit it. You said you weren't jealous, and . . ." My voice rushes up, sharp and hot as the tears I can't stop. "Say it! You're jealous!"

"Of course I'm jealous. I'm infernally jealous!" He throws his arms up, knocking multiple posters crooked on the wall behind him. "How do you think it felt to hear about your first time with somebody new? After you blew me off to be with her? Did you think I *wouldn't* be jealous? Also— what about you? You're jealous of Stevie. Can you admit that? Because you clearly don't like discussing him, either, and it's pretty unfair that I should feel obligated to act less excited to be with him all because you can't deal—"

"How could we ever be friends when you act like this? You're being so selfish, Henry!" The words splinter out. He looks at me, his eyes huge behind his glasses, and I guess . . . yeah.

This is it.

We're fighting.

"*I'm* selfish?" he screams. "Are you kidding? All I've ever done is what you wanted!"

I blink. "That's not true."

"Oh, it isn't?"

"We're a team sport. The only one that mattered until crew. It's not like Mandarin was at the top of my to-do list this summer. But I was determined to get in, wasn't I? I would've for you."

Henry gazes at me. His throat clicks.

And then he says, "Coming out to you was the scariest thing I've ever done in my life. I was terrified of you rejecting me. Terrified of us changing, of losing you. But the biggest reason I held back for so long wasn't due to any of that. It was . . ." He inhales sharply. "My sexuality was this big secret, right? Thrilling, and scary, and amazing all at once, and there were times when not being able to let you in like you wanted, give you a chance to know all of me, was crushing. But I held back because being gay was the one thing I thought you and I didn't share. One thing that got to be mine."

A blast of cold stings my arms. When did the AC come on? I want to run, but my limbs are so heavy they could drip right off. My throat raw from yelling and swimming and throwing up.

From listening.

"I love you, Jillian," Henry says. "I love you so much. But you're—you're so controlling. You have to have everything your way, everything exactly, with your standards and plans and rules, and when I finally got the courage to come out to you and you came out right back, I swear to God I could've punched you in the face. You think you know everything about me, that we're the same? That couldn't be farther from the truth. Take basketball, for instance. I play pickup games with my youth group friends every Sunday. You just think I'm doing worship stuff because that's what I told you to get you off my back about not reliving my family's trauma. Also!" he screeches. "I like raspberry sauce. It's tangy and sweet and mixes impeccably with the crunchy salty part of the mozzarella sticks, but I've pretended to hate it for years. *Years,* just because I made a face the first time I tried it and you decided I was disgusted."

But . . . that's impossible. I know Henry. *Know him* completely. He's only saying this because . . . okay, what I confessed to him about Purdy is complicated. We're complicated, and when complications happen, Henry shuts down. It's me who churns. My gaze whips to the posters behind him. Deltoids, trapezius, pectoralis. The mucky basement smell fills my mouth.

"I never asked you to do any of that," I croak.

"Really? You sure? Because you make it pretty damn impossible to go against you. See: June. Mandarin." He stabs a finger at his palm twice, for emphasis, then lowers his hands to his sides. Pool shadows ripple over his face.

I've never seen him so furious.

"That's how you feel about Purdy, too, then?" I ask quietly. "I forced you into it?"

"No. Absolutely not." He shakes his head so hard his hair swirls. "Purdy was our idea. That's a fact."

Our idea.

Yeah.

Guess it's clear what that means to him.

The door squeaks. I turn to see a face—Carla's—thrust into the airtight hall, Libby, Pris, and Tyler piled behind her. God. My stomach flips. How long have they been there? What did they hear? Carla's eyes ping between us, and I can tell she feels bad.

"Are you guys done?" she demands. "Coach Johnson's waiting."

Henry wavers. "We can't do this alone."

Stepping back, I say, "We already are."

~~#1 NO FIGHTING~~

~~#2 NO MESSING AROUND???????~~

~~#3 NO MORE RUNNING~~

#4—PURDY FIRST?????????

30.

COACH JOHNSON CALLS MY PARENTS, who call me to insist I get to the clinic *this instant, Jillian, we mean it,* but I tell them I have a stomachache and hang up. I walk home and get into bed and that's where Dad finds me an hour later, when the light splashing through my windows is pee-colored.

"What's wrong with you?" he shouts.

How could—

Why would—

You could've injured somebody!

You could've died!

My phone gets surrendered voluntarily. He doesn't ask, but I chuck it at him anyway, since he's the only barrier between me and contacting Henry, taking it all back. I don't want to take it back.

I want to sleep.

Reluctantly, Dad accepts my offering. He leaves with my phone, and I fall into the deepest, greediest slumber, weeks of squat drills in the making. Around noon I wake up to pee and discover Dad must've returned to the clinic without me. A Post-it on my bathroom mirror says *Call us <u>the second you get up</u>*. I stick it to my chest so I'll remember. Then I go back to bed.

When my eyes unstick it's past six—six in the evening— and signs of life rattle up from downstairs. Water hisses, pots clank, as my parents get dinner ready. I can smell it too. Soft and burbly, but the idea of eating anything, even as bland as Mom's best efforts, knots my guts. Slowly I get up. Pull on a hoodie. I'm not cold, but the more layers between me and whatever I'm walking into, the better.

My parents do or don't greet me as I pad into the kitchen. I miss it because I've never slept so hard for so long, and my senses are still fuzzy. When my dad goes, "Jillian?" it doesn't sound like the first time.

"Hi." My mouth feels muggy.

"Hi," he says with an expression best described as *carefully neutral*. "Good to see you. We were wondering if we should—"

"Can I have the car?" I burst out.

My parents look at each other. Understandably. Everything is fucked and it's all my doing and this is the first they've seen me bipedal all day—not ideal circumstances for operating heavy machinery. But I can't be here anymore. Every time I shut my eyes upstairs, my bedroom rocks like the river.

Dad rubs his chin. "To do what, exactly?"

"Jill," Mom says, "I think that's—"

"Did you get kicked off the boat team?" Garrett asks. He's at the table, surrounded by the spelling drills and workbooks our parents inflict on him every school break. I suck my tongue, resenting how most of our parents' concerns for him revolve around school. Like, is Garrett not allowed to have other issues? Because he's younger, and doesn't drive yet or date, I get to be the target of all their scrutiny, just for wanting to go somewhere?

Chin stiff with drool, I tell him, "Suspended indefinitely." As in, whether I'll be permitted to row, or use the weight room, or merely attend practice as a *participant spectator,* ever again, remains up to Coach J's discretion, and the other girls in my shell once I prove to them that I'm not "a danger." Practically the only thing she *didn't* do is kick me off outright.

It's infuriating.

She could've spared me the torment of making that decision for myself. With one freaking decree, she could've put Purdy out of my reach for good.

"Honey," Mom says, supremely steady, "I appreciate you asking, but I don't think—if you need to talk to Henry, wouldn't it be better to just take your phone back? I know that"—her eyes slide to Dad—"your dad gave me your phone at the clinic for safekeeping, and there were alerts on the screen. We looked. I'm sorry. But it looks like Henry's been trying to reach you since early this morning. The Purdy Foundation called. Your father and I were wondering if maybe there's a connection."

All I can think to say is, "You're back to calling him Henry."

"Oh, yeah. Your father shared this article with me about the necessity of calling people what they want to be called. And he seems to prefer being called Henry, so." Mom looks proud.

I thumb a tear from my eye. "I'm not going to see Henry."

Maybe I wanted to before—like in Coach J's office. Or when I first dumped myself into bed and couldn't trust myself not to call him. *You're so controlling,* Henry screamed at me. *All I've ever done is what you wanted!* I didn't recognize the boy who said that, or what I told him back. But I know he meant every awful word as fiercely as I did.

"Sorry." Dad cups his ear. "What was that?"

Right. My parents—unless my teammates ratted to Coach J, who would've ratted to them—have no idea Henry and I fought. Still, this is the closest I've come to acknowledging *anything* to them about what's going on between us, and it's seismic. Even Garrett observes a moment of silence.

"*What?*" Dad repeats, tilting closer. So into his joke.

Mom touches his arm. "I'll drive you," she says.

IT'S A STRUGGLE RETRACING the route to Carla's house. I've only been there once, in the dark, weeks ago, but when Mom pulls up to a house the same square shape from before, I recognize it instantly. The drive over was frigid, thanks to the AC. When I get out into the sludgy night I remember I'm wearing a sweatshirt, and slip it off.

Incredibly, Mom accepted my need to come here. Only asked three questions—an improvement from the customary twenty. *What landmarks do you remember? How did you meet this girl, anyway? Are you sure you don't want your phone?* I ball my sweatshirt onto the front seat and tell her I'll be back soon.

But not *so* soon, hopefully.

At the door, my knock echoes impossibly.

Maybe nobody's home? Three cars are in the driveway, including hers. I count, to verify, and when I turn back around the door squeaks. Carla appears in the yellowish glow of the hall, her mouth knotted and watermelon-sticky, hair wadded on top of her head like a frizzy lightbulb.

" 'Call us the second you get up,' " she says.

"What?" I gasp.

She points to my chest.

Oh.

The Post-it. I crumple it up.

Carla falls back, and I see the opening for what it is, stagger after her gratefully. She doesn't wait for me to ask if her parents are home. Doesn't uncross her arms. In the entryway, she pivots so close I almost think she might kiss me, and says, "I am extremely fucking pissed at you."

"I know. A-and I'm so sorry. I didn't mean—"

"Yeah, actually, that's what I'd love to find out. What *did* you mean? Because, okay, aside from the obvious safety violations, which jeopardized not only our lives but, like, many thousands of dollars' worth of equipment earned through endless fundraising, and for Libs and me, our second-to-last summer to row before college, you just—what? Had enough? Decided the sport wasn't for you?"

"No!" I protest. "I . . ." Have so much to tell her. So much to make up for. "I—"

"You couldn't have waited until we docked to act on these revelations? Hudson got in my mouth. Something *touched* me underwater! My life flashed before my eyes and I don't even believe in God." As her voice trembles higher she eases off, smearing at the shaved part of her head that's still greasy with sunscreen from this morning. "I know you threw up," she says, "and I'm sorry, that sucks, but it would've been nice if you'd taken, like, three seconds from your personal meltdown to make sure your teammates were okay."

"Are you?" I ask haltingly. "Okay, I mean?"

She uncrosses her arms, crosses them again, but looser, over her belly. "Yeah," she mumbles. "Yeah, I'll be fine. Whatever. Want some water? You look like shit." I nod—my neck rusty from being kinked against my pillow—and she leads me to the kitchen, which I didn't see on my first visit. It's small like her bedroom. Like the rest of her house, I'm realizing, with a spindly metal table and chairs and windows that overlook the driveway, where my mom's waiting in the car. Photos of Carla and her sister, Devyn, cover the fridge. In one, Carla might be about eleven, brush raised to a painting as splattery as her smock. I wish I could see what colors she'd picked, but it's black and white, printed from a newspaper article. The top comment, circled in blue pen, says *MY KID COULD PAINT THAT LOL* and has 556 likes. The first reply—*But they didn't ;)*—got over a thousand.

"My parents," Carla explains. "Pretty sure they were more stoked about starting an artistic debate than me getting featured in the first place." She pushes a mason jar at me. The glass is staggeringly cool against my palms, reminding me that I haven't fed or hydrated myself at all post-barf. But I drink carefully, knowing I'll belch if I don't. "They're in their studio, by the way. Working on a collage. If we stick to the front of the house, they won't hear us."

Studio? I bite gently at the jar's rim, intrigued by this new species of parent and Carla's reassurance of privacy.

"Is the season ruined?" I venture.

She snorts. "Why, because you're so essential?"

"I'm . . ." Ouch. "You said this was your second-to-last chance to row . . ." But saying this only sparks more. Henry and me piecing together our senior schedules back in April, when doing so felt as inconsequential as checking items off a packing list. Destination: college. Come September, we'll have every class together. No matter who we're dating.

Whether we're speaking or not.

Carla checks her phone. "Coach said we can recombine Girls One and Two into an eight-seater. She'll fill your spot, and Eugene will take over for her in the motorboat. The only problem is cox. Tyler and Maggie Gould will have to trade off, and . . ." She stares at the screen, thumbs poised. Is she conveying all this to Tyler now?

"I'm sorry," I whisper. "Truly."

Carla's crop top says BOOB SWEAT. She leans on the counter to text, all her weight on one leg, flamingo-style. "Yeah. Well. Be sure to tell the other girls, too. I can give you their numbers. You should reach out if you intend to join us on Monday, obviously."

I'm not so sure I will join them.

But I say okay anyway, weak with thanks.

"And," she hesitates, "I'm sorry too. About Henry. That sounded rough."

"It was," I answer, my voice brittle.

Carla takes a breath. "With Bea, when we're together, and things are going smoothly, it's so amazing, because that's one less part of my life I have to worry about. Sometimes I wonder if that's what keeps me going back to them all this time. The stability. So what you guys were saying—what I heard him say to you—kind of makes sense to me."

Stability?

Her and Bea?

But Carla's serious, so I smother the impulse to laugh and nod glumly. Technically, I have no reason to feel superior. Not anymore. Carla and Bea *live* down each other's throats. Henry and I had one fight. Our first ever.

And we dissolved.

I clink the jar she gave me into a sink crammed with bowls and paint palettes, my neck scalding. Of course I was worried about her seeing us fight—that alone is humiliating. But I hadn't counted on her absorbing what Henry said about me. Combine that with my actions at practice, and why would she ever want me? Enough to make her forget Bea. Enough to make me forget—

". . . Henry," she's saying.

I don't remember pressing my fists to my eyelids, but now I lower them with a tremendous sniff. "What?" God, if I fucked up my last shot with Carla, too . . .

"I said, what are you going to do?"

Now I do laugh, but it's a sound I've never made. A laugh that was probably saving itself for a moment like this, practically has to be wrung out of me. She's asking for my plan. And it occurs to me that, other than coming here, I don't have one. Shouldn't *want* one. I'm supposed to be letting go. "Good question." What do Henry and I do now? How will we ever move past this? What if instead of taking this break to sort ourselves out, we never speak again? It's unthinkable. Nothing should be allowed to end.

Carla slides her phone in her pocket. "I appreciate your apology. And I accept it. But now isn't a great time."

Not Henry and me.

Not even high school.

"Bea will be here soon," Carla says.

I have to go.

31.

MONDAY ROLLS IN THICK and thunderstorm-heavy, echoing the congestion in my head as I fumble out of bed and shoulder my duffel. On the walk to school the sky looms greenish black. Mist furs the trees like mold. After a weekend devoid of mercies, I'm relieved to be in the weight room.

Only not, because this place couldn't be more claustrophobic, clogged with sweaty odors, the air somehow both soggy and dry, like what Henry claims gets pumped onto airplanes—

Okay.

Why? Like, of all the ways I could be thinking about Henry, why does it have to be *these* thoughts, stinging at the most random times? How could even the tiniest moments we shared, the ones that seemingly meant nothing—jokes and exciting factoids, questions like, *if the nuclear apocalypse went down today, would you rather know it was coming, or be incinerated on the spot?*—ache so excruciatingly? I shouldn't be thinking of him at all. It's like these stories I found on Reddit once, about people who've lost appendages—their fingers, a whole arm or leg—but keep trying to use them, because their brains won't quit signaling that they're there? Henry's exactly that.

My very own phantom limb.

I'm among the first to arrive, just after Tyler, who avoided me as she pieced back her hair in the locker room. Not that I'm surprised. Aside from Pris, nobody responded to my apology texts. Now I fold my arms over my stomach and navigate the maze of machines to Coach J, who glances at her watch and informs me, Yes, I might as well continue strength training. I thank her for no reason, then approach an erg, delighted in spite of myself that I'm early enough to hog the best one. Or maybe it's that nobody wants to be near me.

Gradually, the weight room fills up. I guess some of the other kids saw a movie at the mall over the weekend, since that's all they're talking about. Pris shoulder checks Angel, who pretends to be mortally wounded, and it just . . . hadn't dawned on me how much I'd come to enjoy feeling like part of their bullshit until I deleted myself from it. Don't even notice I'm staring at Pris until she drops her eyes and I jerk the erg's pulley so hard the burn licks down my spine.

Because, yeah, I don't know what I'm doing here, but I don't know what I'd be doing if I wasn't, either, and after a weekend of lying dazed in bed, my parents forcing me to take my phone back because *it's* yours, *Jillian, how will you learn to limit its use yourself if you don't have it?* practice is my last hope of hammering myself back into a shape I can recognize. Put-together Jillian, with—not a plan. Plans are off-limits. But are goals okay? A routine? I look around.

Carla isn't here.

A blast from Coach J's whistle dispatches kids who are still socializing to whatever stations remain open. As they disperse, trailing smirks and jokes, I scan them to be sure, my resolve faltering.

No Carla.

I move to free weights. I do shoulder presses. Bicep curls. Squats and glute bridges. I get a little exuberant with a weighted jump rope that turns my arms to liquid meat, and that's when Carla slams into the weight room. She's wearing her ELMERVILLE CREW tee and spandex shorts so high and tight that I can see the bottom curve of her butt, the fuzz there when the light hits just right through the squinty basement windows. She whispers a second with Coach J, who shakes her head and directs her to the dumbbell racks. "That's a reason, Kaminski, not an excuse. After practice you'll make up the time you missed. Running laps." Which doesn't seem so awful, until a shock wave rips around the machines.

"Damn," Victor says.

From the corner of my eye, I see Pris signal to Libby, like—*should we do something?* Libby rolls her eyes and launches herself at the pull-up bar, executing three flawlessly.

"Bortles!" Coach J snaps. "Get moving."

• • •

THE TRACK IS ON a hill behind the gym, above the soccer fields Henry taught me to do cartwheels on, and the steps where we watched kids cough smoke during prom. Coach J blows her whistle at me as I sprint through the gate.

"Bortles—"

"Public use! Sorry!"

Carla isn't hard to catch up with. Not that she isn't trying—I'm just faster. But I gag before I can greet her, thanks to the infernal wind slapping her wet hair at my mouth.

"Shit," Carla says. "Sorry, no headband—why are— why—"

"Encouragement. And to thank you for putting up with me when I showed up at your house like the hottest possible mess this weekend. You had every reason to slam the door in my face, but you didn't." Also, strength and conditioning days are half the length of water practices, so it's not like my parents will miss me. I've just got to conserve energy, avoid her stabby elbows, and convince her to give me a second chance.

All while convincing myself I can handle one.

Carla doesn't seem as moved by my speech as I hoped. Our shoes crunch as she gasps for breath.

"You," she says. "Complete sentences. How?"

I grin. "Running's my specialty."

The thunderstorms have passed, but the humidity's not budging. Fog oozes as we loop around and around the spongy track, my kneecaps dripping. Heat wave, day four.

By observing my technique, Carla acclimates. Her breathing loosens, then her stride, too. "Remember how Bea came and got me on Friday?" she asks.

The night I went to her house. When she gave me water in a mason jar, then kicked me out. "I guess so."

"TLDR," she puffs, "I asked them if they wanted to get back together, become official again, I mean, not just friends with benefits, and they said they 'needed to think about it.' That's got to be bad, right? If they wanted to be with me, they just *would be*, wouldn't they? That's why I was late to practice. And it was so annoying, too, because I was depressed and crying in bed all weekend, so you'd think I would've gotten over feeling like shit, but when my alarm went off, I just . . . couldn't. I couldn't get up." We dig deep into the next turn, passing Coach J, who bellows, "FIVE MORE MINUTES! LET'S GO LET'S GO LET'S . . ."

I remember what she said when Carla showed up: *That's a reason, not an excuse.* "You told Coach J you were too depressed to get out of bed?" I ask, astonished. Aside from snapping at my mom that one time, I've never told an adult anything real.

"Hell no. She thinks I had period diarrhea."

"Oh," I laugh.

Excellent.

The five minutes feel suspiciously like ten, but once they're done, we collapse in a heap. After commenting on what she deems my *impressive show of team spirit,* Coach J leaves us panting at the clouds.

"First time being late," Carla says, "last time being late. I'd take rowing fifty miles over running one."

"Not me." We're in the grass at the center of the track. My clothes cling like wet toilet paper, and yet I'm still able to map out three distinct points of contact between Carla and me. Our ankles overlap. The sides of our heads are pressed just slightly together, which should maybe count extra, to account for every hair, never mind all the places sweat and chafing might've glued together that I just haven't found yet. Heat glazes the rest. A car horn beeps. Kids chatter and squeal, getting dropped off at the soccer fields below.

Carla says, "Literally my entire Yale portfolio is inspired by Bea, and to them I'm an afterthought."

I could tell her she's wrong. That maybe Bea just needs time. If she asks how I know, I'll say, *Trust me.* I also cried in bed all weekend. Hating myself. Hating Henry. Missing him and hating that hurt most of all, for being so open-ended. Even if that's all I'm supposed to be now. *Open-ended.* All desire, no solutions.

Or at least not any obvious ones.

You said you wanted a girlfriend, Henry reminded me. Sitting on a picnic table with him at dusk afterward, the acid burn of lemonade on my tongue. Trying to act like the prospect of being casual with Carla hadn't opened a door in my mind that I still can't shut.

He wasn't incorrect.

Of course I want a girlfriend.

I just also want Carla. I want to embrace her and *nothing* and also know where *nothing* will take me, and how far is enough. Or does the fact that I can't plan anymore mean no stressing over outcomes, either?

I slam my frustration down. The grass is drying rapidly—scratchy with dust. I press my cheek against it, watching Carla stretch her fingers up, the backs of her hands across her eyes, shielding herself from the sun.

"You're not an afterthought to me," I tell her.

Carla cringes through her fingers, torched to the scalp with sunburn.

Thus concludes our daily reminder that *casual* is not in my vocabulary. "We should go inside," I make myself say. "You're getting . . ." God, she's fair. And smells like sweaty clover. Her lips are so close and clamped so tight. "You're going to get, like, a third-degree burn, and then—"

"*Jillian*, I'm blushing."

I lean on my elbow, and Carla grasps my soggy shirt collar in her fist, pulls me over her. My heart gulps in my chest. Not saying she's more delicate than Henry just for being a girl, but—that one time in her bed, she wasn't underneath? My shadow makes her eyes even grayer. Hair fizzed from my ponytail during our run, but as I close in, she doesn't wipe it back like he would.

Our kiss is noisy. There's a sigh somewhere, and straining and lots of tongue, the smack of spandex when she thumbs my waistband.

"I have to go get my sister now," Carla murmurs. "But tomorrow . . ." She smiles.

"Tomorrow."

I poke the tip of my tongue between her teeth.

32.

I'VE BEEN DREADING OUR first practice back at the Preserve, but Coach J nods at me when I board the bus, same as everybody else. Immediately my eyes fasten on Carla, wedged in the back with her sketch pad and the Pride Center dance flyer.

I've been thinking about our kiss since the moment we stopped yesterday. At the clinic, photocopying insurance cards. At home, where my hands helped me remember a different way in the privacy of my bedroom. Now, the sight of her sleepy eyes peeking at me from beneath a new baseball cap, splotched with bleach stains she might've done herself, only unravels me back there.

"Hey," she says.

"Hey." *Casual,* I recite to myself—*CASUAL*—then squeeze beside her.

Pris pops up, mascara melting down her cheeks. "You rowing with us, Bortles?"

I clear my throat, surprised Coach J hasn't told them by

now. "Coach says that's up to you guys. I have to prove I'm not a danger first."

"How?" Pris says.

Excellent question. Coach J's compulsive about safety, so maybe she's devised a test to make sure I'll keep my crises to myself from now on, won't tip or bite or bleed. My quads tremble as I contemplate what tortures might await me at the boathouse. Extra squats? Lifting an entire shell by myself? "Not sure," I answer.

"Okay, but can you hurry up and figure it out? Not that I totally forgive you, but rowing in an eight sounds hellish and I don't want to change my seat. Only problem is you'd have to convince Libby and Tyler, too." She inclines her head toward where they're sitting farther up, Libby with headphones clamped over her ears and Tyler perched practically on the driver's shoulder, like always.

Convince is a strong word. I don't even know if *I* necessarily want to get back in the boat. If not for Carla—and Purdy—I never would've signed up for crew. Or was it Purdy-only to begin with? Then Carla? I don't remember. Like my motivations got so mixed up so fast I couldn't see they were doomed. I hardly remember plunging out of the shell. Only bubbles in my ears, the rabid rush of water. How muffled the world felt.

Before I can stop myself, I say, "What if I told you guys why I jumped?" Carla, who's kept out of our conversation until now, lowers her marker. She asked before—I just wasn't ready to tell her.

Still, I know I'm safe with these two.

So I tell them everything—*everything*—starting with how Henry and I came out to each other on prom night. I tell them about Purdy. I tell them how we signed up for summer activities to demonstrate our *well-roundedness* and cement our future together and how I only have a few weeks left to coax my letter from Coach, which is both no time at all and an eternity. I tell them how for the first time in my life I don't know what my future's supposed to look like, that I'm the most disorganized, chaotic person on this bus, at school, on the entire planet. The girls listen sympathetically. Neither interrupts to ask a question, or reassure me I'm not that messy, or make any sort of face to indicate the enormity of what I'm saying. Once my heart rate has wound down enough to not be concerning, Pris says, "Pretty sure I got a bunch of spam emails about that scholarship. Sounds like no joke."

It isn't, but I'm not finished yet. Dragging up every last bit of my courage, I reveal the last bit of truth I've been holding. Not because it's such a big reveal, but to *me* it's pretty new, and I didn't want to share until I was completely ready. "I'm queer. And—I know that's probably not that surprising to either of you, but—I'd been identifying as gay before, and it never quite fit. I think I mostly went with it because that's how Henry identified, and I felt this pressure to"— *You think you know everything about me,* Henry screamed, *that we're the same?*—"he didn't pressure me. I put that pressure on myself to be like him, because that's how I saw us, and I guess I thought it might keep us close. Queer is better, though. For me." Which makes it all the more terrifying, because if I could've slapped Henry's identity onto me even when I sensed it wasn't right . . . does that mean there's some truth to what he said? Could I also have forced Henry to act in ways that didn't make sense for him, just to preserve our sameness?

I shove the thought away. That's not how I want to remember this moment. I want to remember the triumph. The relief at finally getting this all over with to people other than Henry, even though it's far from the last time I'll have to come out. "It was just a lot for me to process. A lot a lot. So—I actually don't know what happened? But the second I got into the boat, I knew that it was going to go badly, and I tried to row and pay attention to what everybody else was doing, like I was supposed to, but I couldn't. I—I had to get out. I can't explain it. But I'm sorry. Really."

Carla strokes my arm. I didn't realize she'd snuck so close. Our legs squelch on the vinyl seat. "I'm sorry that happened to you. It sounds like a panic attack?"

Pris says that's what she was thinking. "Have you had one before?"

I shake my head. "Not that I know of. Actually, Henry—" I stop. He wouldn't want me telling them about his panic attacks—how I would sit on him or rub his back until it was over. And I don't want to tell them I might never again. "No. I haven't."

"I'm glad you told us," Carla says.

"Yeah, but next time, tell us *right* away when you start feeling like that? No need to share details if you don't want.

I'm speaking solely in the interest of avoiding more catastrophes."

"Noted," I say.

"So what are you going to do about your scholarship?" Carla asks as we stretch in the dirt outside the boathouse. I put the soles of my shoes together and hinge over them, savoring the tug in my thighs.

"That's what we're trying to figure out. It's not that I want to throw all that work away. But the whole point was to attend OPI with Henry . . ."

Carla grimaces, easing into an excessively intricate glute stretch. "You can't go to that school anyway? By yourself?"

OPI? *Without* Henry? "I hadn't thought of that," I whisper.

"Or just"—she flaps a hand—"go somewhere else? You said the money would be good at any school in the state, public or private. Shit, if I could go anywhere . . . like, if Yale didn't exist, or wasn't a possibility . . . there's this university on Long Island. I forget the name, but my cousin studied marine science there. It's on the beach. Oh, or—"

"Carla."

"—NYU! Oh my God, it'd be so cool to go to college down in the city—"

"*Carla.* Remember what Pris said about telling people when I start feeling panicky? Well." I back out of the stretch, hands splayed palm up, like, *This is exactly now.*

She chomps her bottom lip. "Sorry." It's so cute that I poke her. She pokes me back.

"Ladies," Coach J barks.

Right. Flirting might not be conducive to safety, either. We smile up at Coach J until she prowls past us to monitor the others' contortions. Under her breath, Carla says, "She really shouldn't make assumptions about our genders like that."

Cue jumpies. Then more push-ups, which, over the weeks, I have gotten better at, executing forty *almost* in a row before death swoops down to claim me. Then, since Coach J doesn't say I can't, I help extract our shell from the boathouse. Well—not *our* shell. The eight-seater they'll be rowing in while I'm on probation, doubly sleek as our four, and requiring quadruple screaming from Tyler to maneuver. Once we set the shell in the water, some of the others wander onto the dock to gawk. Pris looks nervous, nibbling her pinkie, but Angel says softly, "You're going to do great," then gallops into the boathouse before she can respond.

Pris sighs with exasperation.

"He totally likes you," I say.

"What?" She grasps her pigtails. "Nope. No thank you. Pass. Angel is so immature."

Carla materializes, squirting blue Gatorade into her mouth. "Correct, on both fronts. Angel is immature, *and* he likes you. What?" she says as we blink at her. "Two things can be true."

"And I need a break from this hostile environment, thank you." Pris stalks off toward Coach. But she's smiling.

Boarding an eight is . . . a situation. I stand to the side of the dock so I won't take up more room than I already have, my shoes mushed into the mud. Supposedly the heat wave broke overnight, but there are still mosquitoes to contend with, and temperatures in the eighties, and horseflies buzzing around like mini-drones. The moon a half-assed sliver. Carla waves me over once she's seated, and I reapproach cautiously. Wood boards groan under my feet.

"It's not like you guys would never see each other again," she says.

"Huh?"

"On breaks and stuff. I'm sorry. I know you don't really want to talk about the scholarship anymore, but . . . just go through with it. Get the money for yourself, go to the college that works best for *you,* and let Henry do what he wants. That's why you're here."

I study her sunburnt cheeks, the lips I nibbled, the tongue she pressed into my mouth. *I'm here for you,* I could confess. Not Purdy.

I'm sure of that now.

"Before you said you wanted to be like me and Henry," I say, struggling not to sound defensive. "You said you'd give anything—"

"Right, yeah, but that's not the situation for you two anymore, is it? Listen," Carla says. "You already know they want to give you the money. So, take it and decide later. You can't pay for college out of pocket, can you?"

Of course I can't pay for college out of pocket. My parents don't make much money, but there are other scholarships . . .

Wait. What am I saying?

I'd put myself through that again—all the panic and

doubt and stress over soliciting recommendations, and demonstrating adequate *financial need,* and crafting essays that will present me as worthy without seeming delusional or cocky—over and over, for scholarships that would award a fraction of Purdy's money?

Just to avoid Henry?

Carla twitches at the brim of her hat, her knuckles smudged with oar grease and green marker. She doesn't mean to harass me. I get that. I've seen her small house, her jumbled kitchen, the furniture that looks like it was scrounged from yard sales and flea markets. If anybody besides Henry understands the tough spot I'm in paying for college, it's got to be her.

So.

My tongue sticks. I look over her head, at some oak trees clumped by the boathouse that nobody seems to realize are succumbing to disease. *Decide what to do later,* she said.

Like it's that easy.

It's not, Henry would say. I wish he could be here on the dock with me. I wish he could put his face in mine until his glasses hit my eyelids, and shout, *JIL-LI-AN! What's wrong? Do you need rebooting? That scholarship's supposed to be ours!*

It wouldn't be avoiding Henry. It would . . .

It would be acknowledging that pieces of our plan, and the future I've dreamed of, *can* remain intact.

Even if the whole has changed.

Carla must think a decision of that magnitude could be made no problem. She must think because she's a painter and the best rower in our shell, so good at so many things that have nothing to do with each other, that anybody could fill a new future in for themselves, as fast as she could paint one. I don't know what Henry's thinking right now, if he'd also go to OPI alone, or another school entirely, with or without me.

I've never held a paintbrush in my life.

"Have fun!" Carla thumps my calf. It's not until Tyler climbs into position and the shell begins to back up, everybody's shoulders pulling at the same instant, their faces mashed with concentration, that I realize I never answered her.

My own practice is confined to the boathouse, supervised by Assistant Coach Eugene, who seems completely unfazed by his new babysitting assignment. Fine by me. Only Maggie Gould, glowering at me as she awaits her turn in the eight, is making it weird. In the boathouse, which is basically just a long garage with a dirt floor and mounts for shells on the wall, Eugene hands me a startlingly soft rag and bucket of soapy water.

"Shell cleaning," he explains. "Hulls first, then wheels and seat tracks."

It's not so bad. Even if the boathouse is stuffy, with only one set of doors open. Coach Eugene has set three of the skimpiest shells out already—single-seaters used by other clubs, and while Maggie grumbles about flies I buff their grimy underparts until they gleam. It reminds me of scrubbing Big Purp in Henry's driveway, trading slurps of water from the hose while the sky dripped pink over the orchard. I can't get Carla's words about college out of my head.

It's been five days since our fight. What if my next step isn't deciding what to do about Purdy?

Maybe it's figuring out where Henry fits.

How he fits.

ON THE RIDE BACK to school, I sit with Carla. As usual. I get changed in the locker room, in one of the privacy alcoves with a curtain, and I'm just about to pack up my stuff and catch a bus to the clinic when Carla comes up behind me and says, "Can I show you something?" I nod and go, "Sure!" in this bright, bright voice. So she won't see how close I am to breaking.

She waits for me to zip my duffel, then leads me upstairs, into the fresh air of the regular high school, a startling but welcome change from the subterranean depths we've been inhabiting. Might be a lil late, I email my parents. Traffic jam. Strictly as a precaution. Since Mom drove me to Carla's over the weekend, my parents seem to have allotted me some breathing room. It won't last.

But it's nice.

"Where are we going?" I ask, intrigued and a little turned on, though the track's the other way.

"Hmm," she says, all mysterious. "Where do you think?"

I don't know. If we're going to have sex—wait, *are* we going to have sex?—I'm not exactly brimming with knowledge about where that could be accomplished at school. I mean, obviously kids hook up here. We've all heard the stories. There are janitors' closets that lock from the inside, and secret teacher conspiracy rooms. We take a shortcut through the cafeteria, where grates have been pulled down over the hot-lunch counters, out a door that leads to the senior lounge, a hallowed place. Couches have been pushed against the wall, the TV that loops the student-run TV station through the school year blacked out. We turn down the social studies wing, same as my desperate hunt for Mr. Winn back in May. We pass the same cabinets of wire jewelry, the giant paint-ing of hers that I stroked in wonder, all the way down to the same classroom where I first told Carla my name.

The door is propped open. She nudges the stopper with her foot so it'll shut the rest of the way, then takes my hand, pulling me into a room that smells like dust and wax. We kiss on the mouth once, and I'm going in for another when she darts her tongue over my parted lips, saying, "Not *actu-ally* what I was going to show you."

"Okay," I say, confused. "What, then?"

She gestures with her chin at the riot of easels in the cen-ter of the room. Some are empty, while others hold canvases in various sizes and states of completion, the smallest no wider than my laptop screen. Slathered red, with vertical slashes of purple and black painted so thick they're practi-cally 3D. I move closer, my hair heavy on my neck. "Did you make this?"

"How'd you guess?" she asks with a tiny smile.

"Well, it's . . ." Not so much a painting as a high-impact

collision. But I blush, pleased to have spied a connection between this work and the other one enshrined in the hall. "The ridges tipped me off. And the red. I—I don't really get abstract art," I ramble as she sidles beside me and plucks up a paintbrush, rubbing her thumb over the bristles. "But—"

"Look closer. What do you see?"

Hesitating, I glance at her. "Is this a test?"

"Bortles. *Look.*" She swirls the paintbrush on the tip of my nose.

I swat her away, then turn obediently back to the canvas, my heart beating faster. "The purples hold my eyes more than the blue. The colors themselves are sharp, but they're blended delicately, layer on top of layer, so it's hard to tell where each begins. Kind of like a bruise before it's healed the whole way. Or how the sky's looked recently." I hold my breath, praying that made sense. At the very least, I avoided making her painting sound like a menstrual product this time.

"Exactly." Carla aims the paintbrush at the canvas, thumb pressed to the end of the handle. Bristles up. Her fierce conductor's grip. "There's no such thing as a truly abstract painting. It's a myth. Our brains insist on making sense out of whatever's in front of us, even if it's just colors or shapes or . . . Sorry." She lowers the brush. "This probably isn't what you had in mind for today."

"No! It's interesting."

"Yeah, well. Bea doesn't really seem to think so. Not that I blame them. Like, to me, art is this amazing, explosive, hands-on thing, but that's because I'm the one doing it. To them, it probably does seem like I'm just staring at a canvas all day." Carla watches me closely. Maybe for some sign that I'm bothered by all this Bea talk, which I am. A little. But I've certainly shared enough about Henry to return the favor. "You know," she says, sponging the bristles distractedly at her palm, "I'm glad you apologized to us. And that you're still coming to practice, even if you can't row. It would've been so inconvenient to change my entire opinion of you."

"Opinion?" I laugh.

She makes my blood feel magnetized.

I don't have to tell her I'm rewriting my entire opinion of myself.

"You never struck me as a quitter. And you're obviously extremely uptight? Which, I'm not going to lie, stressed me the hell out at first. But I can see how that works for you."

Henry scrubbing his eyes on his shirt when he wrenched away from me. The screech of his sneakers as he shoved out the door.

I quit him.

Quit us.

Now every time I think about what she said on the dock—about Henry and me renewing our friendship to pursue futures that are not together or separate, but every conceivable shade of *in between*—my shoulders, already achy from too many push-ups, tighten desperately. Carla sets her bag on the counter and takes out her battered sketch pad, the same packet of markers she uses on the bus.

"To be clear, when I asked if you liked my painting, I

wasn't serious. Or, not fully serious. Of course, it's nice to get compliments, and good art has aesthetic value, but I want my paintings to challenge people. If they don't, then . . ." She flips open her sketchbook, shrugging. "I'll be a dentist."

The poster is almost finished. I watch as she shades a stringy *T. rex* bicep darker green. My parents will be expecting me soon.

But I can't seem to leave.

"What's the aesthetic value of that?" I ask, pointing to the poster.

She giggles. "A for effort, but that question is irrelevant."

"Irrelevant how?"

"This poster isn't a *work*, for starters. It was never meant to be—it's an ad. The difference between art and design is that design is focused on achieving results. Like getting you to buy a product." She flips the sketchbook around so the *T. rex* is facing me. "Or go to a dance." Her head's bent over the drawing. It's the word *dance* that tips up like an eyebrow, both a suggestion and a statement, a question and not.

My body responds with a deluge of palm sweat. *With me,* I wait for her to add. *Jillian, will you go to the dance with me?* She must see that "achieving results" has been the definition of my life thus far. I stare at the *T. rex*'s toothy smile. His teeny pride flags.

"And art?" I warble.

She grins. "Art exists."

I linger boldly around the art room a little more, periodically consulting my transit app for bus updates. Finally, at nine-thirty, I tell her I have to go.

"Bummer," Carla says. Then, "I've got to finish this painting by the end of the week, and I know you've got to help your parents out anyway, but maybe . . ." She fidgets uncharacteristically, rolling a marker between her palms. "Saturday night, if they won't be around . . ." Red creeps up her cheeks again, that sunburn flush. She's asking . . . oh. Wow. Forget the dance.

She's asking when we can hook up.

A billion thoughts attack at once. Of course my parents wouldn't mind her coming over. But—are they going to *stay*? How will I explain her? Am I ready for this? My body shouts yes, but what if I freak out again?

"I—I'll ask them," I say.

33.

I DON'T MEAN TO look at Henry's post. It's just there, waiting for me when I open Instagram after practice.

Henry and Stevie, their faces just touching. Henry's glasses are crooked, and so are the apple trees poking into the picture behind them, no match for the acreage of Stevie's curls. Stevie's wearing makeup—mascara, blush subtle enough to mistake for a filter.

"Party at Jillian's," Angel whispers in my ear.

I clamp my phone to my chest. "Oh my God, shut up! It is so not a party. My parents said—" Well, initially they agreed to let me have Carla over this weekend. But then Carla told Pris, who started dropping ten-ton hints that she'd love to escape her brothers for a night, which Angel overheard. So now they're both invited, too. There are going to be four of us—*four of us*—packed into my dinky bedroom and getting harassed by my parents, who are giddy at the prospect of hosting some good old teen debauchery for once, prom night round two, no matter how forcefully I remind them we're only watching a movie. *I know exactly which one,* Carla said when she slid next to me on the bus yesterday, grinning fiendishly. *You're going to hate it.* Which is fine.

But.

Does this mean Carla and I *aren't* having sex? She genuinely just wants to hang out?

The whole thing's starting to feel faintly apocalyptic.

Angel bounces away, swinging his duffel at Victor, who threatens to kick him in the taint. I go back into the locker room, where Pris is brushing out her hair. "Hey," she says to me. "Waiting for Carla?"

I shrug, careful to tuck my smile away. I'm pretty sure Pris and at least Libby have started to sense there's something going on between Carla and me, but can't decide exactly what. It's exciting to be part of the mystery—even if I'm not sure what any of it means, either. "She left already."

"Mm-hmm." She squirts antibiotic goo on a finger, then offers the tube to me. I dab gratefully and pass it back. Ritualized callus care. I'm not even rowing right now and my palms are crusty. "Want to hit up Starbucks before you go to Albany? Victor's driving."

"Sure, one sec."

Once she takes the hint and wanders off, I lean against cool tile, thumb back to Henry's post. The caption's in Hangul, the Korean alphabet, which Henry barely knows. Beneath it, he added in English, *(he helped me write this lol)*. Scrolling lower reveals floods of comments and hearts. Mostly from youth group friends and Henry's cousins back in Georgia, complimenting Stevie's makeup and how atrociously handsome they both are. *Ohhhhh,* Yuna wrote, *hi cuties!!!!!*

His mom liked it.

Which, okay. Could be because she's a mom.

But there's no denying this post might be a step in Henry's ingenious coming-out strategy. Another bread crumb he's left his mom as he tiptoes toward sharing his news with her.

Or he told her already, and I just don't know.

Either way?

I'm ridiculously proud of him.

And I want to let him know. I want to remind him I love him, and need him, and how smart he and Stevie were to take a picture in the orchard with the light turning gold like it only does on August evenings, so pieces would shine in their hair.

My thumb hovers over the heart.

"Jill!" Pris calls. "Coming?"

I toss my phone in my bag and hurry after her.

IT RAINS AGAIN THURSDAY. Rains even more torrentially on Friday, and while I'm not out in the shells with the others, I'm feeling just as moldy. Eugene, stumped about what to do with me now that I've swept, soaped, and polished every inch of the boathouse, subjects me to what he calls "dry land"—exercises completed not in but standing beside a shell that's been hoisted onto supports. That way, I

can practice feathering without jeopardizing lives. Or gouging a very expensive oar into the dirt. Rain clops against the
metal roof while I force my wrists level and flick. Powerful,
but calm.

Like I'm either.

While everybody dozes on the bus ride home, I scramble through a barrage of worst-cases for tomorrow. But my
parents promised to stick to their room and remain as un-
obtrusive as possible. Dad even said so in a text, which is
practically a binding document. Garrett will be at a friend's
house. Which leaves . . .

I dart a glance at Carla. Mouth slack, marker packet
carefully inserted between her cheek and the bus window—
firmly asleep. I swipe quickly to an incognito browser and
google *How do girls have sex with each other?*

My answer?

There is no answer. Only options.

Which vary.

Tremendously.

Ergo, I'm panicking. Carla asked me what I liked before. I know she'll be cool if I ask her—but whatever she
wants, I want to do it *right*. Also—and this I truly had not
considered—the most comprehensive website points out that
STDs aren't strictly a penis-and-vagina-sex phenomenon.
Girls can give them to each other, too, and while I'm confident I can have that conversation with Carla—just like I can
tell her I maybe want to take it slow, that I might not be ready
yet for fingering or full-on nakedness or oral—it's daunting
to think about. All the awkwardness and not-knowing, the

excitement and risk, that can be bundled into one new experience, with one new person.

Carla's raincoat crinkles. She slumps away from the window, her damp forehead nearly resting on my shoulder as she murmurs, "How do I impress your parents enough that they'll forget their probably not-so-great opinion of me?"

I laugh feebly. "You'll be fine, trust me."

"You don't know that."

"I do, actually. Look, you might not believe me, seeing as the one time you saw them they actually were losing their shit at me, but it's basically impossible to piss off my parents. Unless you're not a registered voter or supported the war in Afghanistan or something. Slip in a reference to underage drinking, and they'll embrace you like their own."

I feel Carla's gaze on me—not the way I sometimes felt Henry's, like a loose hair tickling, but wide open. "You're full of shit."

"I wish. 'Acceptance' is Stephanie and Richard's entire brand."

Carla tips closer, and a drop of sweat rolls off her forehead, clings to her lip. "Can't register to vote yet, but otherwise I might have this covered."

"You totally do," I say, and then she does touch her head to my shoulder, lets it rest there momentarily before turning back to the window. *Ask her,* this voice inside me urges. *Just ask her if she wants to have sex.* Not that her answer can't change between now and tomorrow night, but . . . it'd be easier managing my expectations if I understood hers. Besides.

MY PARENTS WILL BE HOME.

Getting caught with her would be one way to come out to them. They'd love that. It would be easy.

And utterly mortifying.

But I can't ignore the impulse now that it's knocking around my brain. When *do* I tell my parents? What would I want that to look like? What do I want to say? As the bus bumps through an intersection, I slouch lower in the seat. I flick through my phone, and though the advice about coming out is just as gentle and affirming as the advice about queer sex, none of it gets at what I really need to know. After you sleep with this girl. After she's gone home. When your parents say, *You two seem awfully close,* and you see her at practice for the first time that Monday, sunscreen striping her cheeks, and fully clothed . . .

What happens next?

34.

MIDWAY THROUGH MY SECOND I Love's slice, I realize how hard my parents are trying not to ruin this for me. After Carla arrived, then Angel and Pris, we assembled in the kitchen, where my parents have restricted themselves to inquiries about how the fiery death of our planet's been treating us, and declaring us heroes for waking up at four-thirty every morning when all the best research agrees a growing teenager requires eight to ten hours of uninterrupted sleep. The others are delighted, but I'm clenched to the max, waiting for Mom to ask who's got a boyfriend or girlfriend. Or who needs condoms. Or why I didn't invite Henry to stop by when I picked up the pizza and he slid it across the counter without looking at me, his lips gnawed to shreds.

I almost told him about seeing his post with Stevie. I almost asked how Mandarin was going, and if he'd made any progress on conquering the tan lines that plague him every summer, or whether he'd been spending too much time indoors with Stevie and his big important college class to bother. Then I remembered what he said about playing pickup games. I noted the deep brown of his biceps, and the volcanic blush overtaking his face, and grabbed the pizza box and scurried away. He didn't call after me.

Neither of us said a thing.

At last, my parents start heading to their bedroom. Mom says to knock if we need anything.

Dad cannot refrain from adding that that includes rides.

"Absolutely," Mom adds. "You drink, we'll drive. Oh, but pot smoke gives me a terrible headache, so if you intend to partake we'd prefer if you went outside—"

"*Okay,*" I say. "Good night!"

Thankfully my bedroom is upstairs. I'd rather start the movie, but Carla, Pris, and Angel fan out, scrutinizing everything. "We're looking for trophies," Pris explains, energetically poking through my stuffed Pikachus. "Ears. From your victims. Or are you more into teeth?"

"*I* said it would be teeth," Angel argues.

"Hilarious, you guys."

Honestly, I don't obsess over my room. Our lease has so many restrictions—no paint, no tape or tacks or sticky stuff on the walls—that my decorative efforts are minimal by default. Except with Carla and the others here, the sparseness does seem kind of sad. The daisy sheet set I never minded Henry seeing suddenly reminds me of the underwear I wore when I was five. I'm tugging my blankets up when Angel comes over.

"Dude, one more question."

I go rigid. He's been having a hard time processing my parents.

"If my mom let me smoke around her . . . how are you *not* high twenty-four seven?"

"Too much pressure," I say.

"*Pressure?* But—"

"Lay off, Angel," Pris says.

Carla whistles at my climbing ribbons. "You won all of these?" I nudge up beside her. She's wearing shortalls, and the prickle of her bare leg against mine makes me weaker than three hours of rowing.

"They're not official," I admit. "Like, from real events. The gym just holds these little contests sometimes."

"Sounds official to me," Pris says. She's admiring my bookshelf. And it's hard because those books are all Henry. And these ribbons, they're Henry, too.

Carla commandeers the TV remote and movie-selection privileges, precisely as threatened. Her choice turns out to be some horror anime about a disease that turns humans into living pustules that explode without warning, which everybody but me wants to watch. Not because it's disgusting. On the contrary, it is extremely disgusting.

But also so Henry.

Angel smacks off the lights. There's a critical lack of seating in my room—and my desk chair can't accommodate four people—so Pris and Angel pile onto my bed, and Carla and I take the floor just beneath them. The movie starts. Doctors get doused in gunk while I agonize over whether to hold Carla's hand. I decide to let my pinkie do the sneak-ing. Stroke her knuckles so gently it's a wonder she feels me at all, but her hand opens, just enough for me to slip mine inside. Her palm is calloused from the oar, coarser than mine, and when I think of how that might feel elsewhere, my nipples stiffen.

"Did you want to . . . ," I whisper, afraid of talking over a good part, but Carla turns right away, the pewter-y TV light flickering across her face. "Go somewhere?" I suggest, the words all mangled.

"*Is* there somewhere we can go?" she whispers back.

Okay. Okay. "Yeah. Yes." Yes, I nod, tipping my head at the door. We pick ourselves up against a backdrop of ex-ploding human boils. Quiet. Discreet.

"*Wash your hands!*" Pris screams.

Carla thwacks her with my pillow.

Out in the hall, I groan, "My mom says that."

"It is good advice."

So we detour to the downstairs bathroom, which is both the responsible choice and painfully clinical, like scrubbing in for surgery. Probably this should be where I broach the subject of boundaries, and where I think mine are, how it might not be wise to jump straight into oral anyway, given the elusiveness of dental dams—but then we're drying off, and my feet are propelling me forward. I grasp the handle to the sliding glass door so it won't squeak and glide it open to let her slip ahead of me, into the sweltering backyard. I shut the door and follow, the grass squishy between my toes.

"Dark," Carla says.

Only, not so much, because I can see her walking backward with hands thrust in her shortalls pockets, a smile hovering at her lips. The tent gleams, and my jaw tenses, stuck between this frantic hope she won't notice and a wish that she *will*, that she'll ask to go inside and I'll unzip the flap, climb in after her. We'll touch and make out, mark a new place for ourselves out of what was once mine and Henry's. Spiders will tiptoe overhead, their shadows magnified.

"Cool tent," Carla says. "Your little brother's?"

I could tell her what this tent meant to me and Henry. The nights we camped out here watching YouTube pranks in seventh grade and discovered a year or so later that fooling around in sleeping bags was a greater challenge than expected, like two packing peanuts rubbing together. This is the site of all our beginnings. Even if at first coming out felt like an ending.

Only, as much as Carla doesn't mind me confiding in her about Henry, I don't know.

These memories feel like just mine.

"Come on," I say, taking her by the hand. Away from the tent. Not because I really don't want to hook up with her where I used to mess around with Henry, but because I'm trying to find the space in myself for all those experiences to live comfortably.

The grass is slipperier by the swing set. My heel skids, and I yelp. The swing Carla flops onto soaks her ass. I don't realize we're still holding hands until she pulls me toward her.

I climb onto the swing. Onto her lap—straddling her. She

cracks a joke about the combined heft of our thighs bringing the whole thing down, which makes me giggle harder,
because she's as nervous as I am. Soon our laughter fades.
We grin shyly at each other.

"Your move," Carla says.

My move.

The air is so warm. We're holding hands. I'm sitting on
top of her, as scared as the first time, a galaxy of possibility
jammed in my throat. I think of the rules Henry tolerated
until he couldn't anymore. How tempted I still am to make
up new ones for Carla and me, or at least ask her, before we
go any further, if she does want to be my girlfriend.

But.

My next move isn't overthinking an encounter with
Carla to oblivion.

It's *this*.

That's enough.

The night is bruise-colored and I'm shaking too hard to
undo her shortall straps. Carla does them for me. My zip-
per, too. She murmurs, "This is all right?" And I tell her yes,
then say I just want to use our hands on the outside for now,
if that's okay. "Yeah," she says. "Of course." The rest is all
pressing, panting, don't stop don't stop don't stop oh, until
our wrists cramp and we have to. It's grueling. Our hair gets
in each other's mouths. The swing set groans like an old
ship, and Carla keeps repositioning my hand.

My first orgasm was an ambush. Seriously. A sit-up con-
test, little sixth-grade me so intent on winning I mistook

my shorts rubbing between my legs for the swell of victory, until I screamed and the teacher came running. Only Henry knows this story. Only Henry would dart his tongue in my ear and whisper, *Gym class?* when parents were lurking, just to tease me. Only he would understand if I told him, *Having sex with a girl is exactly like that.*

Gym class.

Because I'm not grieving Henry. Or obsessing over what will distinguish this new future from the one I thought I had. There's this feeling inside me, building and building.

And it's too good to wonder.

WHEN WE SNEAK BACK into my room, the movie's still playing. Pris and Angel are on the bed, though I can't tell if they're really holding hands or if the flicking from the TV just makes it seem like they're touching. But I clamber onto the bed, and Carla joins me. Angel slides to the floor, where he immediately begins grabbing at Pris's ankles, spitting like a cat. She tucks her legs up and burrows against my shoulder. Carla rests her head in my lap, dangling her arm off the bed to stroke Angel's curls.

"Are boys always like this?" Pris whispers.

I smile. "You get used to it."

"Ugh," she says.

Carla's head is heavy in my lap, her mouth against the inside of my thigh, the skin there damp from her breath and what we just got back from doing. I'm still shaky. My nipples are so hard they ache from my bra and the AC cutting across them. I close my eyes and remember Carla laughing against my mouth.

Pris throws her arms around me, yawns hugely into my ear. "How you feeling?" she asks, sly as hell, like I don't know exactly what she's referring to.

"Happy." I don't know how else to explain it. Like this is how kissing and touching and all that intimacy stuff is really meant to feel, and all those other times I thought I was happy I was only . . .

With Henry.

Or maybe it's both deeper and astonishingly less complex than that. Henry made me happy. And even if it was a different sort of happiness from the one Carla just gave me—a joy not linked to any attraction I might've felt to his body—that doesn't make what we had any less significant.

Or real.

It doesn't mean we can't be us again.

Somehow.

As the movie goes on, and we drift asleep one by one, I send up a silent prayer for Henry. A telepathic DM. *Wherever you are, whatever you're doing . . .*

I hope it feels like this.

35.

ON MONDAY, I DUMP my bag in the first available locker and rush to the weight room. Carla's here, chatting sleepily with Angel and Pris in the refrigerated air as Angel attempts to describe a meme he saw of a cat falling off a table. "A *cat*," he repeats, waving his speckled arms, "*falling off a table*. It's majestic. Most of the words are in Spanish but I'll show you after . . ." So far, nobody's noticed my approach. But I think I prefer that. When you're composing yourself, every second counts. Here I am at five a.m. at school in the middle of August voluntarily. About to talk to the girl I had sex with.

The first girl I had sex with.

Hi, I'll say. *What's up?* Or, *How was the rest of your weekend?* Perfectly normal. Perfectly hopeless.

That's how it is when your own heart's trying to kill you.

Carla and I didn't text over the weekend. Haven't spoken at all, in fact, since she left my house Saturday night, her cheek dented red from falling asleep on my knee—not for lack of trying on my end. I texted her twice—to make sure she got home okay. Then again to see if she was free to meet up on Sunday. Not to hook up more—well, unless she wanted that, too—but just to hang out, rewatch the movie in earnest, preferably at her place to block my parents' snooping. But she didn't answer. So I did laundry Sunday night, and the stretches Coach J prescribed to unglue my hamstrings, and contemplated texting Henry before our silence scars too thick to heal. Only, none of the words I typed sounded as good on the screen as they did in my head.

My shoe squeaks. The weight room's empty enough that this qualifies as an event—a dozen heads snap up. Carla glances over her shoulder.

And smiles.

"Hey," she says.

"H-hey." My hands grasp my hips. Carla's pale beneath her hat, which becomes more obvious the closer I get. Smiling back, I sink my fingertips deeper. "How was the rest of your weekend?" I ask, instead of, *Are you okay? Was I that bad?* Her smile falters. She flicks her gray eyes at Angel, who's doing a bad job of not gawking at us.

Right.

Time to go ahead and call this reunion as miserable as I feared.

"My weekend," Carla repeats, like she wants to be sure she understands the question. "It was okay." She brightens. "Did you see the poster?"

"The poster?"

"For the Teen Night dance. Technically you need the principal's approval to post anything around school, but I snuck one up on the bulletin board by the locker rooms. It's vacation. And, like, nobody comes down here."

My smile cracks wider. "True."

Progress.

Coach J arrives and we scatter to our stations. I pump dumbbells and do war with the erg. Hair clings to my neck, and I'm pretty sure there are visible sweat patches on my gray T-shirt, but the strain in my body barely registers. After practice, I wipe down with a towel and change quickly. Carla hung back to talk to Coach, but she should've returned to the locker room by now. She's not by the sinks. Or toilets. Still, I peer under each individually, checking for toothpaste-white Converse. I backtrack to the lockers where girls are changing, respectfully pinning my eyes elsewhere as I ask, "Have you seen Carla?" They all shrug and shake their heads.

I give up and hoist my bag onto my shoulder. Carla was supposed to have finished her painting last week, but there's a chance she went to the art room. I pass the Teen Night poster, tacked squarely between the sports schedules and muscle group diagrams. Whatever printer she used flattened some of her colors—the violet stripe of the rainbow, the T. rex's Jurassic green—but otherwise, the effect's as glorious as it was in her sketchbook. My stomach tightens at the date. August 25 isn't that far away.

Upstairs in the gleaming lobby, I bump into Pris and Angel, shrieking as they press icy bottles of Gatorade to each other's bare shoulders. "Guys," I say. "Did Carla come through here?"

They both stop.

"Oh," Angel says.

Pris says uncertainly, "I think I saw her go outside. . . ."

Thank God. After aspirating my teammates' sweat in the weight room, air would be so, so good. I go to slip past Pris, but she darts in front of me.

"Maybe stay with us?" she suggests.

Angel adds with a twitchy grin, "Starbucks?"

Um. Okay. "Why are you guys being weird?"

They look at each other.

My chest wrinkles. "What?" What could Carla be doing that they wouldn't . . .

"Jill," Pris calls. "Seriously—don't—"

She does try to stop me—this grab at my duffel strap—but then Angel says something like, "Pris, just let her be." On the sidewalk, sunlight axes my face. The coolest morning we've experienced since the heat wave broke. The sky this bright, canned blue. Puffy clouds and birds that won't shut up. No sign of Carla. I walk a little farther, around the perimeter of the school where the hedges, green when vacation started, crisped under the sun. Her Camry's not in the senior lot, where we're officially entitled to park now. Maybe she did leave already?

Then I round the corner, and she's there. On the brick wall by the entrance to the gym.

Making out with Bea.

Her hands are on their waist. And Bea's between her legs. And when Carla slides off the wall the rough brick snatches at her shorts, making her squeal. She lifts Bea off their feet and swings them around—does all of this without breaking the kiss. As Carla sets Bea back down, our eyes meet over their glossy hair.

"Oh," Carla says.

The old me would've run. But this Jillian says calmly, "Hey. Sorry." Bea turns. They're just so cute. Their round cheeks and thick black braid that they thumb idly, like, *Why is this girl watching us?*

"Hey," they say. "Jill, right? You're on the crew team."

I nod.

"It's just 'crew,'" Carla corrects her. "Crew implies team, so if you say both, you're being kind of redund— Never mind." She plucks at the front of her workout shirt, anguish pulling at her face. Bea's mouth wads. They must think I'm still staring, but I'm really looking just past and to the left of them, at where Henry and I sat and watched them together at prom. Those are the steps where Henry stroked my knee. The steps where he caught me staring at Carla, her wrinkly dress where I dreamed of resting my head. *I'm not scared,* I told him.

I'm not.

Because I don't necessarily think it's so awful to desire some control over who I am, what my life should look like. I think it's possible to accept certain things can be beyond my power to define, while also sticking true to what is. When

Carla says, "Wait," whatever I've been holding on to—my expectations, and control, all my frustrations and hopes for what we could, or should, or would be—cracks gently apart.

"No worries." I mean it.

She shouldn't feel guilty. At least, I don't want her to.

But there's somewhere I need to be.

IT GETS MUGGIER the longer I walk, but the bus only takes me so far, and heatstroke is the least of my concerns. My stomach is whirling. Everything is whirling, the buckled steps to Henry's house and the driveway and all the shriveled plants in their pots. But then he answers the door, and says, "Jilly?"

I wrap my arms around myself.

"Are you crying?" he asks.

"No." I gulp. "You?"

"Um"—he gropes for his steamed-up glasses—"it's literally eight a.m.? Your knocking woke me up. I haven't had time to cry about anything." Fair. This transformation into a predawn creature has seriously warped my sense of *early*. I don't say anything more—not why I'm here, or how he's been, since that pic he posted with Stevie firmly attests to that. I don't even remind him of the word he told me once for animals that are most active in the morning, which is *matutinal*.

My legs are quivery. They fold, and my butt hits the top step. After a second, Henry pulls his arms inside his Under

Armour hoodie and sits beside me, both of us careful not to touch except for the brush of his empty sleeve.

"Carla kissed Bea," I say. "Still is kissing her. I don't know."

A car winds down the orchard road. Henry squints at it before saying, "Sucks."

"No, it's fine. I actually—it was kind of inevitable, so." I look to him. His lips are as torn up as they were when our paths crossed over the weekend, but his jaw looks leaner, his chin and cheekbones radiant in the ragged morning light. My eyes have traced halfway up his face before I identify the culprit. His bangs shaggy as ever but his hair clipped tight on the sides, like it never was before. "Nice haircut," I say. "Very . . ." Handsome. But more than that. "Grown up."

He smiles. "Stevie."

"He does hair, too?"

"So you did see my post." Henry looks smug.

"Well—"

"Relax, I get why you didn't comment. He's gorgeous, right? Like, total Sandra Oh vibes? And I'm not just saying that. You should see his bedroom. Plastered with pictures of Sandra Oh."

"Do his parents . . ." I hesitate, not wanting to make assumptions. "Do they—"

"Know he's into makeup? Sort of. I guess one time they caught him, but he was able to pass it off as just trying some looks for the school play. It's his sister Bekah's stuff anyway. As for this"—Henry plucks his new bangs—"Stevie helped me pick the style out over the weekend." Bashfully, his fingers drift to the shaved part. "He's upstairs." He says this like, *FYI.* As in, *keep your voice down.* Or, *don't be surprised if he wanders out here.* I smile past it. Stevie sleeps over.

Henry's seen his bedroom.

"Hmm," I say. "So your mom lets *boys* spend the night?"

Henry elbows me, and I scoot closer. He stops stroking his hair. I want to confess how horribly I missed him. How terrified I was that we might never speak again. But now we are speaking.

So.

"The other night," he says tentatively. "At I Love's . . . I wasn't trying to blow you off or anything. I just didn't know what to say."

"Me neither."

His glasses creak as he adjusts them, looking anguished. "But I really wanted—"

"I know. Me too. But, I mean. Taking a break was my idea, you know? So in a way, I guess it was kind of my responsibility to end it, too. You were just respecting my space, which is way more than I probably would've done. Or have done." I don't realize I'm covering my face until Henry lowers my hands. We press our noses together, and it's prom night all over again, the tent amber-colored, damp with shadows.

I say, "You never wanted to go to prom, either, did you?"

"Nope."

"But I made you."

"Yup."

"I'm sorry," I whisper. Our mouths so close.

It could be a kiss to end all others. A kiss that says, *I love you,* and *forgive me,* and *I can't imagine burning another day up without you.* The kiss I'd be longing for if both of us didn't sense at the very same time, in this very moment, that we're beyond kissing now. Henry nods, his bangs chafing slightly against my forehead. And I know I'm forgiven.

We move apart.

"It was wrong of me to blame you for not speaking up for yourself," I say. "I just . . . It's like, I was always thinking so big about our future, you know? I didn't see how in trying to control that, I made the present, who you are, and who I was, what we were to each other, so small."

Henry inspects his palms. "For the record, it wasn't all awful. Maybe your way didn't always leave much room for me to be my whole self, but for the longest time, it felt safe, too. Especially with my parents acting like they were, fighting all the time, forcing me to be peacemaker—it was honestly a relief leaving everything else about my life up to you. You're so determined, and capable, and strong. Sometimes it was like—like your conviction made me feel invincible by association. And I loved it. It's just that . . ." He shrugs shyly. "I'm not *always* going to need that from you?"

"I get it," I say. "And that's not what I want to ask of you anymore, either. Like, building all your decisions around me and stuff. I do want you. The real you."

"I'm glad." Henry blushes slightly, ducking his head. "And, yeah, you were probably right about me being . . . one-track-minded about Stevie. I'm working on that." He sucks his sweatshirt string. "You're not the only one who struggles with new things. Which I probably could've communicated better if I wasn't screaming at you that day, so. I'm sorry, too."

I laugh. "It was a *fight*, Henry."

"Still—"

"Next time we'll have an intermission."

"Okay, right? A mandatory five minutes of counter-arguments." He grins, and I stuff his sweatshirt hood over his head, and his sleepy boy hair and sleepy boy smells. "Anyway," he says, not pulling it down, "you've accepted my haircut. What's new with you?"

His eyes widen exponentially as I catch him up on my activities these past couple of weeks.

"Well," Henry says when I'm finished, "you're clearly not who I thought you were, either. Casual hookups? Enjoying a *team sport*? How uncouth."

I scowl, embarrassed but also sort of proud. "I'm into crew, I think? Don't get me wrong, I hate the wakeups. And the river smells, and I'm covered in bug bites, and I don't know if I'll want to join next year. But I've met some cool people."

He fidgets. "And . . . Purdy . . ."

"I'll ask my coach for the letter," I say. "Make no mistake, I'm finishing the season. There's only a couple weeks left. I just have to prove that I can be trusted to get back on the water—"

He grips my hands. *"Jillian!"*

"—but I think . . . yeah." I squeeze his back. "Yeah, I think she will write it. I've gone to practice every day, helped out around the boathouse—she even complimented my team spirit the other day. I'll email Purdy and tell them when to expect it." Because honestly, there's no reason not to keep this going. If I can throw myself at Carla, have a blast with her, see her kiss Bea and survive, there's no telling what I'm capable of enduring when it comes to Henry and me. Like maybe reconciling after two weeks of not speaking is just the start. I rest my head in my hands, looking out at the orchard. The air dewy with apple smell, though the trees aren't doing much but being green right now. "Besides," I go on, "we don't . . . Just hear me out. We don't *have* to go to OPI together. I mean, if one of us decides that's not the best choice, personally."

For a second, Henry glazes. His gaze the same sort of wobbly it gets when we contemplate the depths of the ocean, or if there's another word that means *synonym*.

Slowly he says, "You're right."

His look of wonderment makes me giggle. "How proud are you of me for coming to that realization?" No need to mention that Carla helped. Honestly, the fact that I *believe* it is what counts. Because, yeah, maybe the future isn't all design.

It's a bit of art, too.

"Um, considering you once rewrote a week's worth of chemistry notes after your pen died because you couldn't handle half of them being in blue ink and the other half in black? I'm wildly, wildly proud. And impressed." Henry nods. His glasses slip, and I catch them before they tumble down the steps. We grin in astonishment.

"Don't act like you haven't rewritten notes, too," I say. "Continuity is important. My point is that we have time to figure this stuff out right away. We have time. Like, the entire fall." Putting somebody else's glasses on for them is impossible, but I do my best, hooking and re-hooking the nubby tortoiseshell ends around his ears until I'm sure I've got them right.

He readjusts them immediately. "And if we decide that it *is* the best choice . . . ?"

"Good for us. But in the meantime . . ." I let out my breath. "No more rules."

"None." He nods harder.

We clonk heads trying to rest them on each other's shoulders at the same time.

36.

CARLA FREEZES WHEN SHE SEES me striding toward her. "Jillian?"

It's dark—just after five, the bus's headlights tunneling through the fog, hazy as it is thick. Most of the others have boarded already. Pris looks out at us through the smeary window, her mouth stuffed with McMuffin.

"Can't talk long," I tell Carla. "I have to find Coach."

"Sure, um. Over there?" She leads me to a picnic table on the parking lot median, where students inexplicably aren't permitted to congregate during the school year.

"I'm so sorry about this," she says once we're alone. "But . . ." She wads her hair into a bun, lets it tumble to her chin again. "I don't know. I'm not over Bea. I'm not saying we'll get back together, but . . . like . . . I should've told you stuff was moving in that direction. I guess I tried to justify it since you and I were always just messing around anyway, and you're not over Henry—"

"I don't have those kinds of feelings for Henry," I

interrupt. "Not romantic ones. For a long time, I did. But now I—I'm positive I don't. Not anymore."

"Right," Carla says. She flicks a pebble off the curb with her toe. "Yeah. I shouldn't have presumed."

It's okay, I tell her. Then, grinning, "I accept being your rebound."

She grins back. "I was totally your rebound, too. Don't lie."

If freeing up the emotional bandwidth I needed to move on from Henry counts as that, then, sure. But whatever she and I had, I'm not too concerned with how to define it anymore. Brief, but in its own quiet way, pretty damn loud.

Carla nudges me, the motion whistly thanks to her windbreaker. "My rebounding services could still be available. That is, if yours are."

"Hmm. Tempting." But I shake my head. "I want a girlfriend. Somebody official, and exclusive. Not that this wasn't great. Just, I think that's the next step for me." Maybe it's rigid, but dating, and relationships, and sex *are* parts of my life I get to have control over. I'm determined to have my say.

Besides, if Henry's not the boy I made him out to be, I don't have to worry about the girl I'm with next filling the Henry-shaped hole inside me anymore, either. In the forty-eight hours since we reconciled, he's already spilled about how unlike me Stevie can be—so easygoing it's stressful. *He doesn't digitally shelve games he's already beaten, Jillian. They're all just sitting on his Switch's home screen. Every game. At once! They aren't even alphabetized. . . .*

He's learning to cope.

Ergo, I can date whoever I like. Well.

Whoever will want to date me, too.

"We can stay friends, though," I add hopefully.

Carla readjusts her duffel. Her sunburnt cheeks have started peeling, and she coaxes up one wisp and then another. Long, whispery strips. Like what I said requires careful consideration. "Depends on whether you get us out of that eight."

I laugh, aware she's only sort of kidding. "That's what I'm talking to Coach about."

Only, that'll have to wait. We're the last ones on the bus, and Coach J's rattling off names.

"Joseph."

"Here."

"Castellini."

"Here."

The back filled up, so we claim a seat as close to our usual one as we can, but it's where the wheel is, so my knees are jutting to my chin, my feet on the hump. Carla offers to switch with me.

"It's all right," I say.

I like the window.

The ride to Canning is always quiet. But this one seems especially hushed beneath Coach J's barking, my duffel strap grinding a rash into my neck, and Carla's knee pushed against mine while she draws. Her hair still smells like my pillow. The sky's full of tiny stars.

"Bortles."

"Here," I say.

37.

"SMILE WITH YOUR LIPS CLOSED," Stevie instructs.

I roll my eyes at Henry, who's seated beside me on my bathroom counter, sport jacket draped across his lap. He rolls his eyes back at me, and I poke him with a toe until he retaliates ferociously, trying to trap my foot between both of his. Without consulting each other, we put on matching Poké Ball socks.

"Please stop wiggling," Stevie says. Impressive manners for a jock.

Garrett whines, "It tickles!"

"You have to get used to it. Mind over matter. Now smile."

Amazingly, Garrett complies, and Stevie continues lining his lips creamy beige. Of all the ways I could've repaid Garrett for giving me Henry's number that night, I wasn't expecting this. Nor were my parents, who were still cooing reassuringly at us about how *makeup isn't only for girls,* and *we fully support you exploring your creativity in this way, Gar!* literally seconds before Henry and Stevie arrived. Henry didn't introduce Stevie as his boyfriend—they're intent on taking things super slow, and neither of us is out to our families yet—but they're not exactly subtle. I could see my parents doing the math, filing away questions to inflict on me later.

Or not. Somehow the temporary breathing room they granted me just keeps on expanding. Like deep down, they do suspect what's going on. That'll make it easier to catch them up when I decide it's time. But for now I'm into exploring my queerness for myself.

"Okay." Stevie gestures for my mom's absurdly ornate hand mirror, which Henry passes to him. "Ready?"

"Yes," Garrett whispers, his eyes shut tight.

Stevie turns the mirror around.

My brother studies himself: his mouth pinkish nude and eyelashes gobbed with mascara, fluttering against his cheek. At last, he looks up. "I love this."

Stevie beams.

"I look incredible." Garrett turns to me. "How incredible do I look?"

"Extremely, Gar," I say truthfully.

Henry jumps in. "You picked exactly the right colors."

"Wait, I almost forgot. Shut your eyes again." Stevie grabs a spritzer bottle from his makeup bag and mists Garrett's face. "To help the makeup set. It'll last upward of twelve hours, but don't do anything wild, like sleep in it. You'll break out. And ruin a pillowcase or two while you're at it. Trust me, that mascara *clings*."

Garrett slips off the closed toilet seat, where he's been at

Stevie's mercy for the past thirty minutes. "I'm never washing my face again."

Stevie cringes. "So, actually—"

"Never!" he cackles, rushing from the bathroom to show our parents.

Stevie calls after him. "Practice touching your eyes! Then we can do eyeliner next time! Just, you know, wash your hands first." He sighs, pressing his palms to his cheeks. "Your brother's cool, Jillian."

"I wouldn't go that far."

Henry taps my knee. Garrett took so long that there's barely any time left for Stevie's own transformation—smoky neutrals offset by a very maroon velvet tux—and for me to put on my own dress shirt and pants, and suspenders. The shirt and pants are mine, left over from who knows what school function, but the suspenders I scavenged from Dad's closet just this morning. I'm not sure this look works on me. I mean, I've never worn anything but a dress to a formal event before, and I came extremely close to recycling my prom dress for this.

But.

Examining myself in the bathroom mirror, listening to the boys snap their discarded T-shirts at each other in my room, I note how the suspenders accentuate the curve of my breasts, and the dress shirt stretches tight over my rowers' shoulders, achy and traumatized from my first week back on the water. It's exciting. There are so many ways to explore what queerness looks like for me.

Downstairs, my parents mob us with their iPhones.

Literally, they snap enough pictures of us on the porch to repurpose my entire baby book. Lots of Henry and Stevie standing shoulder to shoulder, and then some of Henry and me, in that ridiculous prom pose, only gender-swapped—my hands resting on his hips. Absolutely none of this is necessary, seeing as they already have photos of us like this. Except in those, we weren't cracking up. And one of these might actually belong on my wall.

The photos continue as we proceed toward Big Purp. Stevie whips open the back door for me and curtsies.

"Your chariot, madam."

I laugh. It's just so much—but now that I'm putting sincere effort into getting to know him, I'm on the verge of deciding Stevie isn't *irredeemably* terrible. Even if him being with Henry still makes me jealous.

But that's another thing Henry and I are working out. Like, we do get jealous of each other sometimes. And maybe we just have to accept that that's going to be a little bit of what we are now.

Like me taking the back seat. I'm getting used to that, too.

Smiling broadly, I say to Stevie, "Thanks, dawg."

TURNS OUT THE PRIDE CENTER teen committee took the Queer Paradise theme extremely seriously. When we arrive, the hangout area is awash in rainbows representing every possible version of pride: gay and genderqueer, trans and ace, and some I'm not so familiar with and that I'm eager to look up once we get closer. There are bowls of Skittles, and rainbow Goldfish. The curtains are fastened shut, the dimness lit by blinky LED effects to erase the daytime outside. As for the center itself, it's basically what Henry described— more like a grandma's house than any official-seeming building, with creaky wooden floors the color of honey, and tattered mismatched sofas, a picture window whose seat is smothered with laughing kids and heaps of books. The place is packed already, so it takes us a while to find an empty space. Stevie throws his jacket over a furry blue armchair to claim it.

"Are you wearing anything that isn't velvet?" I ask, screaming over the music.

"No," he says.

Noted.

"Velvet is Stevie's fabric," Henry says.

"*One* of my fabrics," Stevie corrects him. "You'll see." Henry grins, and they kiss lightly on the lips.

I swallow. A square area has been cleared in the middle of the room. A dance floor. I scan it nervously, picking out Pris with her arms around Angel's neck. They disentangle just enough to wave at me—"Jillian! Dance with us!"— and knock into this other group of kids I recognize from Pauline's. Henry comes up next to me. We've been here five minutes, and already this dance far exceeds the last one we attended. There's only one thing I need to happen tonight. One thing, to make the past four months worth it.

That's when I spot Carla. Standing off to one side with light strobing off her, her sunburnt cheeks streaked with glitter. Making me ache.

Henry pokes me. "Go," he says.

"Maybe," I whisper. But the second it's out, my eyes meet Carla's from across the room. She smiles. My heart tightens.

And I think I am going to ask her.

I *know* I'm going to ask if she'll dance with me anyway.

Because queer homecoming is more than a prom do-over. It's about having fun with crew, enjoying it for its own sake, even though I definitely suck. It's getting an email from Purdy stating I've been cleared for the final selection process pending Coach's letter, which she promised to write as long as I can get through Labor Day without killing anybody. It's having your best friend come out to you and making you realize you've been needing to do the same, and sort of letting that rip you apart for a while until you see that okay, yeah, we have changed. The future's not so clear. But while uncertainty can be terrifying, it isn't always wrong.

Sometimes it's better.

"Okay," I say. "We're friends, so I'll ask her to dance. But not yet."

Henry frowns. "Jilly—"

I hold out my hand. "Henry Yoo, will you dance with me?" This is what I need.

He doesn't hesitate, just slips his glasses off and into his jacket pocket. Presumably, so they won't tumble off or get crushed, but—it's a start. With or without them, he looks dazzling. Nothing like the sad, anxious kid I dragged to prom in May. As Stevie steps back, Henry tucks his hand in mine.

"One hundred percent," he says.

Acknowledgments

Before embarking on this project, I'd always heard that the second book was the toughest, and after years of willfully dismissing such wisdom, I am here to confirm it. Yes! The process of writing this very challenging book during a very scary pandemic was among the most excruciatingly stressful experiences I've endured. But it was also joyous and beautiful, and here's to the friends and family who helped make it so:

My amazing agent (amaze-ent!), Danielle Burby, who fights tirelessly on my behalf, offers endless encouragement, and never withholds a nudge when I need one. I am so lucky to have you in my corner. Thank you.

Thanks also to my incredible team at Labyrinth Road: Liesa Abrams, my wonderful editor, who made a home for my voice and whose exquisitely thoughtful feedback helped shape this story beyond what I ever imagined it could be. Thank you for pushing me to go deeper, to say more, and for allowing space for my characters' messiness (and my own). A million additional thank-yous to Emily Harburg, editorial assistant, who provided invaluable notes and suggestions and graciously answered my frantic emails. You've both made me a better writer.

Thank you to everybody at Penguin Random House who helped get Jillian and Henry out into the world: Trisha Previte, Salini Perera, and Barbara Bakowski. And thank you to Ivan Leung, who helped bring Henry to life.

Huge, immeasurable thanks to my friends Faye Chao, Laura Barisonzi, and Erin Reale, who for some reason keep putting up with me; and to Rossana Coto-Batres and Jesse James Crawford, who allowed me to agonize over an early draft of this novel at their lovely new home in the midst of a *very hot* upstate New York summer. To my Write Club buddies, Jenna Marie Hallock and Jason Seligson, whose friendship and feedback I cherish: Jenna, thank you for suggesting this book's gorgeous title. And, Jason, thank you for doing Pokémon trades so my Machoke could become a Machamp and you could get a Scizor. Fifth-grade me is trembling with joy.

Thank you to my family: Mom and Dad, of course, and Dan, Grace, Mike, and Allison—let's all hang out and play *Cuphead* soon, okay?

An extra-special thank-you to my spouse, Kel, whose wisdom, courage, support, and love make nothing feel impossible, even when I insist otherwise. I love you.

Thank you to my therapist, Amy, for all the help you've

given me, including that time when we were doing a remote session and I cried so hard my dog threw up.

Finally, thank you to all my students. Every single one. It's an honor being your teacher. I wasn't kidding when I said this book is for you.

Underlined

A Community of Book Nerds & Aspiring Writers!

READ

Get book recommendations, reading lists, YA news

DISCOVER

Take quizzes, watch videos, shop merch, win prizes

CREATE

Write your own stories, enter contests, get inspired

SHARE

Connect with fellow Book Nerds and authors!

GetUnderlined.com • @GetUnderlined

Want a chance to be featured? Use #GetUnderlined on social!

Art used under license from Shutterstock.com

1407